THE NEXT TO DIE

"Do you know this Lora's surname or the year in which she was killed?"

"No," Petronella said, "but I perceive that you do."

"Aye. Lora Tylney. She died six years ago. A feather was found near her body. One was also left near Diane's." Robert and Sir Walter might discount this as coincidence, but Susanna could not. Robert and Sir Walter were hiding something. For some reason, they wanted Diane's death glossed over and forgotten. Susanna did not like to think that either Robert or Sir Walter, or any of the friends of their youth, might have been guilty of a murder six years ago, but she had to consider that chilling possibility . . . and one other.

"Is it likely there are more victims?" Susanna asked. It was a particularly unpalatable thought.

"More women who look like me? Dead women?"

"Aye." That a woman of a certain description might have been slain every St. Mark's Day since Queen Mary sat on the throne was horrifying to contemplate, and yet Susanna knew she must.

By her grim expression, Petronella saw the logic of Susanna's conclusion. Perhaps it was one she had already come to on her own. "It is possible," she allowed.

"We must try to discover if it is so," Susanna said. "If we learn enough, we may be able to put an end to these killings . . ."

Books by Kathy Lynn Emerson

FACE DOWN IN THE MARROW-BONE PIE

FACE DOWN UPON AN HERBAL

FACE DOWN AMONG THE
WINCHESTER GEESE

Published by Kensington Publishing Corporation

Face Down among the Winchester Geese

Kathy Lynn Emerson

KENSINGTON BOOKS

KENSINGTON PUBLISHING CORP.

http://www.kensingtonbooks.com

KENSINGTON BOOKS are published by

Kensington Publishing Corp.
850 Third Avenue
New York, NY 10022

All Kensington titles, imprints and distributed lines are available at special quantity discounts for bulk purchases for sales promotion, premiums, fund raising, educational or institutional use.

Special book excerpts or customized printings can also be created to fit specific needs. For details, write or phone the office of the Kensington Special Sales Manager: Kensington Publishing Corp., 850 Third Avenue, New York, NY, 10022. Attn. Special Sales Department. Phone: 1-800-221-2647.

First Kensington Printing: April, 2001
10 9 8 7 6 5 4 3 2 1

Printed in the United States of America

1

The one-eyed Spaniard shoved the door with such force that it slammed against the inner wall. As he advanced into the room, lingering vibrations dislodged a stack of elaborate animal-head masks and sent them tumbling to the terra-cotta tiles. Undeterred, he continued on his course, passing within a hand's span of the pageant wagon in which Lora Tylney hid, trembling, fearful of discovery.

When the gaudily painted wood-and-canvas tower had been drawn into the great hall a few hours earlier, four golden-robed damsels had been inside. Now, while revelers throughout the palace and grounds enjoyed the subsequent banquets, dances, and masques Queen Mary had arranged to celebrate St. Mark's Day, only one chamberer sheltered within, crouched low and concealed by the thin walls and lightweight frame but convinced that if she so much as twitched, she'd cast a shadow or otherwise betray her presence. She was no innocent, terrified for her virtue, but neither did she intend to pleasure more than one man this night.

"I saw her come in here, Appleton." The Spaniard's slightly accented words slurred, betraying a recent consumption of inordinate quantities of Xeres sack. As Lora had reason to know, Diego Cordoba's features were handsome, in spite of the eye patch, but they already showed the effects of his dissipated life. His one good eye was bloodshot even when he was sober.

"Admirable wench." Robert Appleton pronounced each word with studied care, for he was also deep in his cups. "Think you she'll have us all?" Stumbling into the room after them were their boon companions—Pendennis and Marsdon, Elliott and Lord Robin.

"This doe set out to lure a herd of bucks." Cordoba chortled at his own bawdy fancy. He staggered a bit as he turned in a circle, surveying the contents of the cluttered, dimly lit storage room. " 'Tis plain she knows the surrender's sweeter after a chase."

Annoyance temporarily drove away the worst of Lora's trepidation. How could he say such things about her? Had it meant nothing to him that he had been her first lover? She continued to hold herself as still as possible, though pain lanced through her from a stitch in her side. She was short of breath from running so fast, and could do nothing to calm the frantic beating of her heart, which she feared was loud enough to betray her presence.

"Search everywhere," Lord Robin commanded. "If she's here, we will find her."

Pressing trembling fingers to her lips to hold back

any sound, Lora considered the chances of escaping rough handling tonight. Another time, she might have welcomed into her bed any one of the bold and lusty fellows who pursued her, but not all together, and not here. She was no common woman. She was a chamberer to Queen Mary. She had her standards.

"*Madre de Dios!*" Cordoba exclaimed.

Scarcely daring to breathe, Lora clasped her knees to her chest and buried her face in her arms. He sounded as if he were right on top of her hiding place. She could almost smell the sweet Spanish wine on his breath.

"What's amiss?" By his voice, Walter Pendennis was some distance from the pageant wagon.

"Thought I had her," Cordoba grumbled. " 'Tis a fine figure in a gown I've embraced, but all of terracotta and paint."

Closer at hand, someone started to laugh. Francis Elliott, Lora thought. Another handsome fellow, one who always wore stark black to contrast with his golden hair.

"Can you not tell the difference? My friend, if you cannot, then you are much the worse for drink."

"I'll know the woman when I hold her," Cordoba bragged. "She's softer than this."

Lora heard the thump of his hand against the costumed figure he'd captured. In her mind, she saw his fingers exploring her own contours, felt his wet mouth seeking hers. A little thrill ran through her. There was something about the Spaniard she could not help but find exciting even in these circumstances. If they stumbled upon her, perhaps she could persuade him that having her all to himself would be much sweeter than sharing. Could she convince him to send his friends away?

"I warrant our quarry's paps are softer," Appleton

declared in a loud voice. Lora heard a tinkling sound as he blundered into something decorated with bells.

"Aye. Nice and round and tasty. Ripe as new apples."

Cordoba had reason to know, since he'd been her lover for the last several weeks, but this bragging offended Lora. Her cheeks flamed as she buried her face deeper in the fabric of her sleeves.

The stiff material of the trim rustled softly at her slight movement. Lora's muscles tensed. Had they heard? The sound had seemed loud as a cannon shot to her. She expected to be dragged from her hiding place at any moment.

"Think you the Tylney lass superior to the king's mistress?" Lord Robin posed the question. Then someone tripped over yet another obstacle and swore loudly, almost drowning out the salacious chuckle that preceded Cordoba's answer.

"How are we to say? King Philip would have the head of any man he thought had made advances to his lady love. His wife, now—he'd gladly be spared bedding her."

Poor Queen Mary, Lora thought. She'd been a dried-up old maid of nearly forty when she'd married the king of Spain. He was eleven years her junior. 'Twas no surprise he looked outside the royal bedchamber for sport.

The screech of unoiled hinges warned Lora that one of the courtiers had opened a chest. Did he think to find her inside? If so, he was cup-shot indeed!

"Methinks Queen Mary has noticed how the king looks at her." The volume of Peregrine Marsdon's voice indicated that he was some distance away. Lora knew him less well than the others, but had often admired the breadth of his shoulders and the gentleness of his smile.

"Lora Tylney?" Cordoba sounded befuddled.

"The duchess," Appleton corrected him.

Not one of them was in full possession of his wits, Lora concluded, else they'd never carry on such a conversation. 'Twas dangerous to speak openly of the king's private concerns. Hope grew in her that they'd forget what they were looking for and wander off. Mayhap they would go and bother the duchess of Lorraine, she thought spitefully. Queen Mary had given her husband's alleged mistress apartments on the ground floor of nearby Westminster Palace, conveniently accessible from the gardens.

"As trim a pair of ankles as I've ever seen," Elliott declared. Once more a voice seemed to come from directly behind Lora's hiding place. She made a small, startled movement before she managed to hold herself still again.

"Aye," Pendennis agreed. "I noticed her ankles during the dancing. What color do you suppose her hair is?"

Lora caught her breath and held it. They kept catching her unaware, wandering back and forth as they were. Right now at least two of them were much too close.

Appleton muttered his answer. 'Who can tell with the absurd headdresses women wear? And what does it matter? All colors look the same in the dark."

"I am partial to dark-haired maidens," Pendennis said. "And I like to keep the candles lit."

"Maidens, is it? And where do you think to find a maid here at court?" Cordoba's sneering words irritated Lora all over again. She had been a maid until she met the dashing Diego. That she'd been as eager as he to change that state was irrelevant.

They might have remained there, debating the matter at length, had not a new voice, one unfamiliar to Lora and shaking with barely controlled anger, interrupted them. 'What business have you here, gentlemen? This is no place for your games.''

"Ah, Master Keeper," Lord Robin greeted the newcomer. "And you, sir? Do I not know you?"

"A humble clerk in the office of the Master of Revels," came the mumbled response. If the keeper was not shy about challenging his betters, his companion saw the folly in it.

But Lord Robin's reaction to being censured was mild. He merely complimented the keeper on the evening's diversions.

"Save your flattery, m'lord." Lora heard age in the voice now, as well as a certain testiness. "Best get you gone from here. The Master of Revels will not be pleased if any of these props or set pieces are damaged. Nor will the king."

No other argument could work so well as that one, Lora thought. Cordoba owed everything to his overlord and the Englishmen were all courtiers who'd come to court to curry favor with the Spaniard who'd wed their queen. They hoped to win back what they'd lost nearly four years earlier by siding with the late duke of Northumberland in his rebellion against her.

Aware that, for the moment, she was no longer being sought, and driven by an overwhelming curiosity, Lora crawled slowly toward the opening at the back of the mock tower. Meant to allow the pageant's damsels to enter unseen and remain hidden, it was covered by two velvet panels that hung without gaping. Cautiously, she reached out with both hands and parted the edges.

Two men were framed by the narrow opening. Appleton looked bleary-eyed and appeared to be a trifle bored. His tawny-colored velvet coat, decorated with strips of black satin, was sadly rumpled, and his hose were streaked with dust from the storeroom. Cordoba, nearly the same height but heavier, fiddled with a green satin eye patch that matched the sleeves attached to his green-and-gold doublet. Lora hoped the nervous gesture meant that he, too, was tired of the chase. She could not see the other courtiers, though she could hear them.

The keeper and the clerk proved no match for Lord Robin. Outnumbered and outranked by the courtiers, they soon departed. Then Cordoba began to turn and Lora hastily dropped the curtains back into place. Once again, she held her breath, hoping he'd not noticed the small movement.

"Presumptuous fellows," Appleton muttered.

"Say rather they are brave men," Pendennis argued. 'Willing to risk our wrath to protect those things in their keeping."

"I have no interest in these toys. I only want the woman."

"But our quarry seems to have eluded us, gentlemen." Elliott's deep and resonant tones made him sound less impaired by drink than the rest. 'While you spoke with the keeper, I discovered a back exit. Doubtless the lass slipped out that door just as we came in the other."

Lora waited in an agony of suspense. Would they believe she was gone? She heard more murmured words, then the blessed sound of retreating footsteps. The level of light diminished. A heavy door thudded closed.

Silence reigned in the cavernous storage room.

Cautiously, after waiting for what seemed an interminable time and hearing nothing more, Lora emerged from her hiding place. She moved toward the door, then stopped abruptly, startled, when it began to open.

Had it been a trick? Had they returned for her?

She'd already started to retreat in the direction of her former hiding place when a whispered voice called out. Her fear ebbed as she recognized it, vanished when she saw that he was alone.

"Your humble servant, m'lady." He made her a courtly bow.

"You need not m'lady me, sir," she said lightly. "I am only plain Mistress Tylney from Lincolnshire."

"It pleases me to think of you as my lady and, here in this setting, illusion must always take precedence over what is real."

When he reached for her, she went willingly into his arms. One man she could accommodate. But he only kissed her gently, then set her aside. Disappointed, she pouted. "Do I not please you?"

"Are you so eager to lie with me, mistress?"

She turned away, then cast a teasing glance at him over her shoulder. At the flash of intense emotion she saw in his eyes, she felt her own excitement increase.

"If you want me, I am yours." She moved closer to the tower. "In here. 'Twill be more comfortable than the hard terra-cotta tiles."

She heard him come up behind her, expected him to turn her in his arms and embrace her with a lover's enthusiasm. Instead, his forearm abruptly cut off her supply of air as it pressed into her throat.

With a horrifying certainly, she understood. He did not mean to make love to her. He intended to kill her.

A harsh whisper, close to her ear, was the last thing she heard before one abrupt movement snapped her neck.

"Whore," her murderer said. "No better than a Winchester goose."

2

Church bells pealed as Susanna, Lady Appleton, pointed to the patch of ground she wanted her gardener to till. She found herself counting until the dolorous ringing stopped at forty-one, the age of the person who lay dying in a nearby parish.

Susanna had been in London only a week, just long enough to learn to distinguish the bells of All Hallows in Honey Lane from those of St. Lawrence in the Old Jewry. With some one hundred churches in the city, there was nearly constant tolling. In time, she hoped to become accustomed to the clanging, and to other intrusive city noises. The constant din from beyond her gate disturbed her concentration. Street cries pierced the air from dawn till dusk, and the noise of carts rumbling by on Catte Street was well nigh deafening.

"Put the leek bed there, Lionel," she said in a brief respite from the clamor.

It would lie between the new-built trellis and the raised beds of her physic garden, in which she had already planted a few of the selected seeds she'd sent for from Leigh Abbey, the Appleton family seat in Kent. It was a gentlewoman's first duty to keep her household healthy and for that reason Susanna needed fresh supplies of a variety of medicinal herbs.

Lionel went to work with a will, using first a shovel and then his little four-pronged fork and a trowel. At seventeen, he was all angles and sharp corners beneath his heavy canvas apron. Susanna devoutly hoped he was through growing. She got a crick in her neck looking up at him now, and she was uncommon tall herself.

While he worked, Susanna surveyed the remainder of the garden she was restoring in the small yard behind the house her husband had leased. Both garden and house, a long, narrow, three-story building with a garret above, had been neglected after the death of their owner. His widow had retired to the country.

Fortunately, Robert had given Susanna enough warning of their impending move to London for her to send servants ahead. Three men and one woman had worked diligently for a fortnight to sweep out all the old rushes, wash the floors and walls, air the house, and put in supplies. Faggots and billets of wood and a cauldron of coal had been safely stored in the cellar by the time Susanna arrived with three more servants, one cat, and enough furniture to fill the house.

From Leigh Abbey had come everything from tapestry hangings and curtains to beds, chairs, and tables, to candles and candlesticks. In addition, Susanna had loaded two wagons with chests and boxes containing clothing, books, and her own herbs and potions. One look at this garden and she'd sent back at once for seeds and for Lionel, who had started as a gardener's boy some years before and worked his way up to the post of second gardener at Leigh Abbey.

Already the two of them had unearthed the remains of open beds, raised above the level of the path on oak boards. Rosemary still grew in among the bricks in the garden wall and there were signs that a central walk had once been bordered by low-growing lavender. If Susanna had her way, both plants would once again flourish here.

A frown darkened her features. There was not as much width as she'd like in this garden plan. Lionel would scarce have room to kneel on the path and reach into the beds and weed. She would have to pay him something extra, she decided, for the ache he was sure to have in his back when he was done. And provide him with a soothing poultice. One of catnip, perhaps. Or lady's slipper.

Susanna drew on a pair of three-fingered gloves to protect her hands from cuts and scrapes and reached for a digging tool. She did not mind getting dirty, but she had seen too many small injuries become infected through carelessness. She did not plan to die before her time.

As she unearthed weeds from an overgrown patch of ground, Susanna found signs that a few primroses, periwinkles, and violets had flowered the previous month. A single bluebell was just about to open and she saw that, with care, she might yet have a few cowslips and some broom. One of the surviving rosebushes was also hardy enough to flower, together with honeysuckle. There could be nothing sweeter, she thought, than the combination of scents of those two

flowers on an early morning in June. Perfect to help
dispel the appalling miasma that seemed to hang over
London, a pervasive stench made up of many parts,
none of which she was inclined to try to identify.

For all her delight in a pretty, pleasant-smelling
garden, however, Susanna put usefulness first. Some
of the herbs she would plant had odors fully as appalling as that coming from the kennels in front of each
householder's door. Other plants, though they were
aromatic when crushed, did naught to scent the air
in their natural state.

She frowned at the raised bed, where boards would
divide each plant from the next in separate squares.
Space was limited. She ran through the list of those
herbs she customarily grew for medicines and sighed.
There would be no room for them all. She would
have to send for supplies from home, and buy other
medicines from the apothecaries. That there were so
many apothecaries, offering a wide variety of both
herbal and chemical remedies, was one of the few
advantages she could think of to living in London.

Borage, she decided, could be sown this afternoon.
In June she would make conserves of the candied
petals, but before the plant flowered she would gather
leaves, using the green herb to make medicines. Borage was an ingredient in several soothing compounds.
One eased sore throats, another inflammations of the
eyes, and a third was good for itching. She would have
to send some of the latter to her friend Magdalen, who
was much troubled with skin rashes.

Susanna smiled to herself, thinking that perhaps
Magdalen would not suffer that affliction quite so
often now that her first, unsatisfactory husband had
shown the good sense to die and leave her free to
remarry. Henry, Lord Madderly, would not have been
Susanna's choice for a mate, had she found herself

in a similar situation, since with him came two wild-head sons, but Magdalen seemed content with her decision.

A sharp voice calling "Lady Appleton" and a jangling sound penetrated Susanna's reverie. She turned, startled, to see the plump and red-cheeked figure of her housekeeper hurrying toward her. From a ring at her waist hung keys to everything from the spice box to the front door. They bounced madly as Jennet advanced.

"Be careful!" Susanna called. The younger woman was about to trip over a gourd-shaped watering pot lying on the path.

Jennet gave a little hop to avoid it and continued on. "Someone has come to see Sir Robert." She took a moment to catch her breath. "A stranger."

Susanna lifted a questioning brow, knowing there must be a particular reason why Jennet had not simply told this person that Sir Robert Appleton was not at home.

" 'Tis a lady, madam. Wearing a visor."

Brows arching higher, Susanna waited for further disclosures. Women might choose to conceal their features for any number of reasons. Some wished to hide the ravages of disease. Poor Lady Sidney, who had nursed Queen Elizabeth through smallpox just last year, now had a face so horribly scarred that she could not bear to have anyone look upon it. Other respectable women, those who wished the freedom to attend an innyard performance of a play without being recognized, also went masked.

"She will not give her name." Jennet worried her lower lip with her teeth.

Though the words remained unspoken, it was clear Jennet thought their visitor was another of Robert's mistresses, like the woman who had arrived at Leigh

Abbey the previous winter with a babe in her arms, claiming the child was Robert's. Susanna's husband had at the time been out of the country, on a mission to Spain for the queen.

There had been a reason for Susanna to acknowledge the baby girl's paternity. She had therefore sent mother and child to live at Appleton Manor in Lancashire. Soon she would have to inform Robert, who had only recently returned to England, that he was a father.

"Show our visitor into my solar," Susanna instructed. "And offer her a little ale or some wine. I will come directly."

A good scrubbing would be necessary to remove the dirt from her face and beneath her fingernails. Susanna considered taking time to change into more formal attire, but decided that the loose-bodied gown she wore for comfort would have to do for this uninvited, unexpected caller. A fresh apron would cover the worst of the garden dirt.

As she washed at the hand pump in the yard, a single church bell tolled, signaling that death had come in the next parish. This ominous note underscored Susanna's one doubt about confronting the stranger. Would her interference create problems for Robert? Indeed it would if the woman were his mistress!

Susanna did not deceive herself. Robert had never been faithful to her. On the other hand, he'd always been courteous enough not to flaunt these illicit relationships. He did not bring his lemans into her home or even keep them in the same town.

There had been times during the nearly ten and a half years they'd been married when she had talked herself into being grateful to such women. Their services had allowed Susanna to maintain a civil friendship, at times even a partnership, with her husband. If she sometimes wished for more, she'd learned to still that foolish desire and channel her energies into more productive efforts.

Susanna gave herself a shake as she finished her ablutions. Best not to dwell on such things. Robert would never change. And there was a more likely reason why a mysterious visitor had turned up on their doorstep. Robert was one of the best of the queen's intelligence gatherers. On a few past occasions, Susanna had been helpful to him in his endeavors. That she might be so again had, in part, prompted her decision to speak with the masked woman who awaited her above.

If the stranger had come to deliver some secret into Robert's keeping, she might not like being confronted by his wife, but Susanna could see no alternative. This woman had come to Catte Street. Susanna had not sought her out. It was even possible Susanna was supposed to act as Robert's intermediary. That would certainly explain his unprecedented decision to lease a house.

In the past, he'd kept lodgings at court, or taken rooms in a nearby inn when his presence was required near the queen. Not only had Susanna never been asked to join him, she'd been discouraged from leaving Leigh Abbey. He'd seemed to prefer she stay in the country while he danced attendance on royalty.

Why, she wondered, did he suddenly wish to appear a devoted husband? A futile effort, most like, when it was no secret that her guardian had arranged their marriage.

A good wife would not question what her husband did, but even though Robert had been twenty-seven when they said their vows and Susanna nine years younger, she'd never been a biddable bride. She had an education to equal any man's and a mind of her own.

Still, she owed Robert loyalty. She knew from experience that he did nothing without a purpose. That purpose, most often, was to serve the queen. As Susanna climbed the narrow back stairs to her bedchamber, she just wished he would deign, once in a while, to share his plans with her.

Ignoring a looking glass, she quickly changed her apron, then ventured through a connecting door to the solar. The woman waiting for her there rose from the cushioned window seat and sketched a curtsey. Her only reaction to the fact that she was being greeted by the mistress of the house and not the master was a flash of surprise in the dark eyes behind the mask.

She was tiny, making Susanna feel like a giantess. Dark hair showed beneath her headdress, and her face was pale beneath the black half mask. Little else was visible. Gloves covered her hands, though she wore an ornate mourning ring on the outside of one. A widow? That seemed likely. Her cloak concealed the cut and condition of her clothing, but Susanna caught a glimpse of black fabric.

"My husband is not at home. May I be of assistance to you?"

"I think not." The woman's speech was soft, difficult to hear, but just those few words betrayed foreign birth. She was French, or perhaps a Fleming.

Her effort to leave was forestalled by Jennet's arrival with a tray heavy laden with food and drink.

"Come, madam. Let us be at ease together," Susanna invited. "You wished to speak to my husband, but he is not here. I do not know when he will return, but you are welcome to wait."

Reluctantly, the woman resumed her seat and

accepted a cup of ale. Jennet busied herself pouring, offering an array of sweets, anything that would allow her to remain in the solar.

Susanna waved her away. The woman might hesitate to confide her business with a third person in the room. She need not know Jennet would remain just on the other side of the door, her ear pressed to the oak paneling.

The stranger nibbled at a piece of marchpane, but she took nothing else and offered no explanation for her presence. Unnerved by her steady regard, Susanna reacted by staring back, her blue eyes boring into that darker gaze. Two could play at this game. After a few minutes, Susanna's guest betrayed her nervousness by crumbling the last piece of marchpane on her plate. The fine trembling in her hands indicated she might be afraid.

"You are troubled, madam." Susanna was not without sympathy. "Tell me how I may assist you and I will attempt to do so."

Instead of answering, the woman rose abruptly. "You cannot help me." Her voice was louder now, and husky, as if she might be in the throes of some deep emotional turmoil.

Susanna spoke to her departing back. "What shall I tell my husband when he returns?"

At the door the stranger turned. She lifted the visor briefly, to reveal an unmarked and very beautiful countenance beneath. "Tell him he will find me at the Falcon Inn near Paris Garden."

"And your name?" Susanna asked.

The visor fell back into place as its owner whispered her reply: *"Je m'appelle Diane."*

3

Only a matter of weeks, Sir Robert Appleton reminded himself as he dismounted and gave his horse to Fulke the groom to stable.

He glanced up at the house he'd leased from Lady Eastland, feeling a bitter sort of satisfaction that he'd managed to secure it. Although he'd have preferred to be in Milk Street or Bread Street, quiet enclaves of wealthy citizens near to but secluded from Cheapside, this would do. There was a nice irony in its location on the south side of Catte Street, just a stone's throw from the Guildhall, the center of city administration and the place where London's municipal courts met.

Only a matter of weeks, he thought again. Then he'd have everything he'd ever wanted. In the meantime, he had chosen to play the role of devoted husband.

A few minutes later he joined Susanna in the solar. His wife looked unusually domestic, sitting by the westward-facing window that she might catch the late afternoon sun while heming a pillow slip. She glanced up when he came through the door, her expression so bland that he was at once suspicious.

"Good afternoon, my dear," she said.

"Susanna."

Something had happened. Instead of asking questions, Robert gave himself time to think by crossing the room to a tapestry-covered table. A light repast awaited him there, but he ignored the cold meat and bread and poured himself a goblet of Rhenish wine, drinking half of it down before he turned to study his wife.

As she bent over her stitches, one errant lock of dark brown hair escaped from her embroidered cap. She never could keep it all tucked in.

Robert's gaze swept lower, noting that she'd dressed with unusual care, her attire more formal than was her wont when at home. In place of the loose-bodied gowns she preferred, she'd donned a tightly laced bodice and the matching kirtle, both of fine honey-colored damask. The sleeves were slashed and puffed to reveal the white silk layer she wore beneath. The same fabric, embroidered with bright flowers, showed through the forepart of the kirtle.

"You are dressed uncommon fine for housework," he commented.

"I am not likely to soil my garments with such trifling duties as you see me perform here." The sharp edge to her voice confirmed Robert's suspicion that something untoward had happened during his absence. He drained his goblet and refilled it.

In the days since Susanna had joined him in London, she had made no secret of her displeasure at being dragged away from her home. She did not care for cities, not for a stay of any length, and he knew it irked her not to be told how long they would be in residence here.

He had not informed her of a departure date because he did not know one, not for certain. Perhaps he should have explained that, but he did not like feeling accountable to his spouse.

By now, he'd expected her to demand to return home, or else accept her situation and become reasonably content. After all, here in London she had immediate access to all the books she could desire. The tiny yard behind the house contained a garden. She'd begun to restore it. One or two such projects, he'd thought, should serve to keep her busy and out of trouble.

Frowning, Robert continued to contemplate his wife. She studiously ignored him, pretending complete absorption in her needlework. The scene was so patently false that he had to bite back a chuckle. Susanna was a genius with herbs, but she had never had any skill at other domestic pursuits. Given a choice, she'd rather dig ditches than sew.

"Do we expect company?" he asked, still seeking an explanation for her finery.

"You have had company already."

So, something *had* happened while he'd been out. Someone. "Stop mangling that hem," he suggested, "and tell me what is on your mind."

"If you are so uncommon perceptive, perhaps you can guess." Her pale blue eyes briefly betrayed the intensity of her emotions as she tossed the needlework aside and met his penetrating gaze. Something had offended her, and made her angry, too.

Had she learned of his plans? No. Impossible. He played his cards too close to his chest.

With an effort, he kept his voice even. It did no good to lose his temper with Susanna. Though he hated to admit it, she was more than his match in any battle of wit and words.

"Even the most skillful intelligence gatherer must have some clue to begin with," he said. "Come, Susanna. Give me a hint as to what troubles you."

"A Frenchwoman came here asking for you today," she told him. "She said her name was Diane."

Robert froze in the act of pouring a goblet of wine for his wife. Here was a pretty pickle. The name was common enough, especially among Frenchwomen. In the last generation a great many young girls had been named for Diane de Poitiers, the French king's influential mistress. For all that, Robert had not a doubt in the world which Diane had arrived on his doorstep. He'd made a foolish offer, years ago, and it had just come home to roost.

"No surname?" he asked. Not that it mattered. The Diane he knew had never given him one.

"No."

"Describe her then, this woman who seeks me." He crossed the solar and sat next to Susanna on the window seat, handing her the goblet of wine.

"Short. Small of stature. Dark hair and eyes. Very pale skin. A beautiful face. A mourning ring." She sipped the Rhenish.

As he watched her, Robert could not help but make comparisons. The best that could be said for Susanna was that she was comely. She bore an unfortunate resemblance to her late father, having inherited his height and his sturdy build and his square jaw, as well. She was feminine enough, soft where a woman should be soft, and rounded in all the right places. He'd never had any difficulty performing a husband's duties. On the other hand, no one would ever make the mistake of thinking Susanna weak and in need of protection . . . as Diane was.

"Do you know her, Robert?" Her capable hands held the goblet in her lap, clasping it as if she feared to spill the contents did she not hold on tight.

"Only a little."

Skepticism lurked in Susanna's eyes when she lifted her head to stare at him. 'Twas obvious she thought Diane had been his mistress, but for once his conscience was clear. He met her gaze and held it.

"If this is the same Diane, I met her nearly four years ago. Do you recall my last mission to France, at the time when Walter Pendennis was in Paris?"

"How could I forget? You journeyed to France and I made my first visit to our lands in Lancashire."

Robert winced. He preferred not to think about that particular venture or its outcome. Better to focus on Diane. "I was sent to meet with a rebel leader named La Renaudie. He's dead now, poor fool. His mad scheme to take control of the French government never had much chance of success. But he had a mistress named Diane. A widow. La Renaudie and I met at her estate outside La Rochelle."

She'd spoken charmingly accented English, he recalled. And had she not been La Renaudie's woman, he'd have responded to the invitation in her dark eyes. But what did her reappearance in his life at this juncture mean? Simple coincidence? He hoped so, and hoped, too, that she would not make demands on him.

Just at present, he could ill afford to call undue attention to himself.

"La Rochelle was a Calvinist stronghold in those days," Susanna mused.

She understood much more of politics than was normal for a woman. Most of the time, her insight annoyed Robert. In this instance, he found it useful, saving him the trouble of long explanations of French intrigues. Susanna knew already that Catholic and Huguenot factions had spent the last few years trying to massacre one another.

"Before civil war broke out, La Rochelle was a safe refuge. I doubt it is now." He cleared his throat. "If this woman is the same Diane, I once told her she might come to me for assistance should she ever feel obliged to flee her homeland."

"It appears she has taken you up on your . . . generous offer."

"Aye." And her timing could not have been worse. He did not need such a complication. He heartily wished the woman would just disappear, but he supposed that was unlikely. "Did she say what she wanted from me? Money? Introductions?"

Susanna seemed edgy again and Robert wondered idly if she was jealous. He quickly discounted that notion. She'd never shown evidence of the emotion in the past. Most like she was put out because he'd refused to share his plans with her.

Truth be told, she'd disapprove of his current scheme for advancement. Mayhap she'd even attempt to thwart it.

After a pointed hesitation, Susanna answered his question. "She asked that you meet her at the Falcon Inn near Paris Garden."

The location surprised him. Paris Garden was in Southwark, at the edge of the most notorious brothel district in all of England.

"Will you visit her?" Her voice level, her expression unrevealing, Susanna again gave Robert the impression she hid her true feelings.

Once, he thought, he'd have teased and tormented her until she exploded, and likely they'd have ended up laughing at the absurdity of their quarrel, but over the last few years he'd found little humor in anything, and no advantage at all in relaxing his guard with his too intelligent, too perceptive wife. Although he wondered what she was thinking, he had neither the patience nor the inclination to coax her opinions out of her.

"I must try to help Diane," he said. "I doubt she has many friends in England."

"Doubtless she will soon find new ones."

"I met her on a mission for the queen," Robert reminded his wife, hating the defensive tone in his voice. " 'Tis my duty as a loyal subject to pursue this matter."

"A hardship, certes." Susanna no longer tried to hide her sarcasm. She knew that if he went to the Falcon Inn, he would stay the night.

And what if he did? It was not as if Susanna made him feel welcome in her bed.

Only a matter of weeks, he reminded himself again.

Turning his back on his wife, he left the solar without saying another word.

4

Susanna threw her needlework across the room.

What a fool she was! After all these years she should not care what Robert did. Much of the time she did not.

But today his behavior was surpassing bothersome. Meeting another woman who might be his mistress, the second in less than six months, seeing how beautiful they both were, upset her. Combined with Susanna's growing sense that she was being used in some way, that she'd been ordered to London for some nefarious purpose, a purpose Robert refused to share with her, Diane's visit had left her feeling both irritable and frustrated.

"Bodykins," she swore softly when she heard a door slam below. Robert had left the house.

It was not Susanna's way to indulge in self-pity, but just this once she allowed regrets to consume her. She despised waste. As a true partnership, what might she and Robert not have accomplished? Theirs could have been an intellectual union as well as a marital one.

But Robert valued the body more than the mind. He craved physical variety and condemned her that she could not share his enthusiasm. Worse, although he was quick to claim credit for solutions she reasoned out, he made no secret of the fact that he resented her intelligence.

More than once in the early days of their marriage, the women in the duke of Northumberland's household had advised Susanna to bend her will to her husband's, to let him lead her in all things, to hide the fact that she was better educated than he. Just fascinated enough by her handsome new spouse to try, she'd succeeded in naught but making herself miserable and unhappy.

It was not that she disliked physical union between them. That act had proven to possess its own compensations, once the first messy encounter was over with. When Robert began to stray, she'd believed the fault lay with her. But with the passage of time, Susanna had realized that her husband was the sort of man who would never be content with one woman, not even one he loved.

Love had never been part of the bargain.

Leigh Abbey had won his heart. And the lands and revenues that went with it. He did not disdain the earnings from Susanna's herbals either, though he'd had naught to do with producing them.

She still remembered, with some bitterness, the reaction he'd had to her second venture, *The Great Herbal*, a compendium of herbs and their uses. On this one, her name had been listed as compiler, along with the names of three other women. A mistake, Robert had said. What man would respect a scholarly work if he knew it had been written by females? Better, he'd claimed, to remain anonymous, as she had with her first book, *A Cautionary Herbal*.

Better, she'd said, to have taken full credit for that one. She was proud of the work she'd done to warn housewives and cooks of the dangers of using certain plants in food and medicines. For all she knew, Susanna thought now, Robert had convinced her to use initials so he could claim he was "S. A.," author of a book on poisonous herbs.

Disgusted with herself for dwelling on such thoughts, knowing that regrets availed her nothing, Susanna abruptly left the solar for her bedchamber. She called for Jennet as she went, to help her change her clothing. There was work still to be done in the garden, hard honest work that would occupy both her mind and her body. Let Robert go to his mistress! She had better things to do than brood.

5

Robert dismissed his wife from his thoughts as soon as he left the house. Turning east, he strode rapidly past the fair, large church of St. Lawrence Jewry, the entrance to the Guildhall, and Bakewell Hall, the market for London's woolen trade.

Walking was not Robert's preferred way to travel, but today he'd been to Westminster and back already. Vanguard, his horse, deserved a rest. Besides, he did not want to call attention to himself. For that same reason, he instinctively chose a less direct route to Paris Garden.

It would have been quickest to go west, then south, hailing a wherry at Puddle Dock. Instead he turned south on Ironmonger Lane, which shortly brought him to the Great Conduit. Water carriers surrounded it, filling their butter-churn-shaped wooden casks from the outlets, vying for space with goodwives and apprentices. Inside the high, round building, an iron-bound lead cistern held water piped in from Tyburn.

Crowds surged all around as Robert circled the conduit and proceeded eastward along the wide cobbled street. Here the air was redolent of spices from nearby shops, for both grocers and apothecaries inhabited this part of London. That made him think of Susanna again. Why could she not be pleased to be here in the city? Was he not providing her with the opportunity to meet other herbalists? She should be grateful.

The quality of the air rapidly diminished again as he descended through the Poultry toward the Stocks Market. For a brief stretch, as he turned south on Walbrook Street, skinners' shops abounded.

It was no improvement to draw closer to the river. The Thames had an offensive aroma all its own. When he came in sight of the docks, the Steelyard, Dowgate, and the Wine Wharf, Robert glanced east toward London Bridge. He might walk across it into Southwark, but that would mean a long trek on foot on the other side. He turned west instead, entering the garlic market and passing by tenements that crowded the north side of Thames Street.

"Hot mutton pies!" a boy cried out, catching his attention.

Another lad called, "Hot oatcakes."

It occurred to Robert that he was hungry, and straight ahead, beyond Queenhithe, were cookshops. Diane could wait a bit longer.

By the time Robert hired a boat to take him across the river to Bankside, it was dusk. The best time to visit the stews, he thought. From the water, the area looked much as he remembered.

He'd not had any reason in recent times to resort to hired women, but years ago he'd been a frequent visitor. Back in the days when Queen Mary had sat on England's throne, the young bloods of the court had made many a nocturnal foray into Southwark. Robert had fond memories of one house in particular, the Sign of the Smock, where the whores possessed most inventive repertoires.

Paris Garden lay at the western end of Bankside, almost in the open countryside beyond. Paris Garden Stairs were situated between that same Sign of the Smock and the Falcon Inn. Unlike most of its neighbors, the inn was only what it claimed to be.

Robert entered the large parlor and surveyed a familiar scene. Blue-coated boys served wine in glasses and ale in tankards under the supervision of a hostess. At some tables, dice or cards shared space with food and drink. Pausing only long enough to make sure no one was paying him any particular attention, Robert found the stairs. Diane would be in one of the private rooms above.

He did not have time for French plots and counterplots, he reminded himself. All his hopes now resided in a different direction. He would find out what Diane wanted, deal with her, and return home.

He rapped sharply on the elmwood door.

As if she had been watching for him, Diane opened it at once. She was more attractive than he remembered. She'd been young four years ago, he recalled. Now her beauty had matured into something fuller and more compelling.

"*Ma belle,*" he said. " 'Tis good to see you looking so well."

She held out one slender white hand. In a throaty purr, she invited him inside.

6

"Madam?" Jennet stuck her head through the door and, seeing Lady Appleton was alone in the solar, came in. "Is there aught I can do for you?"

Though it was now long after dark, Sir Robert had not returned home. Jennet's mistress had occupied herself in the garden after his departure, coming inside to sup only after the light faded. Now she sat in the dim light of a single candle, no needlework to occupy her hands, no book open before her. Jennet had rarely seen her so broody.

"Come and sit beside me," Lady Appleton bade her. "Keep me from mine own thoughts."

"Are they so troubling?" Jennet complied with her wishes, settling herself comfortably on the wide window seat. The cat, from one of Dame Cat's litters and bearing the name Ginger for her coloring, hopped up beside them, curling once about herself before she settled down to sleep. Jennet absentmindedly rested her hand on the soft fur, finding the steady rise and fall beneath her palm more soothing than a draught of Lady Appleton's daily elixir.

"Troubling?" Lady Appleton repeated. She turned to face Jennet on the window seat, drawing her legs up and resting her hands on her knees as she leaned back against the side of the recessed casement. "Say rather, tempting. I have been thinking about a spell I once read of, a spell for a wedding day. Someone among the guests secretly knots a leather cord in a certain way during the ceremony and utters these words: 'Whom God hath joined together, let the devil separate.' This is said to cause impotence."

Jennet felt her eyes widen. Her mistress was in a strange mood, indeed, not only in contemplating magic, but in speaking of such forbidden things aloud. "What wickedness! And is that not witchcraft, besides?"

"Oh, yes, especially now that we have a new law against sorcery."

Uncertain, Jennet said nothing. It had always been dangerous to dabble in spells. Potions, now, they were another matter.

"This incantation would save many a wife much trouble," Lady Appleton pointed out, "and spare her the bother of children, as well."

"I'd not want to keep my Mark from his pleasure, nor myself, neither!" Jennet exclaimed. She felt color rush into her cheeks as soon as the words were out.

Lady Appleton chuckled. "You are a fortunate woman, Jennet. You married a man of your own choosing."

Jennet looked down at the hand still stroking Ginger as a small, secretive smile played about her lips. Yes, she was happy in her choice. Mark had proven himself a prince among men. Even when she'd told him she intended to travel to London with their mistress, and that she did not want to take the children with her, he'd not argued. Instead he'd arranged for his sister to come and look after them while she was gone.

She missed them more than she'd thought she would. The eldest had been named Susanna and was Lady Appleton's godchild. The second girl was named for Catherine, Lady Glenelg. Jennet's third child, a boy, dutifully named Robert, was still in swaddling clothes.

" 'Twould almost be worth the price of another babe to share a bed with Mark again,'' she murmured.

"There are ways to prevent conception," Lady Appleton announced.

Startled, Jennet gaped at her mistress. Close as the two of them had been over the last few years, they had never discussed anything this personal before.

"Some," Lady Appleton continued, using her most matter-of-fact voice, "are said not to diminish the pleasures of lovemaking for either husband or wife. The great physician Maimonides wrote of a two-step process. Before the act, the man must anoint his pintle with the juice of an onion, or wood tar, or the gallbladder of a chicken. Afterward, the woman must insert inside herself a suppository made with juice of peppermint, or with pennyroyal, or with seeds of leek." Her brow furrowed. "I would advise against using pennyroyal, I do think. The wrong amount might cause much damage."

Ask Mark to rub an onion on his man's yard? Jennet could not imagine herself suggesting such a thing, let alone Mark doing it. "I do not think I—"

"You need not be embarrassed, Jennet," Lady Appleton said. "Knowledge is a good thing." Then she fell into what Jennet privately called her lecturing tone and continued to share the fruits of her research.

"All manner of mixtures have been used by women through the ages in attempts to keep the size of their families small. Some have no effect at all. Some do harm. Beware of potions containing wormwood."

Jennet's initial embarrassment faded, replaced by curiosity. "Do any of these remedies work?" she heard herself ask.

"Some say a mixture of one obol of rocket and one-half obol of cow parsnip, drunk with oxymel, will prevent conception. Oxymel is a vinegar-and-honey mixture."

This was but a recipe for an ailment of an intimate nature, Jennet told herself. No harm in that. But an obol was quite a lot. It took eight drams to make one, and each dram was the weight of sixty grains.

"One might also make pills the size of a bean for this purpose, out of myrtle, wallflowers, and bitter lupines in equal quantities, mixed with water." Lady Appleton smiled at her housekeeper. "These pills are said to be most effective, but I'd not wish to experiment on a friend."

Jennet's answering smile was halfhearted.

"The same is true of a mixture made of three drachmas of rue leaves, two drachmas of myrtle, and two drachmas of laurel mixed with wine."

Six obols to a drachma, Jennet recalled. "I'd not drink that much of anything but beer or ale," she said in a firm voice.

"If you do not wish to use potions at all, there is still one simple way to avoid conception. Insist that Mark spill his seed on the bedclothes. 'Tis messy, but better than breeding too often."

A little silence fell between them.

"I cannot regret having had my children," Jennet said, "though 'tis a great pleasure to be away from them this little while."

"And I must confess," Lady Appleton confided, "that I have never had any great desire for motherhood." She seemed to read Jennet's thoughts in her face. "No, Jennet, I have done nothing to prevent it. In truth, there are times when I feel I have failed in my duty to my husband because I have not given him an heir."

In Jennet's view, Sir Robert's failing was greater. A faithful wife deserved a faithful husband. She did not say so, nor did she admit that she'd once thought Lady Appleton's daily elixir a potion to keep her from breeding. She'd long since learned that mixture was no more than a healthful tonic, an infusion made of chamomile, St. John's wort, and gingerroot.

"I have done naught to change God's will when it comes to having children," Lady Appleton said, her voice sad. "Neither to prevent my chances of conception nor to increase them."

Jennet was already aware that there were ways to increase fertility, but she could not contain a shudder at the thought.

Noticing, Lady Appleton chuckled and shook off her melancholy mood. "Neither of us, I do think, have need or inclination to speak of the treatments for barrenness. Let us raid the cook's store of comfits instead. I have a sudden craving to taste something sweet."

7

Susanna stared at the scrap of paper a burly constable pressed into her hand. Dismay suffused her features as she absorbed what he'd just told her. A woman's body had been found near Paris Garden.

"You say this writing was in her cloak?"

"Aye. In 'er pocket. Soon as 'e read that, crowner's clerk sent me 'ere straight away." He used the old term for coroner, which might have amused Susanna here in modern London if the neatly written words had not directed the bearer to Sir George Eastland's house in Catte Street.

"My husband did but lately lease this property from Sir George's widow," she told the constable, a short, red-haired fellow of indeterminate years, his only claim to distinction a great beak of a nose that had been broken more than once.

"Is 'e at 'ome, then, madam? Mayhap 'e could come and 'ave a look at 'er. Clerk said to fetch what person do live 'ere to see if 'e knows who she be." He'd doffed his hat when she came to greet him and now mangled it between his hands as he spoke.

"My husband has gone ahead to church," Susanna lied. Believable enough. It was Sunday morning. She had been about to walk to St. Lawrence Jewry herself. The truth, however, was that Robert had not returned to Catte Street the previous night, and for that reason news of a dead woman in Southwark made Susanna uneasy.

"The victim. What does she look like?"

"She were dead, madam."

"Her hair, sirrah? What color is it? How tall was she?"

The constable's face blazed bright as his unkempt locks. He mumbled something Susanna did not quite catch, though it sounded like a name. Petronella.

"Do you mean to tell me you know who she is?"

"Nay, madam. Only that she do resemble . . . some-one. Dark 'aired, they be. And little." Running a dirty thumb under his collar, the constable tried to peer into the house. " 'Ave you no man to send for your 'usband, madam? Crowners clerk, 'e'll be wanting to move 'er from where she fell."

The image of a dead woman left lying in the street, where her body could be gawked at by all and sundry, spurred Susanna to a decision. Someone must go, and quickly, for decency's sake.

And if the little, dark-haired woman was Diane? Susanna reasoned that she would cross that bridge when she came to it.

"I will accompany you to Southwark," she informed the waiting constable. "Jennet!" she called over her shoulder. "Fetch my cloak and bring your own."

A short time later, attended by Fulke as well as Jennet, Susanna followed the constable through London's Sunday morning bustle. Her mind raced ahead to what she would find on the other side of the river. No one but the mysterious Diane was likely to have had a paper with Robert's address written upon it. If Diane was dead, what should Susanna do?

Diane had come to Robert for help. Susanna had wondered at the time if the other woman was afraid of something. If she had been slain, it followed that what she had feared had come to pass, and further that if she had asked Robert for protection, he had failed her. To Susanna's way of thinking, that made it the Appletons' responsibility to find out what had happened to her and why, and if possible to see this wrong righted.

As she stepped aboard a wherry for the final leg of the journey to Southwark, and the constable once more expressed his reluctance to take a gentlewoman to the scene of the crime, Susanna was forced to turn her thoughts to Robert's whereabouts. Where was he now? More to the point, where had he been last night? If he had gone to visit Diane, as Susanna supposed he had, he might have been the last person to see the Frenchwoman alive.

Except for her killer.

Unless Robert was—

Susanna attempted to censor that line of inquiry, to assure herself that although Robert might have done many unpleasant things in his time, he was not a murderer. And yet, common sense forced her to be realistic. Anyone could kill, given adequate provocation. She did not know enough about what had happened to Diane to draw any conclusions.

She did not even know for certain that the victim was Diane. As the constable led them past disreputable-looking tenements and lodgings interspersed with a sprinkling of alehouses and taverns, she clung to the faint hope it was not.

Winding dirt alleys crisscrossed narrow streets surfaced with mortar and oyster shells. Up ahead, in single file, a ragtag band of men, twelve in number, came out from between two tall buildings.

"Crowner's jury," the constable said.

A crowd had gathered at the end of the alley, held back by two more constables and a bailiff. Avid, they shouted questions at the jurors and stared as a gentleman emerged from the same location and hurried off without even looking in Susanna's direction.

"Crowner," the constable said. "Master Speedwell. 'E likes to live up to 'is name."

The constable gestured for Susanna, Jennet, and Fulke to precede him into the narrow passageway that had just been vacated. A man she took to be the coroner's clerk waited there, a tall, lanky fellow, clean shaven, with a mole at the side of his nose and a tablet appended to his belt. He moved aside, revealing the body.

Diane was no longer beautiful. Someone had snapped her neck, then dropped her like a broken toy. Marks on her cheeks and forehead indicated she'd fallen face down into the refuse that littered this shortcut between streets.

Pity overwhelmed every other emotion as Susanna moved closer. Whatever the Frenchwoman had been in life, she deserved better than to be foully murdered in an alley.

"Do you know her, madam?" the clerk asked.

"Her name was Diane."

He wrote that down. "The surname?"

Susanna did not know, but she did not think it wise to say so. Someone had killed the woman Robert had been on his way to meet when Susanna had last seen him. Too many possibilities occurred to her because of those facts, none of them pleasant.

A jealous lover, finding Robert and Diane together, could have killed them both. But why leave Diane's body here? And where was Robert's?

She discounted that explanation as unlikely.

Still, Robert had doubtless spent the night in Southwark with Diane. If she revealed that assumption, her husband would become a suspect in Diane's murder. Innocent or guilty, an investigation would hurt his standing at court. She was not willing to wreck all his hopes of future advancement on the basis of supposition.

Could he have killed Diane? What if they'd had a lovers' quarrel?

Susanna forced herself to consider the question rationally, fighting down the emotions that roiled within her. Robert was her husband. She might not love him, might not even like him very much, but she owed him her loyalty, her trust.

And she did much doubt he had the stomach for murder.

Whoever had killed Diane appeared to have come up behind her and snapped her neck. She could not imagine Robert doing that. And surely, if he had, he'd have been more clever at disposing of the body.

Still, he might somehow be tied to the crime. He had known Diane in France, when she'd been involved in a treasonous conspiracy. Susanna abruptly decided that revealing the dead woman's foreign birth would be a mistake. So would encouraging any sort of speculation by the authorities.

"Madam?" The clerk sounded impatient. "Do you know her surname?"

"Aye," she replied, following her instincts. " 'Tis Leigh."

Jennet gave a little gasp of surprise, for that was Susanna's own family name, but the housekeeper said nothing to contradict her mistress. Fulke remained stone-faced, staring in fascination at the dead woman lying in the narrow lane.

Committed to the lie, Susanna elaborated. "She was my distant cousin and a gentlewoman. I will take responsibility for her burial. Where may I hire bearers to carry her back to the parish of St. Lawrence Jewry?"

"There are certain details to be seen to first," the clerk reminded her.

"Let them be seen to, then." She assumed an imperious air. From sad experience, she knew something of the procedure. "Where has the coroner gone? When will he return?"

"He is finished here," the clerk said. "Master Speedwell summoned twelve good men and true immediately upon examining the body. They have declared this was most foul murder by persons unknown."

The coroner had not shown himself to be efficient, simply expedient. Susanna was not surprised by his behavior. She knew coroners were paid from the estates of convicted murderers. If there was no apparent killer, it was likely he'd receive nothing, and although he was required by law to examine the body, call an inquest, and deliver a verdict, it was to his advantage to dispense with the formalities as rapidly as possible.

Susanna surveyed the assorted gawkers assembled in the street. A few bold women ranged among them, as avid for a glimpse of someone else's misfortune as any man. She wondered why they were not in church. Everyone was supposed to attend services in his or her own parish church every Sunday or pay a fine of one shilling for each absence.

"Did any of those good folk see what happened here?" she asked.

"Nay, madam. Layabouts and beggars all. And worse." The clerk motioned to the redheaded constable to disperse them.

Susanna wondered if anyone had bothered to look for witnesses. And unless pressure was put on the authorities by Robert or some other gentleman, little more was likely be done. Susanna could not influence matters. Not directly. As a married woman she had no legal standing.

But she could ask more questions.

"Is it possible my cousin was the victim of footpads?" These surroundings suggested it. This narrow passage must have been very dark just before dawn. Little sun reached into it even now, only enough to reveal the body and the filth and clutter that littered the ground.

Something pale caught her eye and she stooped to pick up a long white feather lying near Diane's leather-shod feet. A quill from a goose. A quick survey of her surroundings told Susanna there were no more in the vicinity, and she'd not encountered many city dwellers who troubled to keep their own flocks of poultry.

"Footpads would have taken that ring," the clerk said. Diane still wore the mourning ring Susanna had noticed the previous day. "And likely her clothing, as well."

And left a feather? Susanna slipped the quill into the pocket in her cloak, meaning to examine it later.

The clerk stroked his chin in an attempt to make himself seem more important than he was. The gesture, Susanna thought, would have been more effective if he'd had a beard.

" 'Tis only luck she was not robbed," he said. "Someone else might easily have come by after her killer left, had not she been found so quick by the watch. Just past dawn," he added. "Constable thought she was drunk at first."

Susanna fixed him with a hard stare. "Why would he assume that?"

"Look around you, madam. This is Bankside. Half the buildings hereabout are tugging houses."

Brothels.

Jennet moved a little closer to Fulke, fastidiously lifting her skirt and petticoat as if to avoid any chance contamination. Even Susanna was startled into saying the first thing that came into her mind.

"Can your men not tell a gentlewoman by her dress?" Diane's garments were of fine black brocade trimmed with lace and silk braid.

"Some whores hereabout have better than this."

More curious than repulsed by the man's frankness, Susanna looked out of the alley and across the wider street to the signs on the whitewashed buildings. One showed a woman's smock. Another featured a cardinal's hat. She blinked and looked again. On closer inspection, the distinctive pink hat bore a striking resemblance to the tip of a man's pintle.

"If this area is . . . active through the night," she mused, "then there is a chance that someone did see what befell my cousin. Can no one question the inhabitants? Ask if anyone saw what manner of man killed her?"

"Not likely they'd tell anyone even if they did, madam." The coroner's clerk sounded resigned.

"So, you do not intend to look for my cousin's murderer?"

"She was in a bad neighborhood and was mistaken for a prostitute," he said bluntly. The unspoken message was clear—the investigation had ended the moment Susanna gave the body a name and claimed it.

From the remaining onlookers, the clerk recruited two stout fellows to serve as litter bearers. It was then that Susanna noticed one figure standing a little apart from the others. Susanna blinked. For a moment she'd thought she was looking at the dead woman come to life again.

Of the same physical type, the stranger also shared Diane's dark hair and eyes. On closer inspection, however, Susanna saw that this woman had a much plainer face, and her clothing, though of similar quality to Diane's, was brightly colored. With another jolt, Susanna abruptly comprehended that the subject of her scrutiny was one of the neighborhood's whores.

Fascinated, Susanna narrowed her eyes and stared harder. As if the woman sensed someone's intense interest and was made uncomfortable by it, she turned and walked swiftly away. Susanna watched her until she went into one of the houses, the one that bore the sign with the smock.

The constable's earlier comment came back to her. He'd thought Diane was someone else at first. Someone named Petronella. Had that been she?

"We are ready, Lady Appleton," Fulke announced, bringing her attention back to Diane's body. Someone had found a dagswain blanket to wrap it in and a door for it to lie upon.

She would prepare Diane's body for burial with her own hands, Susanna decided, and make arrangements for a proper interment in the parish churchyard. Then, if it lay within her power, she would do more.

She would learn Diane's real surname, that a memorial brass might be inscribed with it. She would try to discover why Diane had been killed. And, if she could find a way to identify the killer, she would bring that person to justice, whoever he might be.

Susanna's expression was grim as she left the alley to follow after the makeshift bier. She would have to begin her investigation by questioning her own husband. She did not look forward to the prospect.

8

The woman who called herself Petronella watched from an upper window as the little procession made its way along Maiden Lane. In the near distance she could just hear the commotion of the crowd beginning to gather to watch exhibitions of bear and bull baiting in the amphitheater in Paris Garden. The chief matches were held on Sundays and later, when spectators grew to be a thousand strong, shouts of "Now, bull!" and "Now, dog!" and " 'Ware horns, ho!" would carry plainly to the Sign of the Smock.

Petronella had gone to inspect the victim upon hearing her general description. This was the second small, black-haired woman she knew to have been murdered in Southwark. In both cases, the victim's neck had been broken.

She shivered, well aware of their resemblance to herself. She knew, too, that to be murdered was not an uncommon fate for one in her profession. The patrons of this house were of a better sort than those who visited some other places at Bankside, but they were men, men who often consumed excessive amounts of drink, and for their coin they expected much. Too much, on occasion. All men reacted badly to being refused.

How long ago had that other woman died? Petronella tried to remember. Before or after Easter? After, she was sure. In fact, she thought it had been just about a year ago when the whore who'd styled herself Ambrosia La Petite had been killed. She'd complained of feeling she was being watched for weeks before her death. Her friends had laughed at her. Certes, she was watched, they'd mocked. She'd be a failure in her profession if men did not look at her.

In the last few days, though, Petronella had known that same sensation, a prickling at the nape of her neck at unexpected moments, the sense that malevolent eyes followed her. She tried to tell herself she was no common woman. Not now that the Sign of the Smock was hers. It had been left to her by her godmother three years earlier, and Petronella, even when she'd been plain Molly Bainbridge, had always been allowed to pick and choose her clients.

The woman they'd just taken away had not been employed in any of the brothels hereabout. She had not been in the profession at all. Had she been killed by mistake? The possibility that Petronella herself had been the intended victim was not pleasant to contemplate.

There was no protection if someone was stalking her. She knew that, just as she knew that the authorities never much troubled themselves to investigate the deaths of Southwark prostitutes. She could deal with her fear by staying indoors, but her house was not that secure. By the very nature of her business, she nightly invited strangers onto the premises.

And what if the murderer was not a stranger? What if he were someone she knew, perhaps knew very well? Her hand crept to her throat, fingering the hard, cold amethysts in her necklace as if they were beads in a rosary. She willed a measure of calm to return. A murder had taken place. A stranger lay dead. 'Twas no business of hers. That two murdered women had resembled the bawd at the Sign of the Smock, why, that was surely naught but gruesome coincidence.

Petronella gasped at the sound of a light knock at her bedchamber door. The man on the other side did not wait for her to bid him come in, but entered assured of his welcome, a bold smile on his dark face and a sensual gleam in his eye. When he took her in his arms, his kiss seared her, making her heart pound and her breath come faster, and for a little while she forgot everything but him.

It was always so with this man. He affected her as no other ever had. They dispensed with their clothing quickly and fell into her big four-post bed. With the ease of old lovers, they passed the next hour in most pleasurable sport. But when he lay well satisfied beside her, he seemed to sense her preoccupation. He propped himself up on one elbow to gaze into her eyes.

"Something troubles you." It was not a question.

She sighed. He knew her too well. "A woman was murdered near here during the night. Her neck broken."

"A pity. And yet such things happen."

"There was another woman murdered that same way about a year ago. And these two women were both small. Both dark. Either could have been mistaken for me. I think, perhaps, this woman today may have died in my place."

"Madre de Dios."

"Aye." She caressed his forearm. So strong, her handsome, one-eyed Spaniard. Strong enough to kill.

She hastily repressed the thought. Why would Diego want to kill her? Why would he want to kill anyone? But it was obvious that her revelation had disturbed him. He was scowling quite fiercely.

"Tell me all you know about these women. Why you think you are in danger." He spoke with only the slightest trace of an accent, for he had lived in England for many years.

"One was a whore. The other a stranger, but mayhap of good birth. By her dress, 'twas a gentlewoman who claimed her body."

"Identities?"

"For this morning's victim, I know not. The other was Ambrosia La Petite." She tried to smile at the fact that Mistress La Petite had chosen her professional name on the basis of her build.

She thought Diego would laugh, that he would find a way to talk her out of her fear. "Today is St. Mark's Day," he said instead.

"Aye." The twenty-fifth day of April. "What of it?"

" 'Tis a date seared in my memory. Think, little one, was it exactly a year ago that the other woman died?"

"It could have been. I do not remember."

He stood and began to dress, his manner distracted and his movements erratic. When he was clothed save for his boots, he went to stand at the window and stare morosely down at the street. Petronella could feel his uncertainty from across the room as she began to struggle into her own clothing.

"You must tell me what troubles you, Diego." She came up beside him and turned so that he could tie the laces that held her sleeves to her bodice.

When he had attended to her, Diego seated himself in the room's single chair, a sturdy box-seated, joined piece of furniture padded with a squab cushion. As he pulled on his high leather boots, he spoke without looking at her.

"I knew a woman once. Years ago, when King Philip shared this country's throne with Queen Mary. I was her first lover. Lora looked a good deal like you, with dark hair and dark eyes and pale skin. She was tiny, so small I could span her waist with my hands."

Petronella did not like this talk of another lover. She frowned into a small polished metal mirror on a stand as she used the reflection to adjust her neck ruff. "What happened to her?"

"She was murdered in Whitehall Palace. Her neck was broken." Abruptly Diego stood. He stared hard at Petronella with his one good eye. The other was covered by a black velvet eye patch. "The murder took place on St. Mark's Day."

A chill passed through her. Two women. Both murdered on St. Mark's Day. And with Ambrosia, perhaps a third. "You think these women were slain by the same hand?"

"I think you believe it, do you not, *querida*? But if 'tis true, then you are no longer in danger."

"Not for another year," she whispered, following his logic. So much for her hope that he would make light of her fears.

He paused in the act of pushing a previously missed doublet button through its hole. " 'Tis not your time yet, nor mine to lose you."

The comment increased her uneasiness, but piqued her curiosity. "Was the woman at court a whore?"

"She was a chamberer to the queen."

Another question occurred to her. "How could

someone be killed at the royal court and no murderer caught?"

"There were reasons no one looked very diligently." A long pause ensued. Then Diego seemed to speak more to himself than to her. "Lora's death changed me."

Petronella felt her uneasiness return, but she told herself that Diego's feelings for a long-dead woman were not her concern. And in her profession, she could not afford to feel any emotion, least of all jealousy. She had learned long ago that the only way a woman could gain control of her own destiny was to avoid becoming attached to any one man. Diego was the best of his kind, but he was naught but a paying customer. To allow herself to dream he could become anything beyond that was the worst kind of folly.

9

Sir Robert Appleton traveled by water downriver from Durham House, the Spanish ambassador's residence, to Blackfriars Stairs. Once a great friary, before King Henry dissolved all the religious houses, the enclosed precinct now housed tenements, private houses, and shops. Sir Walter Pendennis's lodgings were in what had once been the friars' buttery. Robert entered from the former cloister, passing through a door near its north end, and climbed narrow stairs to the two upper rooms his old friend used when in London.

Pendennis sat at a writing table, reading what appeared to be a lengthy message. He glanced up when Robert entered, cast a speculative look his way, and went back to his task without speaking. Robert poured himself a cup of ale from the jug on the table by the window, then turned to study the other man.

Pendennis had a new hat, a fantastic creation of buff-colored doeskin slashed to reveal salmon-colored satin and decorated with a braid band and an embroidered badge. Robert was not close enough to see what design had been worked upon the latter, but he'd wager 'twas both intricate and beautiful. His friend had a weakness for fancy clothes.

Before they'd embarked on their present employment, providing invaluable services to the queen, unfortunately for little reward, Robert Appleton and Walter Pendennis had been young men together in the household of John Dudley, the nobleman who'd eventually become duke of Northumberland, then been executed for treason because he'd tried to prevent Queen Mary from succeeding her brother Edward to the throne of England. Northumberland had meant to disinherit Elizabeth, too.

How would it have been if he'd succeeded? Robert often wondered. The duke had wanted to proclaim a royal cousin, the Lady Jane, queen in Mary's stead. Most conveniently, that young woman had been the wife of Lord Guildford Dudley, Northumberland's son. As king, he'd have advanced his friends, including Robert. Privy Council? The peerage?

Thwarted ambition made Robert bitter as he swallowed his drink. He studied Pendennis again with a speculative gaze. It was not so easy to read him as it once had been, but Robert supposed that was true of most of them who'd survived. Pendennis. Himself. Francis Elliott. Peregrine Marsdon. And Lord Guildford's brother, Lord Robin.

Pendennis refolded the paper he'd been perusing and tipped back in his chair. "What brings you to Blackfriars at such an early hour?" he asked, blunt as always.

"Diane St. Cyr." He knew her surname now, for all the good it did him. He also knew considerably more about her relationship with La Renaudie.

Pendennis did not blink.

"She said you were the one who told her where to find me."

"Aye. Yesterday. She came to me looking for you. A contact in Paris provided her with my direction. She would not say what she wanted, only that she preferred to deal with . . . an old friend." He looked wryly amused. "And find you she did, it would seem. What did she want?"

"Of that I am still uncertain. She spoke of her need for money. Asked for a loan, claiming to be destitute, though she had good clothing spilling out of the traveling trunk in her chamber and could afford to demand wax candles of the innkeeper. She hinted at wanting introductions at court, as if she sought a patron or a powerful lover."

"Did you oblige her?"

A double meaning there, Robert thought, but let the barb pass. "I promised to consider her request. In truth, I did wonder if she might be in England hoping to beg, borrow, or steal weapons for the Huguenot cause."

"Or money for the same?"

"Aye."

"I doubt we will ever know now." Pendennis indicated the folded letter. "She is dead. Murdered. Her body was found just after dawn. Only a short time, I think, after you left her bed."

Robert threw himself into the Glastonbury chair that was the only truly comfortable piece of furniture in Pendennis's rooms. He did not like the sound of this. "Did anyone else know she'd come looking for me?" he asked.

"Francis Elliott was with me when she arrived," Pendennis told him. "He offered to help her find lodgings. They left together."

"Elliott took her to an inn in Southwark?" Robert's surprise stemmed as much from the fact that Elliott had not seduced the woman himself, before he let her go in search of Robert, as from the location he'd chosen. Robert frowned. Perhaps Elliott had. In Northumberland's household, he'd always been a great favorite with the ladies.

"You forget," Pendennis said, "Elliott's father lives in Bermondsey. He was on his way there, through Southwark. Why? Was the place not respectable?"

"Well enough, but perilous close to some of our old haunts. You remember the Sign of the Smock?"

"Long Nell's place?" A fond expression came into Pendennis's face.

They had nights in Southwark in common—Robert, Pendennis, Elliott, and Lord Robin Dudley. During that perilous time spent at the court of Mary Tudor, they'd visited many a brothel, together with other lusty courtiers, English and Spanish.

Did Diego Cordoba ever think back on those halcyon days? Robert wondered. He'd encountered the one-eyed Spaniard earlier, just leaving Durham House as Robert was arriving. Cordoba was his primary contact there.

"That was a long time ago," Pendennis said. "What concerns me now is Mistress St. Cyr. Her Majesty's government will wish to know why she was killed. And if her death will have any effect on English diplomacy in France."

"How do you know for certain she is the one who is dead? Who found her? And when? Who identified her?"

"The watch stumbled over the body. Your lady wife named and claimed it. '

Robert had been prepared for the first announcement. The second both stunned and infuriated him. "Susanna? God's teeth, how did she come into this?"

Pendennis explained, revealing that the letter he'd been reading when Robert arrived had come from Susanna. "After telling me all that transpired in Southwark since dawn, she asked me to locate you as quickly as possible."

Silently, Robert cursed, painfully aware that his carefully laid plans might be about to unravel.

"Lady Appleton told them the body was that of her cousin, Diane Leigh," Pendennis continued. "She felt she could not let the woman be buried as a nameless prostitute. On the other hand, she supposed that knowledge of Diane's true identity might endanger some"—he glanced at the letter—"current enterprise concerning the safety of the realm."

"Susanna should not have involved herself," Robert said through clenched teeth.

"It may prove fortunate she did. Mistress St. Cyr's death could cause trouble for us. I must ask you, do you know aught of her murder?"

To gain time, Robert refilled his cup, a large, two-handled container made of dark brown lead-glazed earthenware. He could scarce tell Pendennis the whole truth. He took another comforting sip of a particularly well brewed ale. Confessing where he'd been after he'd left Diane, even if he invented a convincing reason to explain his presence, could ruin everything. But how many lies could he reasonably expect to have believed?

Pendennis had concluded, from Susanna's missive, that Robert had not spent the night at home. No doubt he was outraged on her behalf. Pendennis had what was to Robert an inexplicable soft spot where Susanna was concerned. He even admired her intelligence.

Fool.

"I know no more than I have already told you," he said.

"When did you leave Mistress St. Cyr?" Pendennis asked.

"Shortly before dawn."

"To go where?"

"Does it matter?" He leaned back against the linenfold paneling and met Pendennis's eyes. "The woman was still very much alive when I last saw her."

Pendennis was the first to look away, busying himself with the papers on his writing table. Robert drained his second cup of ale right down to the dregs.

It would be fatal to his plans to admit he'd gone to Durham House to attend mass as a means of ingratiating himself with the Spanish ambassador. Although it was legal to celebrate the Papist ceremony in the embassy, English citizens were expected to attend Anglican church services. Those caught hearing mass and convicted were fined one hundred marks for a first offense, four hundred for a second. For a third offense, a man's goods were confiscated and he was confined to prison for the rest of his life.

Even if he argued that he'd only gone to gather information, Robert knew his actions would be frowned upon by those in power. If they learned his real reasons, he'd be hanged, drawn, and quartered for a traitor.

No, he was not prepared to tell Pendennis where he had been, not even if remaining silent made him a suspect in Diane's murder.

His old friend regarded him with a sad-eyed stare.

"How did she die?" Robert returned his empty cup to the table and resisted the temptation to fill it again. A guilty man would know the manner of Diane's death. His question might allay Pendennis's suspicions.

"I have no details beyond the fact that 'twas clearly murder."

"It might be wise to confiscate her belongings. We may find answers there."

"Aye. As you say. And they may as well be delivered to Catte Street, since your lady wife had the body taken there."

"Shall we adjourn to Catte Street, then?"

A curt nod was his only answer.

Robert brooded while Pendennis gave orders to his servant, sending the fellow off to the Falcon Inn. Susanna might have done them a good turn, he conceded. In giving Diane an identity, she had hidden the fact that the dead woman was French. The local authorities would not pursue the matter. With luck, any lingering questions could be buried right along with the remains.

10

Lady Appleton had just finished washing the mysterious stranger's body with perfumed water and was wrapping it in a winding sheet when her husband and Sir Walter Pendennis arrived at the house in Catte Street, entering the great hall through the central opening in the floor-to-ceiling pierced wainscot screen.

That screen was supposed to block drafts from the street door. It did not, in Jennet's opinion, do a very good job. Then again, 'twas not much of a great hall, nor was this simple dwelling the grand house she'd hoped to find when she'd been told they were going to London.

'Twas plain both men expected the sight that met their eyes. A temporary table, a board supported by trestles, had been set up so that Lady Appleton could prepare French Diane for burial. Would she be chested? Jennet wondered. Even a plain wooden coffin was costly, though she'd heard rumors that such things could be rented here in the city—used for the funeral service, then returned to the coffinmaker at graveside.

Why even bother with a funeral? She wondered who Lady Appleton thought would attend. No one knew this woman . . . except Sir Robert.

Both men doffed their bonnets for a moment to show respect for the dead. They replaced them as they approached the table, faces solemn, to examine the body more closely.

When her mistress stood aside to let the two men look their fill, Jennet slipped into the background, blending with the shadows beneath the stairs, retreating to a position from which she could watch and listen without calling attention to herself.

Nothing in Lady Appleton's expression gave away her thoughts. Jennet was sure she herself would have shown a great deal of displeasure had her Mark been standing in Sir Robert's boots. 'Twas no pleasant task to wash and wrap a dead person. Even less bearable if the deceased was the most recent mistress of a wandering husband.

Determined to remain unnoticed, that she might listen to whatever would unfold, Jennet held in check the ire she felt on Lady Appleton's behalf. Sir Robert's wife was perfectly capable of taking him down a peg or two, if she chose to do so. That she was biding her time likely meant she had good reason to wait.

As Jennet continued to spy on the three people by the trestle table, she realized this was the first time she'd been privileged to observe how Sir Robert behaved when both Lady Appleton and Sir Walter were in his company. The situation might prove most enlightening. Jennet looked first at her mistress. Lady Appleton's stance seemed a trifle more relaxed, indicating that she was relieved Sir Walter had come.

Because he would take charge? Or because there was something more personal between them?

Jennet shoved the foolish thought aside. Lady Appleton had no notion how the man felt about her.

Sir Walter gazed at his friend's wife like a lovesick lad, an expression that vanished the moment Sir Robert glanced his way. It was perfectly obvious to Jennet that Sir Walter, a man Sir Robert acknowledged was the pride of the queen's intelligence gatherers, after Sir Robert himself, was thoroughly smitten. Pity it could come to naught. Not, at least, while Sir Robert lived.

While the two men studied the body, Jennet compared them. Dark and light, she thought. Sir Robert was black of hair and often black of mood, tending to brood when he felt himself slighted. Sir Walter was fair-haired, with locks of a sort of sand color. His beard was a shade lighter. As tall and broad shouldered as Sir Robert, he was rumored once to have been a valiant challenger in the lists, but as long as Jennet had known him, he'd shown only the effects of soft living. A slight paunch distended the already padded front of a fashionably long, salmon-colored doublet that matched the lining of his hat.

Sir Robert, Jennet had to admit, was hard as steel. Body and soul. That ought to make him more desirable to a woman, but in truth she thought the softer man would be easier to live with. Certainly Sir Walter smiled more often.

"Do you know her surname?" Lady Appleton asked. "I would like to see Diane buried under her proper identity."

"St. Cyr," Sir Walter told her. "A widow. But it may be best to conceal that for the present."

"You seek to hide her nationality?" Lady Appleton did not seem surprised, but the idea puzzled Jennet.

Something to do with Sir Robert, she supposed. He'd gone to France at least once on secret missions for the queen.

Frowning, Jennet began to gnaw her lower lip as Sir Walter announced that 'twas best to let Diane be thought an Englishwoman.

Reluctantly, Lady Appleton agreed to continue her ruse. "Had she some particular enemy? Someone who might have followed her here from France?"

"None we know of." Sir Walter stepped back from the table. "Her neck was broken," he observed.

"Nothing was stolen. She still had her clothing, and money on her person, and jewelry." Lady Appleton looked from one man to the other, but neither offered any comment. "I know not if it has significance, but I found a feather near the body." She produced it from atop a small, flat-lidded chest, where she'd also placed the dead woman's outer garments and a mourning ring, and held it out to Sir Walter.

"A goose feather," he murmured. He exchanged a sharp glance with Sir Robert.

"What does it signify?" Lady Appleton asked.

"Nothing."

"You are quick to say so, Robert."

"Because there is naught here to pursue."

Lady Appleton seemed about to protest when she was interrupted by a brisk knock at the front door. By rights, Jennet should have gone to answer it. She stayed where she was.

"That will be Mistress St. Cyr's traveling trunk," Sir Walter said. "If my man brings it in here, we may all examine the contents."

"I will so instruct him," Lady Appleton said.

Jennet held her breath and kept very still, afraid her keys would jangle and give away her presence. With luck, the two men had forgotten all about her.

Lady Appleton had not. She glanced at Jennet on her way to the door, but said nothing to call attention to her.

"Do you imagine there is a connection?" Sir Robert asked the moment his wife was out of earshot.

"It does not seem likely. That other matter was some six years ago. And yet, I do not like this . . . coincidence. Mistress Tylney's neck was also broken. And we found a feather then, too."

"Lord Robin thought it was a quill for a pen."

"And Cordoba showed us that it came off one of the pageant wagons. No one thought it had any. . . significance."

"It did not," Sir Robert said in firm tones. "And there cannot possibly be any link between Lora Tylney's death and Diane's. Bury the woman quickly," he advised, "and with her any hint of scandal, old or new."

They fell silent as Lady Appleton returned with Sir Walter's servant behind her. Assisted by a porter he'd hired to convey it from Southwark, he'd brought a solid oak chest nearly five feet long. A nice piece, Jennet thought, covered with shaved hide and banded in iron and closed with a large padlock.

She looked back at the two knights. A pity they'd not said more, but she had some information, at least, to share with Lady Appleton. If she understood aright, there had been another woman killed in like manner to French Diane. Jennet wondered who this Lora Tylney had been. And what she'd been to Sir Robert.

"Go for the coffinmaker," Sir Walter instructed his servant when the porter had been paid and dismissed. "Bring back a modest sample of his wares."

As soon as the fellow had departed, Sir Robert and Sir Walter made a study of the lock. Sir Robert used the small dagger appended to his belt to open it, a task accomplished with an ease that surprised Jennet. What a useful talent for an intelligence gatherer, she thought.

Inside they found only clothing and jewelry. Expensive clothing and jewelry. Jennet moved closer, forgetting that she wished to remain hidden. The kirtle Sir Robert removed first was made of fine white satin that must have cost, at the least, ten shillings a yard. Beneath it lay another of crimson satin lined with crimson sarcenet. And below that a gown of damask. Jennet did not dare estimate the cost of the latter, save to swear 'twould keep ten families in food for a year.

Once he'd removed everything from the trunk, Sir Robert began to search for hidden compartments, slitting the canvas lining with his dagger. He found nothing. No secret panels. No concealed pockets. A thoughtful look on his face, he lifted the damask gown.

Jennet could not hold back a gasp when she realized his intention. Just before he sliced into the fabric, Lady Appleton caught his wrist. "That is not necessary," she said.

"She must have hidden letters or other papers somewhere. They may be secreted in her clothing."

"Then we will pick out the seams and look, but there is no need to slash and destroy it."

With a mocking bow, he yielded the garment.

"Jennet," Lady Appleton called softly.

"Yes, madam?"

"Fetch scissors."

For the next hour, they picked apart seams while the men again searched the trunk, inside and out. Lady Appleton made the only discoveries. The first, which Sir Robert dismissed as unimportant, was that a small triangle of fabric was missing from the clothing the Frenchwoman had been wearing when she died.

"Caught her sleeve on something and it tore," he concluded.

It was a very even tear, Jennet thought. It almost looked as if the piece had deliberately been cut out of the black brocade.

Then Lady Appleton found a folded sheet of paper hidden in the lining of a dark brown wool cloak. She opened it, skimmed its contents, and announced it was a bill of exchange.

"What is that?" Jennet asked.

Sir Walter answered, winning Jennet's gratitude and an even greater degree of liking than he'd claimed before. It was not every gentleman who took time to explain things to a servant.

" 'Tis a way of getting money at the end of a journey without the necessity of carrying coins." He took the parchment from Lady Appleton and examined it. "The traveler, in this case Diane St. Cyr, deposited money with a local merchant, in this case a goldsmith in Paris, who gave her in return this paper. It is directed to a correspondent here in London. When Mistress St. Cyr presented this bill of exchange to him, that London goldsmith would have returned to her a sum only slightly less than what she deposited in Paris."

" 'Twas a very great sum," Lady Appleton remarked.

Who would claim it now? Jennet wondered, but she did not ask, only watched Sir Walter tuck the paper inside his doublet. She had other questions, as well. The search of the dead woman's belongings had brought them no closer to discovering Mistress St. Cyr's reason for coming to England, nor had they unearthed a motive for someone to kill her.

Jennet and Lady Appleton repacked the traveling trunk while the two men talked quietly in a corner of the hall. Jennet could not overhear a single word. Her annoyance was simmering by the time Sir Walter's man returned with a coffin.

"I will arrange for the burial," Sir Walter offered. "What is the vicar's name?"

"Busken," Lady Appleton told him. "But what are we to do with her trunk?"

"Keep it, dear lady. For what you have done for her, you deserve the finery. Remake the garments for yourself."

When Lady Appleton would have objected, Sir Robert cut off her protests. "Pendennis is right, Susanna. We have earned these goods."

No matter that the clothing was much too small to fit Lady Appleton, Jennet thought. No doubt Sir Robert expected her to sell it and give him the profit.

"She must have kinfolk. Heirs. Is there no one in France?"

Sir Walter promised to make inquiries, but insisted Lady Appleton keep the trunk and its contents, no matter what he found.

" 'Tis fine cloth," Jennet ventured when the two men had left.

"They will not search for her relatives," Lady Appleton said. "For some reason, they want this matter to end here."

Jennet sighed deeply. She knew her mistress well. Injustice made Lady Appleton angry. She was both perturbed and offended by the idea that murder might go unpunished. If neither the authorities nor Sir Robert did anything about it, then Lady Appleton would doubtless try to find out who had killed Mistress St. Cyr, especially now that she perceived herself to have profited from the woman's death.

"One mysterious murder," Lady Appleton mused. "No obvious motive." Her voice trailed off and she gave her housekeeper a sharp look. "What did you overhear, Jennet, while I was out of the room?"

Jennet hesitated, torn between reluctance to involve herself again in tracking down a killer and the pleasant sense of self-importance to be derived from assisting her mistress. At least a full minute passed before she repeated every word that had passed between the two courtiers.

11

"I must speak with the proprietor of this establishment," Susanna Appleton said to the formidable male person who opened the front door of the Sign of the Smock. He had fists the size of hams and thighs as big around as small trees.

Insolently he looked her up and down, from the top of her hooded cloak, past the visor she'd found in Diane's trunk, to the tips of her sturdy boots. He cast the same speculative gaze over Jennet, but seemed less interested in her. "I have heard of gentlewomen visiting brothels," he said, "but they do not customarily bring maidservants with them."

The previous day, after Jennet revealed what Robert and Sir Walter had said to each other about an earlier murder, Susanna had intended to begin her search for information by questioning her own husband, but Robert had left with Sir Walter and he'd stayed away. She could only guess how long she would have to wait before he deigned to return to Catte Street.

The only certain means she could devise to learn more was a return visit to Southwark to locate Diane's look-alike. With luck, Susanna thought she might find a reason for Diane's murder that had naught to do with Robert.

The woman had fled into this . . . house. Doubtless she worked here. 'Twas possible she was the constable's Petronella. The brothelkeeper would know.

Jennet disapproved, arguing that Susanna risked her reputation should she be recognized. Hence the visor. Jennet had also wanted to bring Fulke and Lionel and hire a man or two more for protection, but Susanna had overruled those objections, determined to arrive with as little fuss as possible. Faced with an impertinent giant, she had belated second thoughts.

"Will you let us in or not?" she demanded, relieved to find that her voice sounded normal.

Apparently deciding it was not up to him to bar the way of any who wished to enter, the sentinel stood aside, admitting them to a strangely appointed vestibule. He locked the door behind them.

Instead of the narrow, empty corridor that led into most dwellings, here was a goodly chamber. On the far wall were charcoal sketches of women in fine gowns and headdresses, the sort of studies artists did as preliminary work when they were commissioned to paint portraits. Susanna wondered if these had been executed by some patron of this house in lieu of payment in cash. Beneath the drawings sat a table, account books and coffers neatly laid out on top of it.

Beyond the reception area was the great hall, at present uninhabited. Susanna had never seen a room with so many chairs in it, let alone so many with seat cushions. The chairs were painted in bright colors,

as was a cupboard laden with a variety of fine wines
and dozens of Venetian goblets. Elaborately woven
tapestries graced the walls, showing scenes from classi-
cal antiquity. If a few more unclothed bodies graced
these depictions than Susanna would have seen in
the decor of a private home, she did not find them
offensive. In fact, she thought the quality of the
arraswork most excellent.

It had seemed to Susanna that early on a Monday
morning would not be a busy time in an establishment
such as this one. She'd chosen the hour of her visit
for that precise reason. Now, however, she wondered
if everyone but the manservant was still asleep. The
house was very quiet around them as he led the way
up a winding stair.

A narrow corridor ran the length of the upper level.
What an extraordinary number of private chambers,
Susanna thought as she passed door after door. Only
one stood open, at the end. Jennet at her heels,
Susanna entered a room any housewife would envy.

"The proprietor," their guide announced. He shut
them in when he left.

Susanna could scarce keep the surprise out of her
voice. "Why, you are the very one I seek!" The last
thing she had expected was to find a woman of no
more than four-and-twenty in charge of this place.

"Who are you and what do you want?" Attired in
a nightgown, a loose, wrap-over, floor-length garment
made of crimson satin with wide bands of black velvet
down the fronts and around the hem, the woman
was just breaking her fast with ale and manchet bread.
She did not seem alarmed or even irritated by their
intrusion, only wary.

Acting on impulse, Susanna discarded the visor.
"I am Lady Appleton," she announced. "I saw you
yesterday morning when I came to identify the body

of Mistress Diane . . . Leigh. She was a woman who looked a good deal like you."

A sudden stillness was the brothelkeeper's only response.

"There seems no reason for Diane to have been murdered, since she was not robbed. One possibility is that she was attacked in error." Susanna met and held the other woman's eyes, dark eyes much like Diane's. "You bear such a close resemblance to her that I cannot help but think she might have been mistaken for you."

Slowly, deliberately, the brothelkeeper bit into a chunk of bread and chewed. She did not speak until she had swallowed. "Why should I discuss this matter, or any other, with you?"

"Because it is in your best interest to do so. If someone was trying to kill you, will they not try again?"

"I am safe." A wry smile kicked up the sides of her mouth. "For another year, at least."

Susanna came farther into the room with Jennet trailing reluctantly behind her. "I do not understand you."

"This particular sort of murder seems only to occur on the twenty-fifth day of April. Today is the twenty-sixth."

"Do you speak of Mistress Tylney?" she asked. If so, this was unexpected, and a tie to Robert that Susanna could not like.

With calm, intelligent eyes, the brothelkeeper studied her guests. After a long silence, she seemed to come to a decision. "Sit," she invited, gesturing toward a cushioned chest. "It seems likely to profit us both if we share what we know."

Susanna obliged, using the time it took to cross the room for a more detailed survey of her surroundings.

The level of luxury continued to surprise her. So did the display of good taste. The wainscoting on the walls consisted of small oak panels decorated with roundels showing faces in profile. The plaster ceiling was covered with intricate geometric patterns. The furniture, like that belowstairs, was painted—crimson on the stools and benches, gold for the chests and coffers, bright blue on the tables and cupboards.

Jennet sniffed disdainfully as she settled herself at her mistress's side. The stony stare she directed at their hostess was full of disapproval, particularly of the nightgown and the woman's long, black hair, which was both unbound and uncovered.

"I have many questions," Susanna said.

"As do I."

"I will endeavor to answer them, Mistress? . . ."

With a faint smile, the woman confirmed Susanna's earlier guess. "I am called Petronella."

Susanna lifted a brow. "Called?"

"It is the custom for women in my profession to take names that sound foreign. 'Tis a popular misconception among our clients that French and Italian women, and even those who are Dutch or Flemish, know more interesting diversions than those who are native born."

"So the name is deceptive?"

"Or tells much in itself."

Susanna nodded. "Yes, I see. My given name is Susanna."

"The virtuous heroine of Old Testament times."

"And a popular choice among those of the New Religion."

"Even as those who cling to the old faith still name their daughters Ursula and Werburga after local saints."

Her hostess was obviously an educated woman.

With a degree of surprise, Susanna realized that she was inclined to like her. "You implied there have been other murders. Will you tell me about them?"

"A member of my profession was killed last April. I confirmed the date last night. She is buried in the single woman's churchyard here in Southwark. Another woman was slain several years ago. Lora, she was called. Both of them and your friend shared the same physical description. All had their necks broken. And all died on St. Mark's Day."

"Do you know this Lora's surname, or the year in which she was killed?" Susanna had little doubt Petronella spoke of Lora Tylney, the name Jennet had overheard.

"No," Petronella said, "but I perceive that you do."

"Aye. Lora Tylney. She died six years ago. A feather was found near her body," Susanna added. "One was also left near Diane's." Robert and Sir Walter might discount this as coincidence, but Susanna could not.

Petronella's brow furrowed in thought. "What kind of feather?"

"The quill of a goose."

Bitterness underscored Petronella's next words. " 'Tis possible that was meant as a reference to Winchester geese."

"I do not understand you," Susanna said.

"That is what we are called, those of us who earn our livings in places such as this. Once the Bishop of Winchester owned all these houses and the women who worked for him became known as Winchester geese. The term has other meanings, but that is the most common."

"Was Lora a whore?"

"I asked that very question myself. It appears not. And your friend?"

"A married man's mistress, perhaps, but not a woman who worked in a bordello."

At Petronella's knowing smile, Susanna suddenly felt uneasy. Was it possible this woman knew Robert? The thought unnerved her, but this was not a line of questioning she wished to pursue. Not yet.

"Did Lora die here in Southwark?" she asked instead.

Setting aside the covered flagon that held her ale, Petronella stood. Susanna had seen no signs of emotion before, but now she noted the clasped hands, fingernails digging into palms, and the quickened breathing. Petronella kept her agitation under control only with a great effort.

"She died at court. She was a chamberer to Queen Mary."

That news brought Susanna to her feet as well. There was no longer any doubt that Petronella's Lora was the woman of whom Robert and Sir Walter had spoken. Six years ago, she recalled, England had been preparing for war with France. At the end of April, King Philip had been in England, engaged in gathering troops. To improve his political fortunes, Robert had gone to court and, later, off to fight. He'd been knighted for his bravery in battle.

Robert and Sir Walter were hiding something. For some reason they wanted Diane's death glossed over and forgotten. Susanna did not like to think that either of them, or any of the friends of their youth, might have been guilty of a murder six years ago, but she had to consider that chilling possibility . . . and one other.

"Is it likely there are more victims?" It was a particularly unpalatable thought.

"More women who look like me? Dead women?"

"Aye." That a woman of a certain description might

have been slain every St. Mark's Day since Mary sat on the throne was horrifying to contemplate, and yet Susanna knew she must.

By her grim expression, Petronella saw the logic of Susanna's conclusion. Perhaps it was one she had already come to on her own. "It is possible," she allowed.

"We must try to discover if it is so," Susanna said. "Will you ask among the other houses here in Southwark?"

"I will ask, but here the death of a whore is less than nothing."

"To officials, perhaps, but to her friends?"

"A clever girl lasts but three or four years before she's worn out. Others are not so fortunate."

Appalled, Susanna gaped at her.

"I will ask," Petronella promised again.

"If we learn enough," Susanna told her, "we may be able to put an end to these killings."

"You should look elsewhere, as well," Petronella said.

Susanna felt her insides clench as she realized Petronella must have heard of Lora Tylney from someone who had been at Queen Mary's court. In all likelihood someone known to Susanna. Perhaps well known.

Again she wondered if Petronella had ever met Robert. Again she did not ask.

"Murder must not go unpunished," she said instead, "no matter who the killer is." Only by determining the identity of the murderer could she resolve her own doubts about Robert's involvement.

"Not even a whore's murder?"

"Not even a whore's murder." For a moment something very like understanding flickered between them. Susanna had the feeling she'd just made a pact, a commitment to find justice for all the murdered women.

"Who told you about Lora Tylney's death?" she asked.

The tenuous bond dissolved. "You should leave now, Lady Appleton."

So, Petronella meant to keep his identity secret. A gentleman or a nobleman, that much seemed likely. Someone Susanna knew, at least by reputation. Mayhap someone in Robert's circle of friends, someone she had met. She hoped Petronella's client did not turn out to be Walter Pendennis. She found she could not like the thought of Sir Walter visiting a Bankside brothel, though she could not imagine why the possibility bothered her so much.

"Look you to the court and courtiers," Petronella said. "Leave Bankside to me."

"Will you send word if you learn anything to our purpose?" Susanna reluctantly resumed Diane's visor in preparation to depart.

With equal reluctance, Petronella promised that she would.

Susanna told her new ally where the Appletons lodged, then left the Sign of the Smock and walked rapidly toward Paris Garden Stairs. Her mind raced even faster. Look to the court? And who there could she question, in a casual fashion, about events so long ago?

Petronella had said that Lora was a chamberer, in other words an upper-level maidservant of gentle birth. Who better to ask about her murder than other royal attendants? But with Queen Elizabeth's accession, Queen Mary's ladies-in-waiting, maids of honor, and chamberers had for the most part been replaced. Were laundresses, scullery maids, seamstresses, and the like also changed at the beginning of each new reign? Susanna had no idea. Then she realized it did not matter. She did know one person still at court who had most assuredly been there throughout Queen Mary's reign.

At Thameside, Susanna and Jennet paid their pennies to a waterman and clambered aboard his wherry for the river crossing. Jennet let out a huff as she sank onto the hard wooden bench provided for passengers.

" 'Tis glad I am to be clear of that place."

"Try to keep an open mind, Jennet. The woman will be more inclined to help us if she does not sense your disdain."

"How can you lower yourself to treat her as an equal?" Jennet demanded. "She is a bawd."

"I know what goes on in her establishment."

Or at least she thought she did. In truth, she was curious to learn more. She wondered about Petronella's background and her reasons for earning her keep as she did. The brothelkeeper was not at all what Susanna had expected.

12

Dismissing Robert Appleton's wife from her thoughts, Petronella went about her normal morning business. The premises had to be inspected for cleanliness, to make sure no offensive smells drove customers away. The girls here had clean smocks and clean bed linen and were regularly checked for disease and signs of breeding by Old Mag the midwife.

In addition, those who had broken the rules had to be called to account. Petronella visited the young woman who called herself Celia Clatterballocks. The small cubicle she'd been assigned held naught but a bed, a stool, and two identical pissing pots, one for Celia and one for her customer, a nicety observed in better bordellos like this one. The makeshift walls were no thicker than a screen, yet here the whores had more privacy than most of their profession enjoyed, and Petronella allowed her employees to live in, despite local ordinances against that practice.

"You have been using bad language again, Celia."

Her tone was one of mild reproof. "One of your men complained. We entertain an elite clientele here. None of our customers will tolerate being cursed at or called names."

Sullen, Celia mumbled something her bawd could not catch.

"You may refuse only if 'tis obvious the client is greatly diseased.'

" 'E were cunt-beaten," Celia muttered.

"The word is 'impotent,' and it is your job to help him overcome that problem." Seeing she was not making an impression, Petronella changed tactics. "Your earnings will increase if you follow my rules, Celia. Why, you could take in as much as ten pounds a month per man if you make yourself desirable enough. Some of my girls have even married clients when they were ready to retire."

Her interest piqued, Celia looked sly. " 'Ow?"

Although Petronella had gone through her precepts many times before, she repeated them. "Keep yourself clean and your skin soft by frequent bathing and the use of oils and creams. Use alum between customers to stay dry and clean." Celia made a face. "Wine, then. That will do as much to tighten things up again. And learn to speak well, without cursing."

There was no excuse not to mimic their betters, in speech and dress and manners. Petronella provided dancing masters and tutors for her employees. They were encouraged to study foreign languages, especially French, and could learn to read and write, as she had, if they so chose. 'Twas rare anyone entertained more than a dozen men a night, and Petronella spared her girls the need to demand payment from their customers. Those who came to the Sign of the Smock paid in advance for what they wanted.

As she left Celia, Petronella smiled to herself. She

never said the words aloud, for 'twould break her own rule about proper language, but the same motto held firm in this house as in all the others: "No money, no cunny."

The rest of the morning she spent going over plans for the week ahead with the servants, making sure all was in order for meals with the cook wench, checking that the laundry lass kept up with the masses of linen that came down to her, and supervising the girl scullion and the apple squires, the boys who served wine to Petronella's regular customers. The Sign of the Smock had a gaming room, and also provided singing and dancing for entertainment. Out back a walkway for promenading circled a garden and a small pond.

Later, Petronella had accounts to do. She had nearly finished when Vincent Cheyne, who was not only her doorman but also a friend, came into the room.

"Odd visitor this morning," he remarked.

"Aye. A gentlewoman. Sir Robert Appleton's wife."

"Oh, aye? Which was he?"

"He last came here a long time ago. Some six years, I do think." She stopped speaking, struck by the coincidence. Or perhaps it was not so coincidental. With exaggerated care, she closed the account book.

"Stayed a long time," Vincent said.

"Lady Appleton? Yes, she did." Petronella shifted in her chair to look at him directly. "Strange. I found myself liking Sir Robert's wife. How many other gentlewomen would have visited a bordello in broad daylight?"

"She wore a visor."

"But her very recognizable maidservant did not."

"Arrogant, she was," Vincent commented.

Petronella agreed. The woman gave the impression of thinking herself above her station, and distinctly superior to any whorehouse madam. Possibly she was more companion than servant. Petronella knew little of the lives of ladies, for all she was familiar with ladies' husbands.

"Robert Appleton was one of the courtiers who accompanied Diego Cordoba on his first visit to Bankside." That had been well before the killing of Lora Tylney. Petronella remembered because Cordoba himself had been memorable. He'd been a steady customer all that spring of 1555, when she'd been a slip of a girl of fifteen and new to the game.

She smiled suddenly, pleased to realize Diego had known her before he bedded the Tylney lass. 'Twas even possible he'd only been attracted to the other woman because Lora reminded him of his earlier passion for Petronella.

Vincent's expression gave away none of his feelings. "Appleton and his friends came here often in Long Nell's time."

"Aye. And Robert Appleton was no better and no worse than his fellows." Petronella had known most of them intimately, become acquainted in a professional way with their differing tastes, their little foibles, if not from personal experience then by talking to the other whores. "Appleton continued to frequent the Sign of the Smock whenever he was in London during Queen Mary's reign." She concentrated, calling up another memory. "The last visit was right before Shrove Tuesday six years ago."

Vincent's face darkened. They both had reason to remember that horrible night. Shrove Tuesday, the traditional last revel before Lent imposed its strictures, was the day when London apprentices ran wild, often taking out their high spirits in the brothel districts. That year the Sign of the Smock had been besieged and only the prompt intervention of one of

Long Nell's powerful friends had prevented the place from being burned to the ground.

Petronella shivered. The annual riots were a known danger to one in her profession. She could take precautions. But the annual killing of a woman of a specific description was something else entirely. Was Lady Appleton right? Had there been more deaths than the three they'd uncovered? One a year?

Frowning, Petronella wondered why Lady Appleton was so interested. She had not specified her relationship to the woman whose body she had claimed. Diane, she'd called her. Why had this Diane chosen to walk the streets of Southwark alone in the early morning hours of St. Mark's Day?

Lady Appleton did not seem consumed by grief, or by rage, as might be expected after the death of a near relative or a good friend. There was something more to this matter than the gentlewoman had shared, Petronella decided. Something, she'd be willing to wager, to do with Sir Robert.

Did Lady Appleton think her own husband had murdered the woman? And the others, too? It was possible, she supposed. Lady Appleton must know that Sir Robert had access to both Whitehall Palace and Bankside.

Six years earlier, Diego had, too.

She wanted to dismiss that possibility, but in truth she knew very little about the man's everyday life. And he had confessed to taking Lora Tylney's innocence, if not her life.

" 'Tis not your time yet," Diego had told her, and then he'd said Lora's death had changed him.

Petronella's involuntary shiver focused Vincent's attention on her. "What troubles you, Molly?" he asked.

She managed a weak smile. Vincent was the only

one left who called her by that name. He had been employed in Southwark's stews longer than she had.

"Lady Appleton came to me for information," she confided. Then she told him everything, even confessing her uneasiness about Diego Cordoba.

"There was a woman five years back," Vincent said after a considerable pause for thought. "Little Alice." Petronella's heart skipped a beat. "Strangled, or so I was told. Near Eastertide."

Close, Petronella thought. Too close. "Any others?"

He shook his shaggy head. "May be records in the parish registers."

"I could ask to inspect them." Petronella knew that every parish was required to keep records of burials, including the cause of death in the entry, but the law was haphazardly enforced. Many parish priests could barely read, let alone write. Their clerks were no better educated.

"You do not want to call the church's attention to yourself."

"No," she agreed. "I will ask at the other houses, then."

"I will ask," Vincent said.

"Do you care so much for my reputation?" She meant to tease him, but his expression remained as somber as a Puritan's.

"Heloise, at the Castle-on-the-Hoop, will remember Little Alice."

"I'll leave Heloise to you, and glad of it." The brothelkeeper was a grotesque creature, nearly as wide as she was tall, and that all covered in rolls of fat. The Castle-on-the-Hoop was located at the other end of Bankside, in both geography and prosperity. Near London Bridge, it bounded on Deadman's Place, Maiden Lane, and Bankside, just beyond the

Antelope and the Bullhead. All three of those properties shared a wharf, and all three had seen better days. The average girl working in any one of them serviced thirty to forty men a night.

Several hours later, Vincent returned to report that Heloise did remember Little Alice, and had confirmed she'd been small and dark haired. There might also have been another murder, perhaps three years back, but no one could remember the woman's name or the exact date of her death.

Vincent once more shook his shaggy head. "Hard to imagine now, but I've heard tell that Heloise herself was once a lissome little lass. Not so small as you are, Molly, but none seeing her then could have guessed she'd grow to such great, gross proportions."

Petronella did not care for the implication she might end up another Heloise. Her words came out more sharp than she'd intended. "Someone must check the entries in the parish register. There is no help for it now."

"I will see to it," Vincent promised.

"Good." She patted his cheek. "Send hot water up from the kitchen," she instructed, dismissing him. "I would bathe before the evening's work begins."

As she soaked in her leather tub a short time later, Petronella considered what she had learned. There were still years unaccounted for if there had been a small, dark woman murdered each St. Mark's Day since Queen Mary's time. She would have to search further afield to find those remaining victims.

Whores congregated in other districts besides Bankside. Duke Humphrey's Rents near Puddle Dock were in the Liberty of St. Andrews-at-the-Wardrobe. Then there were the houses in Cock's Lane and along Duke Street, both near Smithfield, where brothels had long operated by paying hefty bribes to officials to look the other way.

She would visit those places, she resolved, and ask a few more questions here in Southwark, as well. Then she would send word to Lady Appleton and they would compare what they had each discovered.

With a sense of amused wonderment, Petronella realized she was looking forward to her next encounter with the gentlewoman.

13

It had been a long time since Lady Mary Grey had last seen Susanna Appleton. Nearly ten years, by her reckoning. Whitsunday, the twenty-fifth day of May in the year of our Lord 1553. At a triple wedding. The most important nuptials performed that day had united Lady Mary's sister, Lady Jane Grey, and Lord Guildford Dudley in the bonds of matrimony.

Susanna had been newly married herself then, wed less than a year to Robert Appleton. She could not yet have been twenty, but she'd seemed old to Lady Mary, a girl half that age.

For a moment, as Lady Appleton made her way through the gardens of Whitehall Palace from the river steps at the bottom of the orchard, Lady Mary let memories of that long-ago day flood into her mind. The weddings had been held at Durham House on the Strand. If she squinted toward the northeast from her chamber window, Lady Mary could just make out the twin turrets flanking its water gate. At the time of the weddings, the mansion had belonged to the duke of Northumberland, Lord Guildford's powerful, frightening father.

How her own father had cursed, Lady Mary remembered, when Jane balked at marrying Lord Guildford. Then their mother, ever more straightforward, had beaten the bride into submission. The Lady Frances had been a great one for such heats until the day she died. Lady Mary had learned early to avoid being noticed. She'd almost been left behind on the day of the wedding.

A short service had been followed by feasting, masques, and jousting. That had all been very exciting to the girl she'd once been, but afterward she and many of the other guests, along with Lord Guildford, had been passing ill of food poisoning. Someone, she thought with the clarity of hindsight, should have taken that as an omen.

Lady Appleton reached the little knoll where Lady Mary waited. "It was good of you to agree to meet with me so soon, my lady," she said.

Lady Mary looked up at her. *Way* up at her. In the last ten years, Lady Mary had not grown at all. She was a bit over four feet tall, a fact made more noticeable by a malformed back.

She knew perfectly well that people called her Crouchback Mary out of her hearing. She was able to ignore that fact because, with her sister Jane dead, executed for trying to take the throne from Queen Mary, and her sister Catherine imprisoned and in disgrace for a runaway marriage, she, the Lady Mary Grey, was heiress presumptive to Queen Elizabeth. If aught happened to her royal cousin, Lady Mary would succeed to the throne of England.

With that in mind, Lady Mary drew herself up as

much as she was able and accepted as her due the obeisance Susanna Appleton made her.

"Sit down," Lady Mary said, indicating a bench in the shade of a fantastically shaped hedge. "You are much too tall."

Lady Appleton sat, but plainly her attention was caught by the beauty around them in the royal gardens.

"No herbs, I fear," Lady Mary said. She knew of Lady Appleton's reputation as an herbalist. In fact, she had read the woman's work on poisons. A most useful book, she'd thought at the time, both for avoiding accidental poisoning and ridding oneself of enemies.

"Can we see the sundial from here? My husband tells me it is one of the wonders of England, having in it no fewer than thirty different devices for telling the time."

"All paths lead to it," Lady Mary said. Broad and gravel strewn, they ran between the flower beds. The sundial, as Lady Mary and the other young women at court had reason to know, also contained a fountain. More than once, an unsuspecting visitor had found himself doused with cold water.

"You have not come here to talk of gardens," Lady Mary said in a preemptory manner. "Your letter mentioned a desire to know of certain events which took place six years ago."

"I need your help, my lady. You are the only person I could think of who was at court under both the previous queen and the current one."

"That is no great accomplishment on my part, but rather an accident of birth," Lady Mary pointed out. "If you seek my influence, you will be disappointed. I am for the most part ignored."

"I do think that means you are like to see and hear all the more, which is exactly to my purpose."

Not easily flattered, Lady Mary regarded her with suspicion, but there was nothing but sincerity in Lady Appleton's face. "What is it you would know?"

"An acquaintance of mine was murdered two days ago," she said bluntly. "I believe there may be a connection to another death, here at Whitehall, some six years ago. Is it possible you remember anything of that event? The victim was one of Queen Mary's chamberers, a woman named Lora Tylney.

"Ah," Lady Mary said. Her interest piqued, she decided to be helpful. "As it happens, the death of the chamberer attracted my attention at the time. Several noteworthy courtiers were involved."

She might herself be short, hunchbacked, red haired, and homely, but Lady Mary appreciated tall, handsome men.

14

The Lady Mary's avid expression boded well for Susanna's mission. When the noblewoman described what she remembered of the incident, Susanna listened carefully, asking occasional questions. By the time she returned to the Privy Stairs, where she'd left Jennet waiting, she'd learned considerably more than she'd expected to. More, perhaps, than she'd wanted to know.

"Well?" Jennet demanded. She hadn't liked being left out, but the Lady Mary had agreed to meet Susanna in Whitehall Gardens, on the day following the interview with Petronella, only if Susanna came alone.

"Well, it becomes more imperative than ever that I talk to Sir Robert." Susanna had hoped to speak with him the previous night, but he had not come home. Again. He would have to show up later today, she thought. Diane's funeral was set for four that afternoon.

"A pity you just missed him, then," Jennet said.

Confused, Susanna gave her housekeeper a sharp look as they descended green-slimed steps to the water gate. The tide was so low that they might have walked from Whitehall to the houses along Canon Row by way of a narrow, muddy, pebble-strewn beach.

Susanna handed over sixpence to a waterman for the west-east journey and the two women settled themselves on cushioned benches beneath an awning while he cast off.

"What place is that?" Jennet asked, pointing toward the north shore. "The great house just in the middle of the curve of the Thames?" They moved rapidly past it, propelled downriver by tide and oars.

"That is Durham House," Susanna told her. "Why?"

"Sir Robert left there by water just as you were making your way into the royal gardens. I do not think he noticed me, but he stared long and hard at you."

"Nowadays the house is leased by the Crown to Alvaro de Quadra, bishop of Aquila and ambassador to England. It is the Spanish embassy."

"I am certain it was Sir Robert, madam," Jennet said. "I recognized his court dress."

Susanna did not reply. Doubtless it had been, though she did not suppose his white-and-crimson doublet was unique. Robert had only recently returned from a long sojourn in Spain on the queen's business, making it logical to assume he had reason to deal with Spaniards. And yet, she'd been under the impression he was through with them, and glad of it.

"What did the Lady Mary say?" Jennet asked.

"That several men were questioned during the investigation of Lora Tylney's death." Susanna lowered her voice so the boatman would not overhear. "Sir Robert was among them." Jennet's eyes widened. "And Lord Robin Dudley." Her mouth opened to form a silent O. "Also suspected were Peregrine Marsdon and Francis Elliott, two courtiers who were in the duke of Northumberland's household at the same time Robert was, though I have never met either of them."

When she hesitated, Jennet prompted her. "Who else, madam? Did the Lady Mary name Sir Walter?"

"Aye, and a Spaniard. A man by the name of Diego Cordoba." The Lady Mary had known nothing more of him.

They rounded the bend in the river. Susanna could see the whole of London spread out before her. And the Southwark shore. Her sharp eyes picked out the Sign of the Smock.

She had not been surprised to hear Robert and Sir Walter mentioned as suspects. It had been obvious from the first that the two of them knew more than they were prepared to share with her. What she had not expected was the keen sense of disappointment she'd felt on learning Robert had been involved in the cover-up of a tawdry murder. And in drunken revels at court.

What else, she wondered, would she discover about her husband in the days to come?

Was it possible she was married to a murderer?

15

His face appropriately solemn, Robert threw dirt into the grave that held Diane St. Cyr. An eerie silence descended on the churchyard as the only mourners— himself, Pendennis, and Susanna—turned away.

When his old friend declined Susanna's offer of supper and left the two of them to go to his own lodgings in Blackfriars, Robert's gaze followed his departing form with real longing. He did not look forward to an evening in his wife's company. Because he had not been home since Sunday, he knew she'd have a barrage of questions. He had a few of his own, but was unsure how to determine what business she'd had at Whitehall without explaining why he'd been in a position to notice her entering the palace grounds.

He'd barely been able to see Whitehall's Privy Stairs from the Durham House water gate, but he'd caught sight of the wherry passing the Spanish embassy and noticed something familiar about one of the women on board. When Susanna stood, the better to view her surroundings, her height and proud carriage, all too familiar, had attracted his attention. Recognizing his own wife somewhere she had no reason to be, he had continued to watch the watercraft until it docked.

Her destination both puzzled and worried him. Susanna was scarce an intimate of the queen. In fact, she had never been presented to Queen Elizabeth. Robert intended that to remain the case. The very thought of two such independent-minded, overeducated women working in concert filled him with dread.

But if it seemed unlikely his wife had gone to Whitehall to meet with the queen, then why had she disembarked at the Privy Stairs? Hours later, that question still nagged at him.

Not long now, he reminded himself. The plan was moving forward. His allies in Spain were cooperating. If he could just keep Susanna from meddling and also manage to divert official attention from this unfortunate business of the Frenchwoman's murder, all would be well. Somehow, he had to prevent Susanna from involving herself further in the matter.

He glanced at her, noting the stiff way she held herself, the stubborn jut of her chin, and realized he had little chance of persuading her to cooperate. His wife was as tenacious as a terrier. His best chance of success lay in counterfeiting amiability and persuading her to share her conclusions about Diane's death. At least that way, when she strayed into dangerous waters, he would have warning before they were both dragged under the waves.

A cat greeted them at the door, stropping against his best hose with utter disregard for their cost. "Get away," he ordered, kicking at the ginger-colored beast. It ran, but stopped to glare malevolently at him from a safe hiding place beneath a cupboard.

"Bring ale to the solar," he barked at Jennet, who hovered nearby, ears flapping. He'd like to banish both housekeeper and cat from the premises, he thought irritably.

Bad enough he had to put up with Susanna.

"A word with you in private, madam," he said to his wife.

Susanna followed him up the stairs meekly enough, but he was not fooled. Either she was angry because he had been the dead woman's lover, or she was prepared to be forgiving, an annoying tendency that took much of the spice out of an amorous extramarital exploit.

"I cannot think why you have concerned yourself in this." Robert began to upbraid her the moment the solar door closed behind them. "Diane was naught to you and little more to me. Far better for the body to have gone unknown and unclaimed."

"Difficult, when Diane had a paper on her person directing any who found it to the house of Sir George Eastland in Catte Street."

"Pendennis did not tell me that," Robert murmured. "An unfortunate oversight. Should have been more careful."

"Who?" his wife asked. "Diane? Sir Walter? Yourself?"

Robert scowled at her. "Diane was an amateur. A novice at intrigue for all her connection to La Renaudie."

"Her killer was no novice." Susanna's intense gaze made him think it possible she had so far lost faith in him as to suspect him of murder.

They were circling each other like fencers, each waiting for an opening, prepared to thrust or parry. No, Robert thought. That analogy was not accurate.

Only he was skilled with a sword. His wife's weapon of choice was poison.

At that moment, Jennet arrived with two cups of ale, handing one to Robert and the other to Susanna. He resisted the absurd urge to insist that they swap drinking vessels. "Leave us, Jennet," he said instead. "We will sup in an hour's time."

"Have you an hour's worth of news to impart?" Susanna asked when they were alone.

"Let us speak honestly together," he suggested, pasting on his most sincere expression.

She lifted a skeptical brow. "A novel notion."

"As honestly as I am permitted to speak," he amended, hoping she'd think he was bound by the security of the realm to keep some matters to himself.

"Very well, Robert. Honesty. I have nothing to hide." She settled herself on the window seat, taking great care with the arrangement of her skirts.

"I have been told you visited Whitehall earlier today. What purpose had you in going there?"

Susanna's fingers stilled on a fold of fabric. "I met with the Lady Mary Grey."

Robert choked on his ale, coughing uncontrollably. 'Twas as well he could not speak, he realized when he finally caught his breath. His shock had been great at hearing that name. He might have given something away.

Susanna could not possibly know his plans. Her face was open, easy to read. He saw in it only her concern for him—she went so far as to get up and pound him on the back to aid his recovery.

This had to be mere coincidence. It could be nothing else. And yet 'twas worrisome.

"The ale went down the wrong way," he said hoarsely.

"Yes," she agreed, and waited, as was her habit

when she wished to encourage others to speak first, filling a deliberately left silence.

'Twas a remarkable effective ploy. Robert pretended to fall into the trap. "What business did you have with the Lady Mary?" he asked, as if he'd only just recalled what she'd said before his fit of coughing. "Why, I had almost forgot she was at court." He grinned, thinking of the Lady Mary's size. "She is passing easy to overlook."

No smile came in reply. "She is a most observant person herself," Susanna told him solemnly. "The Lady Mary likes to know things." She sighed and folded her arms on the table. "There is no point in concealing my intentions from you, Robert, but I must tell you that had you been here, I'd have had no necessity to question the Lady Mary."

"I find your words enigmatic, Susanna." *Question* the Lady Mary? He did not like the sound of that. "Tell me plain what you discussed with the queen's cousin."

"The murder of Lora Tylney."

This time he could not disguise his shock. He gaped at her, incredulous. "How did you—?"

He broke off as comprehension dawned. He and Pendennis had spoken of Lora in this house. Annoyed that he'd not been more careful, he cast a thoughtful glance at the door. No doubt Jennet was stationed behind it even now, positioned to eavesdrop on every word he said.

He supposed it did not matter. Anything she did not overhear, Susanna would repeat to her later. He'd never understood this bond between mistress and servant and did not approve of it, although he had no choice but to acknowledge its existence.

"Come, Robert," his wife urged, refilling the cup he could not remember draining. "You are the one who proposed honesty. You cannot deny that the murder of Lora Tylney and the murder of Diane St. Cyr have several things in common. The date—St. Mark's Day. The feather, indicating a connection to Winchester geese. The broken necks. And most important, the physical description of the victim. I have learned of a third murder, that of a prostitute in Southwark just a year ago. Like Lora and Diane, she was small and dark and her neck was broken. What conclusion can I draw but that one man killed all three women? A man who must be known to you, for he was at court with you during Queen Mary's reign."

Robert's mind was too clogged with questions to allow him to speak. What Susanna had reasoned out was at once less alarming and more daunting than anything he'd feared she would say.

"A killer who strikes but once a year," he finally managed to say. "A killer who follows a pattern?"

"Aye. It makes a sickening kind of sense. There is a sort of logic in it."

"I have never heard of such a thing before!"

"Does that make it impossible to be true?"

"No," he said, short-tempered because he did not care for surprises. Her conclusions were unexpected. He refused to inquire how she knew of the death of a whore.

"Well?" Hands on her hips, Susanna glared at him. "Will you help me discover this killer's identity?"

"Before I agree to anything, you must tell me all you learned from the Lady Mary Grey." Most particularly, he thought, Susanna must tell him if the Lady Mary had mentioned his name.

"Do you agree with my conclusions?"

"I agree only that I must hear more of this matter

before I can decide. Why did you go to the Lady Mary?"

Resigned to telling him, Susanna reclaimed the window seat. "I thought of her because she and her sister, the Lady Catherine, were privy to all that happened at court during Queen Mary's reign. They knew who had reputations with the ladies." She gave him a pointed look, but did not elaborate. "The Lady Mary well remembered the uproar over Mistress Tylney's death. She said King Philip himself took charge of the investigation. And put a stop to it."

"He had good reason to do so. There was no obvious suspect. And he had returned to England to gather troops. He needed every able-bodied man to fight the French."

"Ah, yes. I can see how experience killing an innocent young woman might be useful to a soldier."

"That is not how it was, Susanna. And I must protest that Lora Tylney was no innocent." Robert remained where he was, across the room from his wife, fighting the urge to pace.

"Nor was Diane," Susanna mused. "That was the point of the feather, I presume."

Robert knew he could never hope to deter Susanna if she was resolved to search for Diane's killer. How, he wondered, could he use her quest to his own advantage? The success she'd enjoyed in the past had given her a false sense of her own abilities. If she pursued this matter, she'd focus on it to the exception of all else. It was unlikely she'd discover who had killed Diane. And she'd not have time to inquire into his comings and goings. 'Twould be good to divert her from too keen an interest in his business for the next few weeks.

Feigning capitulation, he forced a smile. "Ask me what you will. I vow I will assist you in any way I

can. Did the Lady Mary remember I was one of the
courtiers interrogated when Lora Tylney was killed?"

"Aye, she did." Susanna gave him a hard look, then
dropped her gaze to stare at her folded hands. "The
Lady Mary said you were one of several gentlemen
in pursuit of Lora's favors. She seemed to think you
. . . intended to force yourselves upon her."

"Susanna . . ."

The warning in his voice went unheeded. "I have
heard of such things, but I had thought better of you,
Robert."

"I'd had a great deal to drink."

They'd all consumed inordinate quantities of Xeres
sack that night. Cordoba had been so deep in his
cups that he'd caught hold of a figure in a gown and
thought he'd had Lora, only to find out 'twas merely
a creation of terra-cotta and paint. Robert had been
none too steady himself, flailing about among the
props and set pieces and boxes of costumes.

"What happened the night she died?"

"I do not remember much," he admitted. 'Twas
true enough. There were gaps in his memory.

"Who was with you?"

"Several gentlemen began the evening in Lord
Robin's chamber. Pendennis. Marsdon. Elliott.
Myself." He did not mention Diego Cordoba, though
it occurred to him now that Cordoba might make a
convenient scapegoat. His preference was to keep the
Spaniard's name out of this, to protect his current
endeavor, but if that was not possible—

Susanna's sharp-voiced question interrupted his
plotting. "Did you pursue the girl? Chase her through
the passages of Whitehall?"

" 'Twas a lark. A game. St. Mark's Day that year
was a festive occasion and Lora Tylney a saucy baggage. She teased any number of men, offering kisses,

hinting at more. I looked for her, as did others, even in the place where she was eventually found dead, the room in which set pieces are stored for royal masques and mummings.''

The morning after the revels, when Lora's body was discovered he'd felt no remorse, no guilt, but now Susanna's silent disapproval made him uncomfortable.

"Did she try to win King Philip's interest?"

"Did the Lady Mary say so?" Here was a new twist.

"She said he had an eye for the ladies."

"You cannot think Philip of Spain murdered Lora Tylney."

"Is he not capable of murder?"

Robert was silent. 'Twould be marvelous irony to let Philip take the blame. He could not be questioned. Even Susanna would not pursue a king to his own kingdom. But would it be wise to accuse the man who held the key to his own future? Robert's plans remained dependent upon Philip, and upon his son, Don Carlos. He dared not risk such a lie.

"Any man is capable of murder, given the right circumstances," he said slowly, "but if you think the same person must have murdered Diane, then you cannot suspect King Philip, for most assuredly he is no longer in England."

"Did you bed Lora Tylney?" Susanna asked.

"No. Never."

She stared at him long and hard. "And Diane? Did you spend the night before her death with Diane St. Cyr?"

"You might as well ask me if I killed her."

"Did you?"

"God's teeth, Susanna! Do you not know me better than that?"

"I wonder if I know you at all of late," she told him. "But I do not believe you killed those women."

"Small comfort," he muttered.

"Mayhap Sir Walter will remember more than you do."

Robert weighed what Pendennis could tell her against what his old friend might discover of Robert's present business. Certes, she must question Pendennis. 'Twould keep them both occupied while he implemented his master plan.

"Doubtless you will pay no attention if I forbid it," he grumbled. "You will go your own way unless I imprison or kill you. 'Twould be a great temptation, my dear, were I the sort of man who could murder a woman."

"Then I am fortunate you are not," she said evenly.

"Talk to Pendennis," he said with a sigh. "I give you leave."

"My thanks, husband." They both knew she had no need of his permission.

Smiling blandly at her, Robert proposed they sup, for he'd worked up an appetite with this sparring. Over the meal, he decided, he would amuse himself by enumerating Pendennis's flaws. Susanna thought Sir Walter pleasant, even charming, for he took care to present his best face in her company. Robert intended to remind his wife that Pendennis had been a courtier, a soldier, and a spy. He'd killed men in battle.

And he'd been responsible for at least one woman's death.

16

In spite of Robert's dire hints about his good friend Pendennis, Susanna felt comfortable paying a visit to Blackfriars. Only hours after her husband's early-morning departure from Catte Street, eager to push forward in her investigation, she sought Sir Walter's help.

Shock suffused his features when he opened his door at her knock and recognized her. "Susan—! Lady Appleton! I—"

"—did not expect to see me here." Susanna finished his sentence for him, then pushed boldly past him into his lodgings. This was a matter best discussed in private.

"I do not—"

"Jennet accompanies me, as you can see." The younger woman eased inside right behind her mistress. "And Robert approves of my plan to speak with you."

"You mean to look into Mistress St. Cyr's murder, do you not? Are you certain such a course is wise?"

"Need I remind you who solved the murders at Madderly Castle?"

Sir Walter's reluctance remained evident, but a faint smile reached his eyes. Her actions in Gloucestershire had earned him his knighthood. They had worked well together at Madderly Castle, Susanna thought. Ever since then, Sir Walter had accorded her a respect bordering on reverence. A most flattering circumstance, if occasionally an embarrassment when his praise became effusive. She could almost think he entertained tender feelings for her.

"You are welcome in my humble abode," Sir Walter said. "May I offer you refreshment?"

Susanna studied his lodgings with great curiosity. A writing table dominated the front room, a clear indication that he worked at home. His chair was box seated, containing storage space. A second table, holding an assortment of edibles and a jug of ale, sat in front of the window. A second chair, this one in the Glastonbury style, had been placed nearby, the food and drink within easy reach. Thus were labor and reward neatly divided.

"We require nothing but information," Susanna assured him.

Through the door to the inner chamber, she caught sight of a boarded bed on four short legs. A narrow shelf at the head held both candles and books. She was not surprised, given his weakness for fancy clothes, to see that two large presses occupied the remainder of the room.

Sir Walter Pendennis was a tidy soul, she decided, or else he had a woman to pick up after him. As she walked across the floor, the faint scents of marjoram flowers and woodruff leaves came to her from the rushes strewn upon it. More evidence of female influence, she thought. Her own preference was for bay leaves.

"We needs must talk of Lora Tylney." Without allowing him to object, Susanna launched into an account of all she knew of the three murders, then summarized the conclusions she'd previously shared with Robert.

Sir Walter listened quietly, taking the Glastonbury chair when she declined his gesture offering it to her. Jennet had moved to an unobtrusive post near the door.

"What do you hope to accomplish by looking into the matter further?" Sir Walter asked when Susanna had finished telling her tale. His long fingers toyed with the copper-gilt pommels at the extremities of the arms.

"Justice."

For a moment Sir Walter did not respond. Then he gave a curt nod. "Your theory that the murders were committed by the same person makes sense. 'Tis clear this person must be stopped. I will help you if I can. What is it you wish to know?"

What he had been like six years earlier. Susanna tried to picture him. Younger. Hungrier. More optimistic. They all had been, back then. In those days, she'd even believed she and Robert could still make a successful partnership out of their arranged marriage.

She opted to ask simple questions first. She had a goodly number of them. Once supper had been served the previous evening, she'd learned little more from Robert. He'd devoted himself to blackening Sir Walter's reputation, as if Susanna did not know full well that soldiers killed men in battle. If Sir Walter had, so had Robert, for they'd fought side by side at

Saint-Quentin. As for Robert's dark hints of a tragedy concerning a woman in Sir Walter's past, Susanna told herself she was content to leave solving that mystery for another day.

"I would learn as much as I can about the death of Lora Tylney," she informed him. "She seems to have been the earliest victim. Can you tell me what was done at the time to find her killer?"

"All that was possible, I do assure you. No one saw anything that was helpful to the authorities."

"And the men searching for her the night she died?"

"Never found her.

"How can you be certain? 'Tis obvious someone did."

"Elliott confessed afterward that he misled us. For pity's sake, he said. When we gave up our search she was safely hidden inside a pageant wagon."

Susanna crossed the small distance between him. "Francis Elliott?"

"Aye." Sir Walter's gaze held a question. "You knew he was there. You just told me that you did."

"Yes." And Robert had mentioned that Elliott had escorted Diane to the inn in Southwark where she'd spent the last night of her life. "Are you saying Elliott knew where Lora was? That he could have found her?"

Sir Walter frowned. " 'Twas six years ago. I cannot remember every detail, but as I recall it, Elliott thought to play the gentleman. He saw some movement, a shadow inside a canvas tower. All the while we searched for her, she was concealed by naught but the thin walls and a lightweight frame."

"She must have been terrified."

"She was no innocent."

"Nor was she a common woman. She was a chamberer to Queen Mary. A gentlewoman by birth."

And Susanna doubted she'd wished to lie with more than one man that night. What woman would?

Walter said quietly, "I do much regret mine actions that night. I am certain the others do also, especially Cordoba."

Cordoba again. How strange that Robert had made no mention of the Spaniard. Then again, he had not said anything either about Francis Elliott helping Lora elude her pursuers.

Robert had chosen to leave out certain segments of the story. Why should he do so? And why those particular pieces of the puzzle? Sheer perversity, mayhap. He did relish any chance to thwart her.

"Tell me more of these two men, Sir Walter. Elliott and Cordoba. Their background. What they look like."

"Elliott hails from Bermondsey, just south of here. His father was naught but a clerk to the Master of Revels, but he rose to favor during King Edward's brief reign. The golden lad, we called him, for the color of his hair and his luck with women. The ladies seem to like his looks."

"And Cordoba?"

"I know nothing of his family. In appearance he was typical of his nationality. Dark. Swarthy. Several years before I knew him, he'd lost an eye while jousting in a tournament at the Spanish court. He always wore an eye patch, but the remaining eye seemed to see all the more. And, as if to compensate, his hearing was almost preternaturally acute, at least when he was sober."

Robert's omission of the Spaniard from his account continued to bother Susanna, but she considered lack of information a challenge. "What reason had Diego Cordoba for being at court?"

"I recall little more than that he was part of King Philip's retinue."

"What had he to do with the rest of you?" Robert, Sir Walter, Peregrine Marsdon, and Francis Elliott all had ties to the duke of Northumberland's household and to Lord Robin Dudley.

Sir Walter shifted uneasily in his chair and would no longer meet her eyes. "Cordoba was of an age with the rest of us. And good company, for all he was a Spaniard. We first met when he came to England for the marriage of his lord and our queen. That was July in the year of our Lord 1554."

"And?" Susanna moved closer and stood staring down at him, certain there was more, something he was reluctant to share with her.

"Until shortly before her death, Lora was Cordoba's mistress."

Sir Walter was still holding back, but the bone he offered distracted Susanna. If Cordoba and Lora had been lovers, then why had he been part of what Robert had called a game? Some peculiar form of vengeance against an unfaithful leman?

"Did Cordoba continue to search for her after the rest gave up?"

"I do not know." Sir Walter's brow was furrowed now. "You must forgive me, but my memory is sketchy."

A weak excuse, she thought. And possibly a lie. As an intelligence gatherer, Sir Walter had been trained to retain the smallest details, since one could never tell what trivial thing might become important, and to conceal his thoughts when the need arose.

Robert, too, was good at hiding behind a blank expression. When he kept hold of his temper, he could tell lies with great conviction. Susanna had sometimes wondered if he did not manage to convince even himself that he told the truth. 'Twas a convenient skill for a spy . . . or a murderer.

Standing, Sir Walter walked to the window to stare down at what had once been the monks' cloister. "We had drunk a great deal before we began our search for Lora and consumed considerably more after, back in Lord Robin's lodgings."

"What happened to Señor Cordoba? Did he remain in England?"

Sir Walter hesitated. "I do not know where he is."

"Can you find out?" She came up beside him and placed one hand on his sleeve.

"I will try."

"And Francis Elliott? Where is he these days?"

"At court. He has a minor position under the Master of the Queen's Horse."

Another connection to Lord Robin. "Can you arrange a meeting for me with Master Elliott?"

"If you insist." He gazed down into her face, his expression somber. "I wish you would not involve yourself further in this matter. You do not know what evil you may stir up."

"I am in no danger." She forced a smile. "I am much too tall."

"This is not a matter suited to jesting," he chastised her.

She sobered instantly. "No. It is not, but it does seem he kills only small, fragile women. I wonder why? Is it easier? Does he dislike the type?"

A flicker of something, perhaps pain, crossed Sir Walter's face before he gave a short laugh and an opinion. "Another sort of woman would be a more sensible choice, for the sheer number of them available. A tall lass, with a porcelain pallor and coltlike features, and perhaps red-gold hair, natural or otherwise, in imitation of the queen."

"Have you known one such and thought to murder her?" The words were out before Susanna could stop them, but she was not sorry she'd asked. And she was not afraid. Jennet's silent presence was her protection.

"I knew one such." Sir Walter's voice contained no emotion, his eyes no light. He seemed to look inside himself rather than at her. "She died by her own hand."

With a visible effort, he shook off melancholic memories and produced a faint, apologetic smile. "I meant only to describe the typical Englishwoman."

Susanna accepted his desire to say no more of the woman in his past and pursued the change in subject. "Are all nationalities so clearly defined?" She remembered what Petronella had said concerning her patrons' preference for foreign women . . . or those they thought had been born on the Continent.

"The typical Spanish lass is full-bodied and olive-skinned. Lora and Diane, with dark hair and fair skin, might have Irish blood in their veins. The average Frenchwoman—"

"Stop, I implore you. No more. And we digress. I do not believe the murderer killed Lora and Diane because he thought they were Irish. Neither do I believe I need fear for my own safety. Given my form and features, I am as likely to have poetry written to me as I am to be murdered by the man I seek."

"We digress indeed." He sighed. "But think a

moment, my dear Lady Appleton. If you are correct that one man killed three women, and perhaps more, then you place yourself in danger, no matter your appearance, simply because you attempt to track him down. To protect himself, such a man is capable of striking out at anyone at any time."

"He must be stopped. Surely you see that?"

"I see a woman who needs must be protected from herself. I beg you, do not concern yourself further with this matter. Let me investigate. Or leave it to your good husband."

Let them cover up murder? Susanna smiled sweetly but she had no intention of allowing either man to dictate to her. "I understand you may have reasons for not wanting to create a stir about Diane's death." The woman had been French, and involved in treason in that country. "But that is no reason not to look into what happened in the past."

He sighed again. "Ah, you will go your own way, no matter what I advise."

"You can help me. You have already said you could arrange a meeting with Master Elliott."

"Will you at least promise to allow me to be present when you talk to him? Or have Sir Robert with you? I do not believe any of my old friends are guilty of murder, but I failed to protect you in the past. I will not be so careless of you a second time."

"I agree we must suspect everyone," she conceded. "And I will not meet with anyone alone."

It did no good to remind him he'd done all he could that time in Gloucestershire, when she had put her own life at risk to catch a killer.

After Sir Walter had escorted her home and left her at her door, Susanna went over their conversation in her mind. He was right. She must be careful. And she must consider everyone a suspect, even Sir Walter. Even Robert.

It was as well, she decided, that she'd kept one thing back from both of them. They were aware she'd talked to the Lady Mary, but neither knew she'd been in contact with Petronella.

17

On the north side of Aldgate Street, just outside the city wall and beyond the churchyard of St. Botolph, stood the Crowne, a hostelry operated by a respectable two-time widow. It answered all Robert's needs. A heated private chamber. Stabling for Vanguard. A cook who knew his spices. And little chance of being recognized, especially if one arrived disguised.

Diego Cordoba appeared at the appointed hour, cloaked and hooded to hide the fact that he lacked an eye. He came directly to the upper chamber Robert occupied, one he had used on previous occasions for assignations with his last long-term mistress, the delightful Eleanor. From time to time he wondered what had become of her. She'd been gone from London when he returned from Spain. He had not tried to locate her. A mistress, after all, was easy to replace.

"Why so much secrecy?" Cordoba demanded, throwing off his cloak. "Notes delivered by street urchins. Coded messages. You have gone willingly enough to the ambassador's residence ere now, and there is an adequate tavern just across the Strand from the embassy."

"The Chequers? That place is a hotbed of political and social gossip." Robert poured two mugs of ale and offered one of the green, lead-glazed, earthenware vessels to his guest.

Cordoba accepted it but did not drink. "You are of a sudden skittish, Appleton. Why? Because of your diplomatic mission to Spain last year, 'tis easy enough to explain away any visit to Spanish territory."

"Not to anyone who knows the results of that venture." He'd been sent to Zafra, in Estremadura, to treat with a number of Englishmen and women who'd left England after Queen Mary's death. They'd accompanied her former maid of honor, Jane Dormer, now the wife of the count of Feria. None had been interested in his offer on Queen Elizabeth's behalf, but the proposal he had made on his own had met with greater success.

"You are overcautious," Cordoba complained.

"And you are not?" When King Philip left England for the last time, Cordoba had secretly stayed behind. It was remarkable, Robert mused, that he had succeeded so well in blending with the English. Cordoba should have been easily identified, not only by his eye patch, but by his swarthy Spaniard's complexion and his faint accent, and yet no one in the queen's government seemed to have the least idea what he had been up to. He'd traveled from one end of England to the other, sometimes passing for a Gypsy, at others disguised as a merchant who'd spent time in sunnier climes. Lately, using the name Ruy Vierra, Cordoba had openly joined the household of Ambassador de Quadra.

"To caution?" Cordoba proposed the toast, his voice mocking as he raised his mug.

They went through an elaborate ritual, drinking the ale, watching each other for any sign of weakness. Cordoba was no fool. He knew this clandestine meeting meant something had gone awry in their plan for the English succession.

"Your name, your real name, has come up in connection with a matter that has the attention of Sir Walter Pendennis. Does he suspect you are in England?"

Cordoba understood Pendennis's key position in the ranks of England's intelligence gatherers. "I have not seen Pendennis since Mary was queen."

An evasive answer, Robert thought, but the best he was likely to get. "Do any of your present acquaintance know you as Diego Cordoba?"

"Who but your own good self would be in a position to recognize me?" Cordoba smiled, but there was no humor in the expression.

"I do not want your real identity to become known any more than you do, but we may have no choice in the matter. Our entire scheme is in danger because my wife interests herself in the murder of a woman in Southwark. Not only has she made a connection between that death and the killing of Lora Tylney, coming to the conclusion that since both women were killed on St. Mark's Day, they were the victims of the same villain, but by sheer ill luck one of the persons she questioned about events six years ago was the Lady Mary Grey."

Robert took a long swallow of ale. Cordoba set his mug aside. "Can you not control your own wife?" Cordoba's contempt was the only emotion he showed. "Order her to desist."

"That would do naught but call more attention

to both of us. And Lady Appleton is nothing if not tenacious. She may ferret out other secrets in this effort to bring a murder to justice, unless she solves the crimes in a timely manner. I propose to help her do so."

"You know who killed Lora?"

"I neither know nor care who killed either of these women, but it occurs to me that if you leave England and it then becomes known you were living here under an alias, suspicion will fall on you." Once Cordoba was safely away, Robert would reveal that Cordoba and Vierra were the same man, a most suspicious circumstance.

Cordoba's face suffused with rage, he advanced on Robert, one hand on the pommel of his dagger. "You accuse me of murder?"

On his guard in an instant, his reflexes born of long years of uncertainty as to who was an enemy and who was a friend, Robert met the attack with sharp words and an even sharper sword. "For the greater good, this step is necessary." He held his weapon at the ready.

"You insult my honor."

"I offer a way out of an untenable situation. Now that Pendennis is interested in the murders, he will eventually uncover your presence in England." Or Susanna might do so on her own. He'd learned not to underestimate her. "All we've worked for, all we've planned, will be at risk if that happens."

Cordoba's hand left the dagger to reach for the earthenware mug he'd abandoned. He drank long and deep, then threw the drinking vessel across the room to shatter against the wall. Green shards tumbled to the rushes covering the hardwood floor. The dregs of the ale, adhering to the plaster, dripped into an ugly stain.

"We have no choice." Robert's temper simmered, though he maintained a reasonable tone of voice. In truth, it would be simpler to accomplish the tasks that remained on his own. He might even use Susanna's new acquaintance with the Lady Mary to lure the queen's cousin away from court and into his clutches.

"How long?" Cordoba asked. "How long until the queen leaves Whitehall?"

Their plan was to snatch the Lady Mary then, when her absence would go unnoticed for some time in the confusion of a move from one royal palace to another.

"The queen is fickle, always changing her mind about when she will journey where, but I hold myself ready to act at a moment's notice."

At the same time, he had taken care to protect himself. Susanna's presence in London would help deflect suspicion during the first crucial hours of the operation.

"I should be here," Cordoba argued. "You will need help to subdue her."

"I will use my man Fulke, if need be. And you can be of as much use, perhaps more, coordinating the meeting between Don Carlos and his bride."

Neither of them said anything for a moment, both contemplating the end result of their scheme. King Philip's only son, Don Carlos, was not a husband Robert would have wished on anyone, but all he needed to do was father a son on the Lady Mary, a son who would then be heir to both England and Spain. King Philip himself had approved the mating of the heiress to the English throne, dwarflike though she was, and his demented son.

"Others will bring Don Carlos," Cordoba said.

Robert laughed aloud. "Do you doubt your ability to handle him?"

Always physically undersized and afflicted with a speech impediment, a fall headlong down a staircase had left Carlos partially paralyzed and blind. To relieve the paralysis, an Italian surgeon had cut a triangular piece out of his skull. Ever since, the prince had suffered from fits of uncontrollable rage.

"Never doubt my abilities," Cordoba said softly, "but it is my reputation you plan to sully."

"There is no other way. If we succeed in this, we will both be well rewarded in Spain. A title and lands should make up for any rumors that linger behind in England." Certes, they'd cure Robert himself of any regrets! "Here is how I mean to proceed. I will recall, upon having been reminded of our old acquaintance, that I recently saw a fellow much like you at Durham House. A few careful questions will reveal Cordoba and Vierra to be one and the same. Then we need only place you in Southwark when this latest murder took place."

"Why not say you were the one to see me there as well?" Irony tinged the suggestion.

Robert frowned. "Better to bribe someone to describe you. Eye patches are not uncommon, but still something a man notices. Pendennis will seek you, find that you have fled, and that will seem to settle your guilt."

"And if I do not leave?"

"You will be found. You will be charged with homicide. Pendennis will dig deeper. King Philip will never acknowledge that you acted with his knowledge and consent. As a spy, as well as a murderer, you will be executed."

"I might, in turn, reveal your activities."

"And for that reason, I have gone to great pains to warn you." Why could the fellow not see reason?

With an abruptness that caught Robert by surprise,

Cordoba acceded to his wishes. "By this evening," he promised, "I will seem to have vanished into thin air."

"Then when we meet again, it will be on Spanish soil."

His movements brusque, Cordoba gathered up his cloak and stalked to the door, pausing there to look back over his shoulder. "I wonder," he mused, "how many small, dark-haired, pale-faced girls abide in Spain? And how safe they will be in years to come?"

18

As Petronella entered the area known as Duke Humphrey's Rents, near Puddle Dock, she sensed someone watching her. She tried to convince herself 'twas imagination. She was in an area of the city strange to her, and a woman alone, but her uneasiness increased until she found the place she sought.

The house was not whitewashed, as brothels were in Southwark, but it had a distinctive hatch door set with metal spikes to discourage sudden intruders. Petronella's old friend Isabel, a buxom, fair-haired courtesan, welcomed her with pippin pie and wine.

"You need not be so extravagant," Petronella chided her, knowing full well that what cost fourpence in the market went for eighteen or twenty in a whorehouse.

" 'Tis already paid for," Isabel assured her, "by a generous admirer, a fripperer in Houndsditch." She giggled. "He seeks to fatten me up. Likes meat on bones, he says."

"You have been here for some time." Long before Petronella took her first customer, Isabel had worked at the Sign of the Smock. If she was now accepting special favors from a secondhand clothes dealer, 'twas a signal she soon meant to leave the business and marry the man.

"Aye," Isabel agreed, "and this is the first visit you've ever paid me. Why did you come, lovey? Not to talk about old times, that's certain." They'd last seen each other when Long Nell died. All Nell's girls, past and present, had turned out to bury her in the single women's churchyard, for she'd been much loved.

Sugarcoating served no purpose. Petronella dished out the few facts she had, though she kept Lady Appleton's name to herself, then added a question. "Is there any reason for folk hereabout to remember a murder on any St. Mark's Day?"

"Aye. There is, though I'd not have given it another thought if you'd not told me about the others. 'Twas in the second spring of this reign. That very day did the queen's grace sup at Baynard's Castle. There were torches everywhere in the streets hereabout, cresset lamps on poles, filled with burning oiled rags so they could be carried in procession later, for after supper her grace was rowed up and down the Thames with a hundred boats about her and trumpets and drums and flutes and guns, and fireworks till ten at night. When her grace departed, all at waterside stood, a thousand people strong." Isabel gave a little sigh of delight, remembering. Doubtless the pageantry had been good for business, too.

"And the murder?"

"A whore, small and dark, as you say. And her neck broken." Isabel thought for a moment, "Mariotta, she called herself."

"Was anything left by the body? A feather?"

Isabel did not remember.

Petronella went back to her own place of business and thought about the things she'd learned. Then she contacted Lady Appleton.

19

Grooms did all manual labor connected to the royal stables. As Master of the Queen's Horse, Lord Robin Dudley's position was primarily ceremonial. Between the two extremes, Gentlemen of the Horse and Yeomen of the Horse shared the remaining duties. Sir Robert Appleton and Sir Walter Pendennis ran Francis Elliott to ground in a small counting room in the Royal Mews in Westminster, just a stone's throw from the place where Her Majesty's favorite mount was stabled.

Elliott seemed glad of the interruption. "I've become a damned bookkeeper," he complained, gesturing to the ledgers spread out before him on a worktable. "Reduced to tracking how many loads of hay we receive when I did not even know at first that a standard load is reckoned by the capacity of a two-wheeled cart extended by lades. Seventy-two bottels," he clarified, referring to the usual-size bundle in which hay and straw were sold.

Robert had not known that either, though he supposed Susanna must. She handled all the day-to-day business involved in making their lands profitable.

"Do you recall Mistress St. Cyr?" Pendennis asked, moving an ornate saddle, a beechwood frame covered with oxhide and decorated with copper studs, from bench to floor to make room to sit.

"The Frenchwoman I met in your rooms and escorted to Southwark? Aye. I remember her well. A lissome lass. How does she?"

"Dead," Pendennis said bluntly.

Robert shut the door and leaned against it. "Murdered," he elaborated.

"A pity," Elliott said, "but what has this woman's death to do with me? When I saw her last, she was well, and looking forward to renewing her acquaintance with you, Appleton."

"She did not seem ... afraid?" Susanna had insisted Diane looked worried when she visited Catte Street.

"No. Now, if that is all you want to know, I have work to do. The fancy has recently infected some of the queen's horses."

This was news to Robert, and cause for concern. As soon as Elliott mentioned the disease, which produced boils inside a horse's nostrils, he noticed the faint smell of burning frankincense in the air, a common precaution against another equine infection called the mourning. The fancy was thought by some to be an early sign of the mourning, in which abscesses formed in the angle of the jaw. These might burst, either internally or externally, and if the disease did not then run its course quickly, wasting occurred because the horse's throat was too sore for swallowing. Robert worried about Vanguard. On occasion he stabled his favorite stallion here in the Royal Mews.

"Any sign of illness among the Irish stud?" he asked, momentarily diverted from their main purpose in confronting Elliott. They were passing fine coursers. The queen preferred such good strong Irish gallopers to the geldings her ladies rode.

Pendennis cleared his throat. "Diane St. Cyr was killed in the same way Lora Tylney was."

Elliott looked from one to the other, disbelief in his eyes. "You jest?" he suggested weakly.

Robert outlined the few facts they knew about the three St. Mark's Day victims and owned up to his wife's meddling in the matter.

Elliott stared at the quill pens beside the ledgers. "Gentlemen, what you say fills me with astonishment."

"My wife wishes to question you," Robert said bluntly.

Elliott's eyes narrowed. "Do you suspect me of these murders? I have no reason to kill anyone."

"Susanna," Robert assured him, "suspects everyone." He glanced once at Pendennis, then took care to avoid the other man's too sharp eyes as he launched the diversion he'd devised. "Now that we three have met again, my memory stirs. Does not logic dictate that the murderer we seek is the one who felt most strongly about Lora Tylney?"

"Cordoba?" Pendennis looked thoughtful.

"But he left England years ago," Elliott objected. "How can he have killed Mistress St. Cyr?"

"It is possible he did not return to Spain. I asked after him when I was there on the queen's business and none did know his name. And of late I have twice seen a man, from a distance, who does much resemble our old companion."

"Where?" Pendennis asked.

"At Durham House. I inquired about him and was

told his name is Ruy Vierra. I assumed I was mistaken, but now that I consider, I believe Vierra may in fact be Diego Cordoba. A disguise?. . ." He let the suggestion trail off.

Pendennis gave him a strange look. "If you had reasoned this out, why did you not report it?"

"Report what? That I might have recognized an old friend?"

"Ruy Vierra is one of the ambassador's clerks," Pendennis said. "I have lists of the names of all those employed at Durham House. Vierra has been there less than a year."

"Even if Diego Cordoba killed those three women, we will never be able to bring him to trial," Elliott mused. "The ambassador will simply send him back to Spain at the first hint of an investigation."

"Not if we move swiftly to question him." Robert reckoned Cordoba had a full day's head start by now. Pendennis would discover the man had fled. He would conclude that guilt had made him go. Then Robert himself would suggest that, having heard questions had been raised about the murders, Cordoba had left to avoid arrest.

What fine irony that 'twas true!

20

"We need," Susanna said, "to make lists."

She and Jennet once again sat together on a chest in Petronella's chamber. Susanna's companion held herself aloof, contributing nothing, still uncertain how she felt about their hostess's profession, but Susanna had decided to treat this visit the same way she would a call upon any ordinary gentlewoman.

"What lists?" Petronella produced paper and pen from an ornate, inlaid box even as she asked the question. She had spent the last hour detailing all she'd learned of other murders in the years between Lora's death and Diane's.

The massive guardian of the gate at the Sign of the Smock, Vincent by name, had assisted in her inquiries, a fact Susanna applauded. Sir Walter's words had made more of an impression upon her than she liked to admit. It was all too possible that the killer, hearing someone had been asking questions, might panic and strike out in order to protect his dark secrets.

"A list of victims first." Susanna moved to Petronella's writing table and jotted down each name as she spoke it. "1557—Lora Tylney, at court. 1558—Little Alice, in Southwark. 1559—Mariotta, in Duke Humphrey's Rents. 1560—an unnamed woman here in Southwark. But for 1561 we know of no one." She brushed the feathered end of the quill pen back and forth across the underside of her jaw as she thought. "The celebrations for St. George fall but two days prior to St. Mark's Day. I have heard the court travels to Windsor for those festivities. I wonder if a woman might have been murdered there in 1561. Perhaps Sir Walter can inquire."

"Is he not a suspect?" Petronella asked.

"Aye, but so is mine own husband. What harm in soliciting their assistance? Besides, Sir Walter has at least some promise of proof he was in another place when one murder occurred. For much of the year the woman named Mariotta was killed, he lodged in Paris to carry out the queen's business."

She wished Robert had so good an excuse, but though he made frequent trips out of the country, he had been, to the best of her recollection, in England on every St. Mark's Day for the last six years. To verify her memory, she'd need to consult records kept at Leigh Abbey.

"The journey from Paris to London and back again may be made quickly," Petronella pointed out. "With post horses and favorable winds for crossing the Narrow Seas, a man might manage it in a week. With careful planning, his absence from Paris might be concealed that long."

Susanna did not like suspecting Sir Walter. She needed him as an ally. But she had to agree with

Petronella's reasoning. Perhaps, she thought, she could discover what the weather had been like in April of 1559. A stormy spring would have made such a trip unlikely. She might request access to travel records, as well. Anyone leaving England was supposed to procure a license to do so.

As she felt a smile creep over her features, Susanna bit back a wry chuckle. Had she learned nothing from that affair in Gloucestershire? 'Twas passing simple to forge such documents. Still, every possibility must be investigated.

"1562," she continued, "Ambrosia La Petite, in Southwark. And this year, Diane St. Cyr, also in Southwark. Now to suspects. Those most closely questioned in the investigation of Lora Tylney's death were my husband and Sir Walter, Lord Robin Dudley, two English gentlemen, Peregrine Marsdon and Francis Elliott, and a Spaniard, Diego Cordoba."

As she rattled off each name and before she wrote it down, Susanna glanced at Petronella. Only the involuntary twitch of an eye indicated the brothelkeeper had greater interest in one man than in the others. Diego Cordoba. Had he given Petronella the information about Lora? The brothelkeeper had not identified her source at their last meeting. She had not known Susanna well enough yet to trust her.

Susanna debated pressing her for information. Cordoba was a likely suspect, at least for Lora's murder. But had he been in England all this while? Most Spaniards had left with their king, shortly after Lora's death.

Sir Walter claimed not to know where Cordoba was. Robert had avoided mentioning him altogether. Both men had behaved oddly when speaking of the man. But why would they attempt to shield him if he was capable of murder?

Too many questions, Susanna thought, and not enough answers. She took a deep breath and spoke bluntly. "You know all five of these suspects, I do think."

Wary once more, Petronella allowed that they were not unfamiliar names to her, but she would admit no more than that. "They are gentlemen of good reputation," she said. "Influential courtiers. A wise woman is careful not to bring charges against such men without ample proof."

And even then, Susanna acknowledged, allegations of murder might prove more dangerous to the accuser than to the accused.

21

"Could you hear it all?" Petronella asked as Diego Cordoba slipped out of the bolthole secreted next to the chimney stack and took the chair Lady Appleton had so recently vacated. She'd removed the lists she'd made, but blank parchment, a quill pen, a bottle of ink, and blotting paper remained on the writing table.

"Aye," Diego said. " 'Tis clear she knows nothing yet of my disappearance, but her husband will soon remedy that oversight."

Petronella began to massage his shoulders. He was stiff with tension, a rare state in the easygoing gallant she had known for so many years.

When he had come to her the previous night, he had brought with him clothing, papers, and other personal belongings. He had not asked if he could stay with her. He had told her he meant to. He'd paid well to ensure that no one knew he had taken up residence at the Sign of the Smock, but Petronella would have hidden him for free rather than let him be apprehended.

She'd enjoy having him with her day and night, Petronella thought, were it not for all the questions he refused to answer. He'd share none of his long-range plans. He'd said Sir Robert Appleton, the very man who meant to accuse him of murder, had given him warning and urged him to flee the country, but he would explain none of his reasons for pretending to fall in with Appleton's schemes.

Diego appeared to have no immediate intention of leaving England, or her premises. Even Petronella's revelation of her relationship with Lady Appleton had not convinced him to move on. His only reaction to learning there were at least six victims had been to remark that Sir Robert had mentioned only two.

"I do not understand why you must take the blame," she dared whisper as she kneaded his muscles. Could Diego be responsible for the deaths of Diane and Lora and the others? Why else would he let Sir Robert drive him into hiding?

"For the greater good." She heard the bitterness in his voice as he turned and drew her into his arms.

She frowned. He did not deny he was guilty of murder. And someone was. Sir Robert, since he was the one who wished to blame Diego?

Her lover stroked the line of her jaw with one finger and she trembled. "Fear, *querida*? Or desire?" He caught her face in both hands. "You are safe as long as I am here with you." His kiss sealed in any protest she might have made.

Petronella yielded to desire, believing him when

he said he meant her no harm. As they lost themselves in the glories of lovemaking, her own wry cynicism told her that the greatest danger Diego Cordoba posed was not to her life but to her heart.

22

Jennet had borne silent witness to her mistress's second meeting with the Southwark brothelkeeper and been reluctantly fascinated by both the woman and her profession. The following day, she had occasion to eavesdrop on an even more interesting conversation.

Sir Robert brought a guest home with him, a man so handsome that for a moment she simply stared, speechless and bemused, at hair as golden as the sun and thick as the finest ermine pelt. Beneath large, mild, gray eyes, given unexpected depths by flecks of black, were a straight nose and a short yellow beard.

Under Jennet's admiring scrutiny, his lips curved slowly upward into the most devastatingly masculine smile she had ever received. His features, she thought, could not have been better sculpted by a master, and his body was a fit pedestal for the face. He was a bit shorter than Sir Robert, of slighter build, but beneath the plain black doublet and hose was a hard, muscular body Jennet could not help but admire.

After fetching Lady Appleton, Jennet watched her betters, as she had once before, from the shadowy recess beneath the stairwell, a vantage point from which she could both see and hear.

"My dear," Sir Robert said to his wife. "May I present my old friend Francis Elliott."

"Master Elliott." Lady Appleton graciously offered her cheek to be kissed, then waved him back to one of the chairs grouped before the unlit fireplace. Sir Robert had already provided their guest with wine and poured a goblet for himself. Lady Appleton declined the offer that he do likewise for her.

"Does it not seem remarkable to you that we have never met ere now?" she asked. "You were in the duke of Northumberland's service at the same time Robert was, and I, soon after, became the duke's ward."

"Aye, madam. A pity, too." Master Elliott had a deep, resonant, melodic voice. He jerked his head toward Sir Robert. "Mayhap this dog would not have won you for himself had I seen you first."

Safe in her favorite place of concealment, Jennet snorted softly. She knew a little of her mistress's past. The marriage to Sir Robert had been arranged by Northumberland. Neither of them had been allowed any say in the matter. They'd not even met until the day of their formal betrothal.

Social chatter quickly dispensed with, Sir Robert broached the subject of murder. "Pendennis sent word just as Elliott and I were about to leave Whitehall to come here," he said to his wife. "One man now seems more likely than any other to have killed both Lora and Diane."

"Diego Cordoba?" Lady Appleton guessed.

Jennet heard a sharp intake of breath but was uncertain which of the gentlemen had been startled. Master Elliott, most likely, since he did not know of her past successes.

"Diego Cordoba," Sir Robert agreed. "Or, as he has called himself these last few months, Ruy Vierra. He remained behind in England after King Philip left six years ago. As a spy."

"Intelligence gatherer, do you mean?" Lady Appleton's tone was arch. Sweet, but tinged with sarcasm, Sir Robert always insisted upon using this less negative term when he referred to his own work for the Crown.

"Aye," he conceded. "Intelligence gatherer. We have not yet been able to trace all his movements. He would have employed disguises. Taken on false identities. Of late he held a minor clerk's post at Durham House."

"And has a warrant been issued for his arrest?"

"Alas, my dear, 'twould do no good. Cordoba, or rather Vierra, has vanished. He must have learned that questions were being asked about the murders and fled in a panic."

A small silence fell. Jennet could almost hear her mistress thinking. She was unsurprised when Lady Appleton expressed doubt. "You have no proof, then. Only supposition."

"Why would an innocent man run?"

"Because he is not so innocent of other matters. You said yourself he was in this country to gather intelligence. What if he simply found out all he needed to know and went home to report to his master?"

"It seems to me too great a coincidence that this

should occur just as you began to investigate the murders."

"You give me too much credit, husband."

"Only that which is your due, my dear."

He was laying on praise too thick. Jennet hugged herself and waited. She was not disappointed.

"It may be you are right, Robert," Lady Appleton said slowly, "but I do think I must continue to ask questions. For mine own peace of mind. And here you have most fortuitously brought me Master Elliott, who may provide me with some of the answers I seek."

While Jennet strained to hear every word, Lady Appleton took both men through the night of Lora Tylney's murder six years earlier. The story was familiar by now. Drunken courtiers in pursuit of a wench. All of them searching the room where scenes and machines for court masques were stored. Master Elliott telling the others that Lora must already have departed.

"And so you can assure me, Master Elliott, that she was still alive when you left that room?"

"Alive and healthy."

Lady Appleton placed one hand on his arm and gazed up at him, speaking softly. "Did you kill her, Master Elliott?"

Jennet held her breath.

He did not seem to take offense at the question, and his words had the ring of truth in them. "I saw she'd hidden, realized how afraid she was, and indeed, I did consider returning alone, to take advantage of her gratitude, but then I remembered how recently she'd been Cordoba's woman, and I did not think such an action would be wise."

"So you have suspected she was killed by Diego Cordoba all along?"

Master Elliott made a dismissive gesture. "He was

always a suspect, but there was no proof. All I can tell you with certainty is that someone went back into that room after we all left together.''

Abruptly, Lady Appleton turned her attention to her husband. "Did Diego Cordoba have opportunity to return that night, Robert? Did he wander off on his own once you'd returned to Lord Robin's chamber?''

"My dear, I scarce remember what I did that night. He and I and Pendennis and Marsdon and Lord Robert, and Elliott here, kept drinking into the wee hours. I slept some part of that time.'' He grinned at her. "No doubt I also made one or two visits to the privy.''

"This is not a matter for levity, Robert.''

"Nor is it possible for anyone to account for every moment of his time, not after all these years.''

Jennet thought Lady Appleton might point out that, six years earlier, during the inquiries into Lora Tylney's death, all the suspects had been asked to do precisely that. And she expected her mistress to ask both men where they had been when each of the other victims was murdered. Instead, she skipped directly to the Frenchwoman.

"Did you ever meet Diane St. Cyr, Master Elliott?''

"Once,'' he admitted. "I was in Pendennis's rooms when she turned up there. Took him by surprise, I warrant, a woman visiting his lodgings.''

"That is no detriment to her character,'' Lady Appleton said stiffly. "I have myself visited Sir Walter's rooms.''

A strangled sound issued from Sir Robert, but he said nothing. Jennet leaned out of her hiding place to give him a hard stare. If he reacted so strongly to his wife's visit to Blackfriars, she wondered what he would think of her trips to Southwark.

"Your pardon, Lady Appleton.'' Master Elliott's

voice was smooth, his demeanor properly contrite. "I did not mean to imply any impropriety, though you must agree that Mistress St. Cyr did not have the highest moral standards. She had no maidservant with her, and she allowed me, a stranger, to escort her to lodgings at an inn. However, I left her long before she was murdered, and in the interim, or so I am told, she came here and spoke with you."

"Where did you go, Master Elliott?"

"Why, to my father's house, in Bermondsey. There I spent the night and returned to Whitehall the next morning by way of Lambeth. I heard nothing of the discovery of Mistress St. Cyr's body until your good husband and Walter Pendennis told me the tale."

"Did she seem nervous or afraid when you spoke with her?" Lady Appleton asked.

"Not that I noticed. She was polite. Grateful for my assistance. Pleased to be safe in England after the turmoil of France."

Apparently satisfied, Lady Appleton thanked Master Elliott for answering her questions. A few minutes later, both men left the house.

"Jennet, you may come out now," Lady Appleton called as she passed Jennet's hiding place and ascended to the upper floor. She was in her solar, already pouring a reviving glass of her special tonic, by the time Jennet scurried in. "You heard everything?"

"Yes, madam."

"A neat solution, presented to us on a platter."

"Aye, madam."

"Robert expects me to abandon my quest and stop asking embarrassing questions."

Little chance of that, Jennet thought. "You did not tell him about the other murders."

"I would have to explain how I learned of them. I

am not ready to reveal Petronella's part in this. Not yet. Perhaps never. I'd not endanger her."

"Then how will you learn if Master Elliott and the rest can prove they were elsewhere when those murders took place?"

"Perhaps Señor Cordoba is guilty," Lady Appleton mused. "I've thought him the most likely suspect myself. But there must be proof, and I will seek it."

"How, madam?"

"I will go ahead with my plan to ask Sir Walter to find out if any murders took place near Windsor Castle in 1561." She sat at her writing table and prepared to compose a letter. "But first, I do think, I must ask him to take me to the scene of Lora Tylney's murder. I would see for myself this scenery storage room where she died."

23

"I wish you would reconsider," Sir Walter said as he led Susanna through the rabbit warren of administrative and domestic offices that comprised the ground floor of Whitehall Palace. Jennet trailed behind them, gawking openly at every new sight. "What purpose will it serve? Why not accept that Cordoba is the killer?"

"In every case?" She had just given him a brief summary of the three additional murders Petronella had uncovered. She had not revealed her source. In fact, she'd let Sir Walter believe Robert had supplied the information. She thought it likely her deceit would come back to haunt her, since Robert at present knew of only three victims, but she could see no good at all in revealing Petronella's name.

Sir Walter glanced her way, noted the stubborn set of her jaw, and capitulated. "I will speak with the Coroner of the Royal Household. He is responsible for investigating any murders that occur within the verge, that is to say within a twelve-mile radius of the body of the queen."

"That will be most helpful."

Three days had passed since Susanna sent her note requesting Sir Walter take her to the scene of Lora Tylney's murder. The May Day festivities had taken place in the interim, making an earlier tour impossible. The area would still be a hive of activity, Sir Walter had warned her, what with returning all manner of scenes and machines and costumes to storage.

They entered a cavernous room, filled with wondrous strange objects. Susanna blinked and came to an abrupt halt. "It is ... overwhelming," she admitted.

"Come, let me show you some of the sights." Sir Walter led her deeper into the room. "When we were first at court during King Edward's short reign, Francis Elliott and I spent many hours here. The Keeper of Machines told marvelous stories about the days when King Henry employed skilled artisans just to design and execute new scenes."

Although this was the place where Lora Tylney had been foully murdered, Susanna found herself falling under the enchantment of its contents. An entire forest seemed to grow from the bed of a wagon more than thirty paces long. Its trees were painted with as rich a variety of greens as nature offered. Nearby was an arbor of gilt pillars wreathed in artificial vines, constructed on another wagon. Next came an elaborate fountain twice as tall as she was and all covered with silver foil.

"There was one pageant wagon, designed for festivities here at Whitehall, that carried thirty men and women," Sir Walter said. "It moved, turned about ... and was so heavy that it broke right through the floor."

The almost musical lilt of his voice was as pleasing to Susanna as his stories. The rhythm of his native Cornwall had reasserted itself in these surroundings. When she realized how much she was enjoying his company, however, she chastised herself for forgetting their purpose in coming here. She started to remind him, but stopped at the startling sight of a ship, white sails set on two high wooden masts and room for a dozen people on the brightly painted deck and half-deck.

"Climb aboard," Sir Walter invited, gesturing to the gaudily decorated galleon.

"How do they make any of these wagons move?" she asked when they had both ascended the rope ladder and were standing side by side at a highly polished, red enameled rail.

"That varies," he said. "The lighter pageant wagons are often drawn by young men dressed in costumes. That forest we looked at can be moved by two stout lads. I remember one time it was used. One fellow was dressed as a lion and the other as an antelope. That tower over there," he said, pointing, "requires a horse to pull it into the hall. The ill-fated wagon I mentioned earlier was towed in by an entire team of oxen."

"And these scenes are used as the backdrop for a story?" Susanna's experience with masques was limited, for she'd never been invited to attend court functions.

Sir Walter nodded. "Most are simple variations of the same tale. A band of fair damsels occupies a castle, or a mount, or a ship. A group of men dressed as Turks or crusaders or pirates lays siege. The women surrender."

"Always?"

In spite of the twinkle in his eyes, Sir Walter's voice

was solemn. "Always," he assured her. "Then other elements are added, for variety. Myth and legend freely mix with comic turns and studied complements. Often there are disguisings."

"When I was very young, my grandmother often spoke of such things," Susanna confided. "She was at court early in King Henry's reign and remembered one time when the king dressed himself as Robin Hood and his courtiers as outlaws, all in short coats of Kendall green. She said they wore hoods on their heads and were armed with bows and arrows and swords and bucklers when they made an early-morning visit to the queen. They only revealed their true identities after Queen Catherine and her ladies agreed to dance with them in the queen's bedchamber."

As a small child, Susanna had thought this sounded most romantic, and had believed that King Henry must truly love his wife. What nonsense, she thought now. Catherine of Aragon had been but the first of Henry's six queens. There had already been two more by the time Susanna's grandmother told her this tale, one beheaded and one dead in childbed.

"Robin Hood is a popular figure," Sir Walter said. "So are the three worthies and the three princes."

The worthies, Susanna knew, were Julius Caesar, Hector, and Alexander. The princes were Charlemagne, Arthur, and Godfrey of Bouillon. "What masque was performed the night Lora Tylney died?"

"Four damsels were inside a tower much like that one." Sir Walter indicated a nearby structure of canvas and wood. "Four masked men, all similar in height and breadth of shoulder and dressed in identical costumes, joined them there as the mumming ended. One of them was King Philip."

Susanna stared at the pageant wagon. " 'Tis passing small for eight."

"In such intimate quarters you may be sure all four lords took liberties with the ladies."

"And the . . . damsels allowed it?"

"What woman dares say nay when it might be her liege lord kissing and fondling her?"

Susanna said nothing, but did not care for the picture he painted of life at court. Or of himself and Robert and their friends.

Sir Walter looked uneasy, as if he wished he had not been so forthcoming. "When people are caught up in a fantasy," he said softly, "it is ofttimes difficult to remember the realities of everyday life."

"No doubt the difficulty becomes more pronounced when all parties are cup-shotten."

Stiffly courteous now, Sir Walter stepped back, motioning for Susanna to precede him down the rope ladder. Jennet waited below.

Reality, Susanna thought as she descended. Just as well to return to it. She had not come here simply to enjoy the company of a charming man.

That Sir Walter had gone out of his way to be pleasant troubled Susanna. She did not want his admiration, not man to woman, even though the attention was flattering. Had he gotten the wrong idea from the fact that she kept contacting him?

Absurdly uncomfortable with that notion, she was glad they were surrounded by other people. Jennet. The current keeper and his staff. Although none of the men working in the room had come near Sir Walter's small party or spoken to any of them, they slanted surreptitious glances in their direction. Susanna would wager they missed little of the interplay between herself and the knight, even if they were too far away to overhear what was said.

"Have you seen enough?" Sir Walter asked.

"I would inspect the tower, though it is not likely to be the same one Lora hid in."

"It might be," he mused. "But she did not die there. She was found in an open space on the floor." He glanced around. "I doubt anyone could say precisely where."

"The man who found her?"

"That was the keeper I spoke of, but he was elderly. He died a year or so ago."

Susanna supposed it made little difference. There was nothing to be seen here, and less, she was sure, at the places where the other women had been found.

"Where did the feather come from?" she asked as she inspected the canvas tower.

"Another pageant wagon."

"The killer did not bring it with him, then?"

"Why should he?"

"I wish I knew. It did seem the feather by Diane's body had been brought there deliberately." She made a rueful sound. "Perhaps the feathers are only coincidence, after all. Tell me again of that night. Do you recall any more, being here again?"

"The rushlights were sputtering."

Susanna glanced at the iron wall brackets. Each one held a two-foot torch. One would burn but an hour before it needed to be replaced. Had the room been almost dark when Lora's murderer returned? She shivered at the thought, feeling pity for a young woman she'd never met. To hide her reaction, she ducked inside the gaudily painted wood-and-canvas tower through an opening at the back.

Experimentally, Susanna sat, clasping her knees to her chest to make herself as small as possible. She could hear Sir Walter moving just outside the canvas walls. He sounded as if he were right on top of her hiding place.

Lora would have been able to hear every word they spoke while they'd searched for her, she realized. Ribald jests. Salacious speculation. That Robert and Sir Walter should have been part of that sickened Susanna.

"Do you want me to trip the mechanism that lowers the drawbridge?" Sir Walter asked. "It is at the front of the tower."

As soon as she agreed, it began to descend. Inch by inch, the opening grew. Sir Walter filled it. As the murderer might have on that long-ago night?

She came to her feet and, with more speed than grace, exited the set piece. "I have seen enough."

"What will you do now?" Sir Walter asked as he escorted Susanna and Jennet through the connecting buildings toward the water gate called Whitehall Stairs. The Privy Stairs, which Susanna had used on her previous visit, were farther upriver.

"I must continue to ask questions."

He sighed and helped her aboard the waiting wherry.

"I have a need to clear mine own husband of suspicion," Susanna added when they were on their way downstream.

"You cannot believe—"

"I will not condemn Señor Cordoba out of hand. I must continue to ask questions until I am convinced of his guilt. By the same token, I must ask questions dealing with Robert's whereabouts on past St. Mark's Days. And Lord Robin's whereabouts. And Master Elliott's and Master Marsdon's. And yours, Sir Walter."

"You may dismiss Lord Robin from your list of suspects," he assured her.

Susanna thought it odd he did not first exempt himself. 'Why?'' she asked. "Indeed, he seems to have been the leader in much that went on at court." He still was, come to think of it.

"He was the nobleman among us, for all that his father had so recently been attainted and executed for treason. He took precedence over knights' sons and the sons of mere gentlemen, but he is also some years younger than the rest of us. Closer to your age than to mine."

"You believe the young do not perpetrate crimes as foul as their seniors?" She smiled at that thought. Young men could be far more vicious. Why else were they so assiduously recruited in wartime?

"I mean that he rarely did anything unaccompanied. All of us were with him that night, but so were several servants."

"I have heard too much about the amount of drink consumed to believe any of you can account for every moment." She remembered Robert's flippant comment. "If naught else, even Lord Robin must have made at least one visit to the privy."

Sir Walter regarded her with a somber, unblinking gaze she found disquieting. "The queen," he said, "will not be pleased if she should hear you suspect her favorite of murder."

He did not have to explain why this would be a particularly sensitive issue. A little more than two and a half years earlier, when Lord Robin's estranged wife had been found at the foot of a flight of stairs, her neck broken, people had wondered if he'd had a hand in her demise. If he had, Susanna had thought at the time, he'd miscalculated badly. True, his wife's death left him free to remarry, but the queen would never have him with such an allegation forever in his past.

"I will be discreet," she promised. Queen Elizabeth could ruin Robert's career if she blamed him for more scandal attaching itself to the Dudley name. "But do not forget I, too, know Lord Robin of old."

Lord Robin's father had been Susanna's guardian, responsible for arranging her marriage after her own father's death. The young gentlemen in his household, a goodly number of them over the years, had gone out into the world trained to be clever, charming, and devious. Some years younger than Robert, Sir Walter, Francis Elliott, and Peregrine Marsdon, Susanna had not known them when she was a girl, but she had spent hours with her guardian's sons, especially Lord Robin. He'd stolen a kiss from her once, when she was thirteen. She'd daydreamed about him for weeks thereafter.

"So, you mean to ask more questions," Sir Walter said, breaking a lengthy silence.

"Aye. I have spoken with Master Elliott already. What do you know of Peregrine Marsdon? Is he in London or at court?"

"Marsdon raises hawks and falcons on his estate in Essex. He gave up playing courtier years ago to devote himself to his birds, and to marrying off a flock of sisters." He smiled at her sudden alertness. "I said marry off, not kill off."

"What do they look like, his sisters?"

"I do not know, but I warn you, if you plan to pay Marsdon a visit, he is not the most sociable of men. He prefers to avoid the company of women. His betrothed left him at the church to run off with another man. And before you ask, she was a tall, thin, yellow-haired lass."

"You do not consider Master Marsdon a suspect?"

"Cordoba's behavior is far more suspicious. But you will go your own way. Come, madam, have at me!" For a moment, he sounded almost jovial. "You must have more questions about my dissolute youth."

"Only one. You were in France in the autumn of 1559. Were you already there on St. Mark's Day?"

"I was sent to Paris soon after Elizabeth ascended the throne and I did not return to England until the following Yuletide. Does that clear my good name?"

"It does if you speak the truth."

When he smiled and made a little bow to acknowledge her point, Susanna realized she believed him. Oh, she still intended to see if she could discover what the weather conditions had been in late April of that year. Petronella had been correct to say a man could journey from Paris to London and back in a week. Robert had often bragged, in the days when he made frequent forays to the Continent, that on a good horse a man could travel a hundred miles in a single day. Such times were also possible with post horses ridden in relays.

But Sir Walter seemed the least likely of all of them to be a cold-blooded killer. He was organized enough, but even that argued against his guilt. If he'd been intent on murdering a woman every St. Mark's Day, then in 1559 he'd have found a victim in Paris. He'd never have disrupted his schedule by returning to England.

More relieved than she wished to acknowledge by this logic, Susanna crossed Sir Walter Pendennis off her mental list of suspects.

24

Jennet's feet hurt. She wanted to go back to Catte Street, sit and put them up, and drink a nice soothing posset. "Do you mean to speak with every man in London who has ever held the post of sheriff?" she asked in a deliberately plaintive voice.

The current sheriffs were William Allen, a leather seller who lived in Bow Lane, and Richard Chamurlayn, ironmonger, of the parish of St. Olave in Hart Street. Visits to both places had yielded naught but a blister on Jennet's left heel.

A great waste of time, Jennet thought.

"Look upon this as a shopping trip," Lady Appleton suggested. "We shop for information."

It seemed to Jennet that they'd walked over half of London already. First they'd gone to the Guildhall. No great sacrifice, that. The place was in sight of the house. But all Lady Appleton had learned there was that this was indeed where any coroner for the city presented the results of his inquests. Master Speedwell was next scheduled to appear on the Wednesday of Whitsun week at one in the afternoon, nearly a month away.

Both coroners and sheriffs kept records of the proceedings of courts held at the Guildhall. That should have made matters simple. It did not. Lady Appleton had been told she could not see these records.

Her first reaction had been to seek an audience with the lord mayor, Sir Thomas Lodge. It turned out he'd served as one of the two sheriffs of London three years ago, but Sir Thomas not only denied remembering anything about the death of an unnamed prostitute in Southwark on St. Mark's Day but grew pedantic when Lady Appleton asked more questions, delivering very little information but using a lecturing tone that raised Jennet's hackles.

In a nutshell his explanation for this lack of helpfulness was that sheriffs were concerned with administration, not the catching of criminals. The watch and constables did that, but each ward had its own watch, and there was little cooperation among them. Unless a thief or murderer was taken during the initial hue and cry, he was rarely caught. No one troubled to pursue a malefactor to another part of the city.

Two more grueling hours passed before Lady Appleton gave up and returned to the Catte Street house. By that time she looked as tired and dejected as Jennet felt.

"I suppose," Lady Appleton said as they reached the comfort of the solar, "that there is little use in trying to locate the constables who found the bodies."

Jennet huffed audibly and limped to the nearest bench. "There are two hundred and forty of them, madam, and they are drawn from the ranks of householders. They change."

"Some are more permanent," Lady Appleton

argued. "Paid to take the place of householders who do not wish to be bothered with such service."

"And how many of them would have noted the death of a whore?" Jennet eased off her shoe and rubbed her ankles, then her toes, and finally her heels. She winced when her fingers came in contact with the blister through her wool stocking.

At once Lady Appleton was at her side, all concern and contrition. "Bare your foot," she ordered. "We must bathe that and apply a poultice," she declared when she'd finished poking and prodding. "I'll not have you risk infection."

Jennet protested, for form's sake, then yielded to her mistress's ministrations. They did not speak again of the day's fruitless quest. Jennet dared hope the investigation was over.

She should have known better.

That very evening a missive came from Sir Walter.

"There was a murder on St. Mark's Day in 1561," Lady Appleton announced. "A young woman fitting the same description as Lora and Diane and the others was killed in Deptford."

"Not Windsor?"

"No, but Deptford is a small village less than a mile from the queen's palace at Greenwich. For that reason, this murder came to the attention of the Coroner of the Royal Household. He has shared what information he has with Sir Walter. The victim's name was Sabina Dowe, the daughter of a local chandler." She tapped the edge of the parchment against her chin. "I think, Jennet, that we must make a trip."

"To Deptford?"

"To Deptford, but that will be but one stop on our journey. First, we will visit Bermondsey, where Master Elliott claims to have been when Diane St. Cyr died."

That meant traveling on horseback. Jennet bit back

a groan. Even more than she disliked excessive walking on paved streets, Jennet hated to ride pillion. The little benchlike seat attached to the back of a saddle was uncomfortable no matter how well it was padded. She'd be bounced black and blue in no time.

"And after Deptford," Lady Appleton said, smiling benignly, "we will continue on to Leigh Abbey."

Where Mark and the children waited. Jennet sighed. Seeing them again would almost make the bruising worthwhile.

25

The distance from London to Leigh Abbey was just
under fifty miles. Susanna usually allowed two days
for the trip, spending one night at a reputable inn
in Rochester. On this excursion, however, she meant
to make two detours and planned her route accord-
ingly.

"Madam, you turn off too early," Lionel objected
when she led them into Tooley Street after crossing
London Bridge and entering Southwark. "The main
road to Canterbury is—"

"Hush, fool," Jennet admonished him. "Lady
Appleton knows what she's about." She accompanied
her words with a sharp thump to the young man's
ribs. Since she was mounted directly behind him, she
could strike him in the side with considerable force.
He subsided, muttering to himself, and kicked the
gelding they both rode to hurry it along.

Susanna considered explaining herself, but
thought it best not to. Fulke was also in their party

and he was as much Robert's man as her own. Fulke had accompanied him on missions to Scotland and to Spain and on more recent trips into Hampshire. He'd told Lionel about his adventures. Lionel had repeated the details to Jennet, and Jennet had told her mistress. Susanna was therefore certain Fulke would report everything she said and did to his master. She resented being obliged to take him with her, but she would have been foolish to travel without an armed escort to scare off robbers and vagabonds.

Relieved to be doing something purposeful at last, yet she cautioned herself against trying to achieve too much all at once. This was a delicate investigation, especially the portion she meant to undertake today. She had accomplished nothing pertinent to the murders since her visit to Whitehall with Sir Walter. Asking questions in London had availed her naught while she waited for a message to travel to Jennet's husband, Mark, the steward at Leigh Abbey, and a reply to make its way back. She'd only managed to talk to Robert once. She'd told him about the other murders, letting him think Sir Walter had uncovered them. He hadn't seemed surprised, or outraged. And they'd quarreled when he'd insisted Cordoba could have committed all the crimes. He did not want to listen to any other possibility. It had been enough to make her doubt his compassion, if not his innocence.

Her excuse for a brief return to Leigh Abbey had been simple enough. Mark had written, following her instructions, that he'd encountered a discrepancy in the amount owed to certain merchants in Dover, where the Appletons bought many of their supplies. Since Susanna oversaw the management of the estate, her presence was necessary to determine which figures were correct. An air of urgency was added by Mark's revelation that these merchants demanded immediate payment. After calling down curses on such impertinent swine, Robert had placed matters in his wife's capable hands, his only instruction that she complete the business as swiftly as possible and return posthaste to London.

Unlike Jennet, Susanna was mounted on her own saddle on her own mare. She smiled to herself as she rode, for it felt good to be free of the city, if only for a short time. Even the air smelled fresher. She knew the River Thames lay just off to her left, beyond the rows of houses, and she could still see the topmost levels of the Tower of London beyond, but the landscape was already changing, showing more green and less grime. The little roan perked her ears and kept up a good pace. By the time they reached the banks of the River Neckinger in Bermondsey, Susanna could almost believe she was in some small rural shire town.

Her first destination, the house of Jerome Elliott, Francis Elliott's father, came as a shock. It was a small, poor place, badly kept. Wooden window shutters were closed, or hung broken from their iron casements. At first she thought the dwelling deserted, but when Lionel slammed a rusty knocker against the elmwood door, a servant opened it a crack.

"I have come to speak with Master Jerome Elliott," Susanna said.

The old servant woman's lips parted in a sly smile, revealing three teeth, all black and rotting. She stepped aside, allowing Susanna and Jennet access to the dwelling.

The interior was a match for the outside, ill maintained and reeking of scents Susanna did not wish to identify. The plastered walls had once been white, the woodwork painted bright colors, but all had deteriorated into a dingy and indeterminate shade. The rushes strewn over plain-colored Flemish tiles needed

changing. Furniture was minimal, only a meager scat-
tering of chests and stools, but there was reading
material. Pamphlets and broadsides on sensational
subjects were stacked on the floor.

She wondered why Francis Elliott had not found
better lodgings for his father. Posts at court might
not be well paid, but a courtier usually found ways
to supplement his income. Perhaps, she decided, neither father nor son was skilled with cards and dice.

She questioned her decision to explore Master
Elliott's background by the time the servingwoman
showed her into the small dark room where Elliott's
white-haired father huddled before a low fire. He
gave no sign that he heard them.

"How old is he?" Susanna asked the servant.

"Three score and six," the woman said.

Sixty-six years. 'Twas an age attained by many hardy
souls, and yet Susanna could count on the fingers of
one hand the number of men of her own acquaintance who had survived past sixty. War took them.
Or disease.

"Is his mind sharp?" He appeared feeble, his body
failing him, but she was in hopes he could still see,
hear, and reason.

"Some days," the servant said, and with that she
left Susanna and Jennet alone with the old man.

Susanna approached cautiously, calling his name.
When she was almost near enough to touch his arm,
Jerome Elliott looked up. Eyes the same color as his
son's were bloodshot and narrowed suspiciously when
he realized he did not know her.

"Who are you? What do you want?" he demanded
in a querulous voice.

Susanna introduced herself and told him she'd
come to talk to him about his son.

Elliott hawked and turned his face away from her

to spit phlegm into the fire. She waited, trying to decide if this was in response to her announcement or a normal manifestation of one of the many ailments with which he must be afflicted. She knew any number of herbs that could ease coughing. For a chesty cough, fennel root mixed with wine sufficed.

"What has Francis done now?" the old man demanded. His voice was hoarse, but he did not cough again. With one gnarled hand he rubbed his belly beneath the blanket that covered his lap and lower extremities.

No one, Susanna thought, lived past fifty without feeling the effects of gout, rheumatic disorders, gastric upsets, and the stone. Toothaches and tympany seemed likely, too.

"Your son has done nothing that I know of," she said. Not for a certainty. She made her voice soothing in the hope of placating him, but the old man's expression turned thunderous.

Taking a deep breath, she asked if his son had paid him a visit on the day before St. Mark's Day. She did not explain why she wanted to know, though she supposed she would if pressed. She half expected he'd not answer her at all, and regretted that she had no force of law to oblige him to cooperate in her inquiry.

Master Elliott grew more agitated at her question, spittle frothing at the corners of his mouth. The blanket slipped off his legs. Susanna bent forward to replace it for him, then backed rapidly away when she realized that his limbs were not shriveled and useless as she'd supposed, but simply bare. Jerome Elliott wore naught but a long linen shirt.

"I wish to help a friend," she said quietly when he'd rearranged the blanket to cover himself. "A woman known to your son. He told her he spent that night here with you, and it is important that I learn if he spoke the truth."

"If some wench doubts his word, 'tis no concern of mine." He glowered at her.

"Was your son here the night before St. Mark's Day? How can it hurt to satisfy my curiosity?"

Elliott's laugh sounded rusty from disuse. "Women! Sinful jades, all of you. Always teasing. Cajoling. Wanting foolish questions answered. What will you do for me, eh? Why should I do you any favors?"

"I will give your servant a recipe for an electuary that will much comfort you, a remedy against the putrid, rotten, and corrupt humors that lie about the mouth of the stomach."

The flicker of interest in the old man's eyes betrayed him.

"Better yet, I will make it up myself and send it." She could obtain all the ingredients in London, even the aloes.

"Expensive, is it?"

"Worth every penny," she assured him, "and the pennies will be mine."

That promise almost won her a smile. "Aye, Francis was here on the eve of St. Mark's Day," his father said. "He comes to plague me. He wants me to die so he can inherit."

Inherit what? If Jerome Elliott had a fortune, he did not believe in spending it on himself. "Did he stay the whole night?" she asked.

"Aye."

"Did anyone visit him here?"

"He's never been one to introduce me to his friends. Ashamed of his humble beginnings," he added in a mutter.

Susanna had intended her question to ascertain if

Diane had visited Bermondsey. Apparently, she had not. "How early the next day did he leave?"

"After he broke his fast."

"After daylight?"

"He's not one for rising early."

Bermondsey was not far distant from Southwark, but Diane had been murdered just before dawn. "Did you see him go? Note the time?"

"He left here well after I was up and about."

The testiness was back in Master Elliott's voice, but Susanna could not tell if he meant to be evasive or had simply grown impatient. Susanna had intruded into his life and 'twas clear he resented her presence nearly as much as he disliked his own son's visits. His tolerance for a stranger asking personal questions had reached its limit.

"Women," he grumbled. "More trouble than they're worth." He bellowed for his servant.

The old woman appeared at once, almost as if she'd been listening at the door.

"Get out," Elliott ordered. "And when you see my son's whore, tell her she chose a weak and foolish man for a lover."

Outside, Susanna drew in a deep breath of untainted air. Jennet, more offended by the way her mistress had been treated than Susanna was, muttered imprecations against nasty old men in general and Jerome Elliott in particular.

"Some men," Susanna observed, "regard all women as whores. I do much pity our erstwhile host. He drives away all those who might be kind to him as he grows older and more infirm."

"I wonder why there is so much bad blood between him and his son?" Jennet mused.

"And is it all on one side? The elderly, or so I have

been told, are prone to peculiar notions about their kin.''

Susanna studied the nearby buildings and after a moment selected the establishment of a haberdasher who displayed his goods on wooden pentices, hinged shop fronts let down to form tables on either side of the door. The shopkeeper's wife, who stood guard over the stock offered for sale, had a clear view of the house Susanna had just left. She looked old enough to have been in Bermondsey for some years.

"Good morrow, goodwife." Susanna pretended an interest in the items for sale, which included a wide variety of smallwares, from sewing silks, buttons, and pens to lanterns and mousetraps. Her true intent was never in doubt to either of them. She wanted information.

In short order she learned that Jerome Elliott had always been surly, always unpleasant to women. His only son visited him often, but never stayed long. On occasion they quarreled loudly enough for the entire village to hear. Jerome thought his son a wastrel. Francis called his father a pennypinching old fart.

"A pity they have such a poor relationship," Susanna said, selecting a packet of pins to purchase. "Have they ever gotten along?"

"He's a hard man, Jerome Elliott is. Drove his wife to kill herself, so they say."

"Francis Elliott's mother committed suicide?"

"So they say. No one saw the body."

Susanna could not decide if the goodwife meant folk suspected Master Elliott of murdering his wife or only of burying her in secret. Since no suicide could lie in a churchyard, such bodies were traditionally buried at the nearest crossroads, at midnight, with a stake driven through the heart lest the departed soul return to haunt the living.

"How old was the son she left behind?"

"Half-grown." The shopkeeper leaned toward Susanna and lowered her voice. "My mother always said that marriage was doomed right from the start. Jerome Elliott was set in his ways when he married her. Helen, she was called. Just a young slip of a thing, she was, a distant kinswoman of his from the north. He wanted a son. She gave him one, but she was never the same after."

She made change and handed over Susanna's purchase.

"Did your mother tell you anything more about the family?" Susanna returned the coins she'd just been given. She had a feeling this woman might recall a good bit on her own. She appeared to be about the same age as Francis Elliott. She might even have known him when they were both children.

"Young Francis left Bermondsey soon after his mother disappeared."

No doubt that was when he'd joined the Dudley household and first met Robert. "And his mother—do you recall her appearance? Was her hair fair or dark? Was she short or tall?"

"A small woman," the haberdasher's wife said, "but she was a gentlewoman, mistress. She covered her hair with a headdress whenever she went out. I doubt any but her husband and her son ever saw what color it was."

26

The road cut southeast, away from the serpentine curve of the Thames, and ran in a nearly straight line from Bermondsey to Deptford. It was wide enough that Lady Appleton's roan and the bay Jennet shared with Lionel could proceed side by side. Fulke rode a little ahead, scouting for danger.

Jennet heard Lady Appleton sigh and saw her cast a considering eye over Fulke.

"Your master is a suspect in the murders of several young women," she said abruptly, addressing both Fulke and Lionel. "In order to prove him innocent, I must discover who did kill them."

"Murder, madam?" Lionel goggled at her. "Again?"

He woofed out air as Jennet's fist once more connected with his ribs.

Ignoring Lionel's comment, Lady Appleton rode a little ahead and placed one gloved hand on Fulke's arm. "I count on your discretion, Fulke. No one must know of this. Not even Sir Robert. Do I have your word not to repeat anything you hear on this journey?"

"Aye, madam. Most willingly."

"And you, Lionel?" She looked back at him but kept hold of Fulke.

"Yes, madam."

"Good. Now, Fulke, you may be able to help me. In your travels with Sir Robert in Spain did you ever hear anyone mention the name Diego Cordoba?"

"No, madam."

"Ruy Vierra?"

"No, madam." He hesitated. "Sir Robert does not like me to hear things, so most times I pretend to be both deaf and blind."

Thwarted in that line of inquiry, Lady Appleton dropped back, riding with Jennet and Lionel once more.

"Think you he is the one?" Jennet asked. "The Spaniard? Or is the murderer Master Elliott?"

"I do not know enough about Señor Cordoba to say. As for Francis Elliott, I do much pity him, knowing now that his mother died when he was just a boy. But, yes, he is still a suspect."

"Sir Robert also lost his mother at a tender age."

"And Lord Robin, though he was older, lived through the execution of his father and one of his brothers."

"Does enduring tragedy make a man more likely to kill?" Jennet asked.

Lady Appleton gave a short bark of laughter, but there was no humor in it. "If that were true, there would be few men living who did not contemplate murder."

"Do you mean to look further into Sir Walter's background?"

Lady Appleton gave her a sharp look. "I know

enough. He spoke of his childhood when he visited
Leigh Abbey." During Sir Robert's sojourn in Spain,
Jennet remembered. "He shared fond memories of
growing up in Cornwall. And Robert has told me of
a great sadness in Sir Walter's life. A woman who took
her own life."

"As Mistress Elliott did?"

"We do not know that Helen Elliott died by her
own hand. The woman we talked to repeated gossip."

Lady Appleton would look into the matter, Jennet
thought. But would she delve deeper into the painful
secrets in Sir Walter's past? Of that, Jennet was not
so sure. She lost her opportunity to ask when their
party caught up with another band of travelers. All
discussion of murder ceased.

Bored, Jennet stared at the small, rectangular fields
by the side of the highway. Some had been planted
with produce, some with woad and madder. She
craned her neck, trying to see around Lionel as the
distant turrets and pennants of Greenwich Palace
appeared ahead. The royal residence was less than a
mile away.

She had seen Greenwich up close en route to London and remembered it as a gaudy place, the bricks
of its exterior walls painted bright red, with the mortar
joints picked out in brilliant white. Every stone window opening had been lime-washed and the battle-
ments were topped with carved beasts holding
painted poles and gilded vanes.

"We turn off here," Lady Appleton said, bidding
farewell to their temporary traveling companions. Just
past an apple orchard, they came to a three-gabled
house with a walled garden and a summer house.
"This is Sayes Court," she announced. "It becomes
the lodging of whatever person holds the post of
Clerk of the Green Cloth, he who is responsible for

the finances of the royal household and for the provision of meat to Greenwich Palace. The current clerk owes Sir Walter a favor, and so we are to be made welcome here. We will spend the night, but between dinner and supper, we will be left to our own devices."

A short time later, Jennet accompanied Lady Appleton into the village proper. What she noticed first was the stench. The smell of pitch and the stink of fish she'd expected, since several fishing boats were drawn up along the graveled beach, but she'd not been prepared for the combined odors of kennels, slaughteryard, and dung boats. They walked straight into the heart of it, where blood from butchers' row ran along a ditch to empty into the Thames.

"Look there," Lady Appleton said, pointing directly across the river. "An even worse place, the Isle of Dogs."

Jennet had heard of it. Those swampy wastes were the haunt of criminals and fugitives. None dared pursue them there.

Deptford was better. A quiet place now that the court was not in residence, it consisted of a parish church, a few shops, a village green, the dockyards, and the kennels of the queen's buckhounds.

Sir Walter had provided Lady Appleton with the location of Sabina Dowe's house. It was a respectable-looking place, but Jennet harbored dire suspicions about Mistress Dowe's character. Had not every other victim been a whore or a woman of easy virtue?

"Jennet," Lady Appleton said when they stood in front of the chandler's shop and its living quarters above, "I will talk to the family. You must make the acquaintance of their servants. A maid, I do think, and several apprentices. Speak with them. Win their confidence. We will compare notes later."

Pleased to have her own assignment, Jennet readily

agreed. She'd been good, once, at tweaking secrets out of maidservants. She doubted she'd lost her touch. Less than a quarter hour later she was comfortably seated in the kitchen, a mug of weak ale in front of her and a scrawny serving wench eating out of her hand.

Two hours after that, she made her report to her mistress.

"Did you have any difficulty getting her to talk?" Lady Appleton asked.

"Not after I swore her to secrecy and told her we were on the queen's business." In the privacy of the best bedchamber at Sayes Court, mistress and maid together ate dried dates and sipped more of the local ale.

Lady Appleton lifted a brow but did not criticize Jennet's methods.

"Mistress Sabina was most secretive just before she died. She hinted that she had a secret admirer. Someone special. Someone at court."

"That is not difficult to believe. A great many courtiers pass through Deptford."

"Did you know that several of the royal musicians live here? And a few minor courtiers, too. And though the queen does not go to Greenwich on St. George's Day, but rather to Windsor Castle, Her Majesty spends a great deal of time at this palace. In between visits, courtiers are frequently there on one errand or another. And messengers travel to and from court because of the shipbuilding here, as well."

Lady Appleton nodded. "No one would remark upon one more gentleman in the area. I gleaned much the same information from the family, though they were reluctant to admit their daughter might have had a lover. I am unsure if they keep their silence because they grieve for her or because they feel shame that she crept out of the house and met a grisly fate. They did not recall seeing a dark-skinned, one-eyed man in Deptford at the time of her murder. Did the servants ever catch sight of such a one?"

Jennet nibbled on a date, debating whether or not to reveal the truth. She hated to admit to any failing, but at last she confessed. "I did not remember that one of the suspects lacked an eye."

"I wonder if he does?" Lady Appleton mused. "Diego Cordoba has also called himself Ruy Vierra, and for years, so Robert tells me, he passed himself off as a Gypsy to wander the countryside."

Jennet wondered how Sir Robert knew that. And why Cordoba would have chosen such a dangerous disguise. Any Gypsy caught by the authorities was deported.

"Do you suppose it is possible Diego Cordoba is not missing an eye at all? Could he have been using the patch as part of a disguise from the very beginning?"

"Why would anyone wear an eye patch if he did not need to?" Jennet asked. That sounded passing foolish to her.

"Nothing would surprise me after some of the idiotic ruses I have known Robert to use. Codes and ciphers," she muttered, as if she addressed some long-held personal grievance. "Robert has used disguises a few times, too. 'Tis common practice, so he's told me, when one travels on the Continent and does not want to be recognized as an Englishman."

At this intelligence, Jennet began to have the darkest suspicions about Lady Appleton's husband. She'd understood from the beginning of this journey that her mistress's primary goal was to eliminate Sir Robert as a suspect. Lady Appleton hoped to find proof at Leigh Abbey that he'd spent at least one St. Mark's

Day there with her. Any St. Mark's Day. It was only needful that she exonerate him of a single murder in order to clear him of them all.

Jennet did not believe she would succeed.

27

Watching Jennet and Mark together was more painful than Susanna had anticipated. This, she thought, was what a marriage could be, what it should be. She felt no envy over the two small girls clinging to Jennet's skirts or the baby boy who wanted to be carried everywhere, but in the relationship between husband and wife there was a deep and abiding affection, a respect Susanna knew would never exist in her own union with Robert.

With a sigh, she turned from her study window and attempted to put Jennet, Mark, and their little family from her mind. On her writing table, she had stacked the account books for the past six years. This was why she had come to Leigh Abbey. The sooner she bent to her task, the sooner she could return to London.

Another sigh escaped her. Robert was in London. And so, she realized with a pang of regret, was her favorite carved oak armchair, the one inlaid with holly. Seating herself in a much less comfortable turned chair, she adjusted the embroidered backing and the matching seat cushion and got to work.

An hour later, frustrated, she pushed aside both the books and the list of events she had compiled. She had wasted her time with this trip to Kent. There was nothing here to prove or disprove Robert's whereabouts when those women were killed.

Standing, she stretched and then, taking the list with her, left the study for her chamber, where she threw herself down on the bed and stared at the green silk tester above her head.

"Bodykins," she muttered.

Her records were both accurate and detailed. Although their primary purpose was to keep track of planting and harvesting on this estate and other Appleton lands, and the myriad of tasks in between, she had also recorded any events of note. Some were personal, some local, and others of national and even international significance.

Susanna had spent most of her life at Leigh Abbey. It had been her girlhood home before her father's death. Robert had acquired it when he'd married her and been content to leave her in charge of managing the manor and home farm. They'd made this their principal residence, but the demands of a courtier's life had from the first taken him away from Kent while she remained behind. Perhaps that was why she'd begun to set down the doings of kings and princes along with her records of the price of grain and the cost of a new kirtle.

The paper crumpled in her hand summarized dates and events in the year Lora Tylney died. In the evening of the eighteenth day of March, King Philip had arrived at Dover, which was seven miles from Leigh Abbey, to begin his second visit to England. Susanna and most of her household had gone to catch a glimpse of the Spanish entourage as it passed by the next morning en route to Greenwich, a most popular entertainment for country dwellers. Had she seen the one-eyed Diego Cordoba? Susanna could not recall him, but she remembered that the king had been recovering from some illness and had worn a hood that left nothing of his face visible save for the tip of his nose.

Robert had already been at Greenwich with Queen Mary and had accompanied the court to London a few days later. He had not bothered to come home first. The next time Susanna had seen him, and then only briefly, had been in July, well after Lora Tylney's murder.

He'd been on his way to France with King Philip, and the queen, Susanna recalled, had accompanied her departing consort to Dover. On the journey from London, she'd spent one night at Sittingbourne and the second at Canterbury. That second night, Robert had been here, slept in this bed.

Rolling over onto her stomach, Susanna smoothed out the scrap of parchment, but she did not need to read what she'd written there. She knew what had happened next. Robert had left England with King Philip and fought for him at the Battle of Saint-Quentin. He'd been knighted for his valor there and might have remained in France a while longer had not word been sent to him of his father's death. He'd arrived in England early in September. He'd not taken time to visit Leigh Abbey, but traveled immediately to Lancashire, and upon his return to London he'd rejoined the court.

Unless he'd been with his mistress in Dover, Robert had been there when a whore named Little Alice was killed in Southwark.

Surging upright, Susanna seized a down pillow and

flung it across the room. What irony, to choose between an Alice and an Alys. And what folly to consider confronting the other woman now. 'Twould be awkward for them both and avail her nothing. Even if Alys would speak with her, she would refuse to help Robert. She might even lie to harm him. Just over three years ago, because he sought to mollify his wife, Robert had turned his mistress out of the comfortable house he'd kept her in and withdrawn the security of his protection. Soon after, she had married an innkeeper, reclaiming respectability, but the last Susanna had heard, Alys did much resent having to work so much harder for her comforts.

Disconsolate, Susanna went back to the list she'd compiled. The bitter truth was that Robert had been in or near the places those young women had been murdered. He might have killed any or all of them. Not in one single year had he been safely ensconced at Leigh Abbey on a St. Mark's Day.

There was no reason he should have been, she supposed, when he was rarely at home for more significant holy days. She could count on one hand the number of times they had celebrated Yuletide together. The only recent year in which they'd done so, it had been because the queen had ordered Robert to join Susanna at Madderly Castle.

As she left the bed and began to pace, Susanna's thoughts drifted further back in time, to the early months of their marriage. They had often been together that first year, both part of the duke of Northumberland's household, but even then she'd spent most of her days at Syon House with the duchess while Robert had been at King Edward's court.

Susanna found herself standing in front of the small looking glass that sat atop her dressing box. She frowned at her disheveled appearance. That one errant lock of hair would keep working its way out from beneath her cap. Impatient, she stabbed at it, shoving it under the edge of the fabric. Like her suspicions, it was unlikely to stay out of sight for long.

She had not known the man she'd been married to when they wed. In the years since, she thought she'd come to understand him, but what if she was mistaken?

Could Robert be the killer she sought? She turned away from her scowling image. She was not afraid of him. That must mean something.

It meant, she realized, that she looked on this quest as an intellectual game. At times, it was not entirely real. She was, perhaps, taking foolish risks with her own safety.

But would she not sense it if she were in danger? Especially if Robert were the source of it? There were many areas of his life she was not privy to, but she had also known him intimately for a long time. In the past, on occasion, he had even confided in her, treated her like a companion and friend, asked her opinion.

When had that changed? It had been a gradual thing, she thought. A growing apart. An increase in resentment toward her. She'd made matters worse during her sojourn in Lancashire. Robert had never forgiven her for saving his life.

But that, she decided, was why she knew he was no threat to her. He owed her a life for a life. And the other women? Was Robert capable of killing them? Susanna did not believe that sort of violence was in his character . . . though deceit was.

He was keeping something from her now. Her best guess was that he'd involved himself in some scheme of which she would not approve. Why else insist she move to London? Why keep her there when he was only rarely in residence in Catte Street? And why blow hot and cold about helping her bring Diane's murderer to justice? When she'd left London, she'd half expected him to tell her to remain at Leigh Abbey. In the past having her out of his way had always suited his purpose better.

Robert's flaws had been obvious to Susanna for many years—greed, jealousy, unfaithfulness. And he'd claimed credit for several of her accomplishments. In the early years, she'd believed the vows they'd made to each other meant something, that she owed him obedience and loyalty. It seemed, however, that their definitions of loyalty differed.

Susanna had been hurt when she'd first learned about Alys, the grocer's daughter from Dover, but she'd pretended to know nothing about her or the house Robert maintained for her. When she'd been in a position to demand concessions from Robert, after she'd saved his life during that business in Lancashire, she had not asked him to give up his mistress. Instead she'd coerced him into signing a remarkable legal document granting Susanna the revenues of several properties in her own right. Ever since, she'd been able to act independently of her husband ... if she chose to do so.

That contract, even though she'd never availed herself of its provisions, had created a barrier between them. Sometimes she regretted having forced him to yield. No man liked to be bested by his wife. He resented her for that, and for the very abilities he used to his own advantage, such as running this estate so profitably.

After Lancashire, they'd quarreled more frequently and laughed together far less. She'd often taken Catherine's part against him when that young gentlewoman had become part of their household. And

then there had been that business in Gloucestershire.
Walter Pendennis had been knighted for solving the
murders at Madderly Castle when Robert felt the
credit should have been his. Since it had been she
who'd actually solved the crimes, Susanna had not
been particularly sympathetic, especially after she'd
learned, from Catherine, that Robert had a new mistress, a Scotswoman named Annabel.

Susanna took another look at her reflection and
grimaced, then stalked out of the bedchamber. She
needed some fresh air. Her thoughts must be mud-
dled, for she'd just caught herself regretting that
Annabel had not been able to keep Robert's interest a
bit longer. He'd left Scotland, his diplomatic mission
there at an end, in February of 1562. He'd arrived
in London in time to kill Ambrosia La Petite.

Robert had been quick to involve himself with
another woman, she realized—Eleanor, the one
who'd borne a child named Rosamond and turned
up, with the baby, when Robert was in Spain.

After the first shock, Susanna had felt anger. That
betrayal had been impossible to ignore, and com-
pounded by the fact that Robert had behaved badly
not only toward his wife but also toward his mistress.
He'd left Eleanor without a moment's concern that
she might be breeding, making no provision for her.
Susanna had quickly remedied that.

Once the proof of Robert's perfidy was out of sight,
Susanna had also tried to put Rosamond and her
mother from her mind. She'd succeeded almost too
well. In all the time Robert had been home, Susanna
had yet to tell him of his little girl's existence. True,
they did not talk much anymore. She had that excuse
for procrastinating. But he would have to be informed
eventually. And he had a right to know where to find
his daughter if he wanted to.

Such an announcement would not be well received. Susanna was certain of that much, though she could not be sure exactly what her husband's initial reaction would be. So far, a cowardice rare to her had kept Susanna silent every time she'd come close to broaching the subject. For one thing, she did not want to have to explain why she'd taken in both mother and child. She was not sure she could. And no matter what Robert's response, she knew she'd have to deal with emotions she usually managed to avoid—feelings of hurt, of guilt, of inadequacy.

When she returned to London, she decided, she would tell him. Would he object to her meddling, thus revealing an utter disregard for his own flesh and blood? Robert had never seemed to care for children and had shown no great desire to father any. Susanna knew most men would have reviled a wife who failed to produce an heir, but Robert had never expressed either criticism or regret.

Not about that.

He might insist they take young Rosamond into their home and raise her at Leigh Abbey as an Appleton. Susanna would think better of him for that attitude, but at the same time Rosamond's presence would be a constant reminder to Susanna that Robert *had* found her wanting as a wife.

Disgusted with herself for descending into self-pity, Susanna entered her garden and inhaled the reviving scents of her favorite herbs. She'd do well to remember that she was married to a man with few scruples and the morals of a civet cat. He was driven by one thing—the desire to attain prominence at court in the form of a highly paid government post and a peerage. That goal had always been more important to him than any woman, wife or mistress . . . and made it unlikely he would ever risk losing it all by being executed for murder.

Someone else *must* have killed Lora and Diane and the rest.

Straightening her shoulders, Susanna renewed the vow that had brought her to Leigh Abbey. Somehow, she would discover the murderer's real identity and clear the Appleton name of any shadow of suspicion.

28

Lady Mary Grey toyed with a little mother-of-pearl scent bottle she wore on a gold chain. No one took any notice of the action. No one took any notice of her.

Except Sir Robert Appleton.

She was aware of his eyes upon her as she moved through the Presence Chamber where Queen Elizabeth gave audiences. Gaudily dressed ladies and courtiers even more fantastically garbed waited to speak to the queen. Everyone wanted something.

As Lady Mary scanned the crowd, she saw a bribe offered to one of the more prominent ladies of the privy chamber. On occasion, the maids of honor also received such solicitations, but it was rare for Lady Mary to be singled out for any purpose. Her influence with her royal cousin was negligible. That she was in line for the throne was merely an accident of birth, much like her stature.

But Sir Robert Appleton was watching her, charting her every move. She wondered why.

Deliberately, she ignored him. When she tired of watching other people, she studied the decor. Every surface at Whitehall was highly embellished. Ornate tapestries depicted scenes as varied as Hector at Troy and the Robin Hood story. Gilded strips divided the ceiling into sections and every inch of each compartment had been carved and painted. Even the floorboards had been plastered over and decorated with intricate designs.

Too . . . busy, Lady Mary thought. If she ever had a house of her own, she would strive for less cluttered elegance—floors of Purbeck marble, simple ribbed oak panels on the walls, and perhaps one or two plain wool hangings of the sort made in London, their blue backgrounds embroidered with red roses.

In her peripheral vision, she again caught sight of Sir Robert Appleton. For some reason, just lately, Lady Appleton's husband had taken an interest in her. Had they discussed her? She tried to imagine it, Lady Appleton and Sir Robert, sitting down to sup, he making some remark about Lady Mary's lack of prospects . . . and height. And Lady Appleton? A word in defense? A shared laugh? Impossible to tell.

Lady Mary had liked Sir Robert's wife. After their meeting in the garden she had reread *A Cautionary Herbal*, once again finding its contents most interesting.

At last Sir Robert made his move, wriggling through the crowd in her direction, his intent crystallized. Reading the determined look on his face, Lady Mary no longer avoided him. Instead her assessing gaze swept over him as he approached.

Sir Robert was tall and broad shouldered, his doublet tailored to enhance the second attribute. His court dress was very fine, grander than his position warranted. The doublet and trunk hose were slashed and adorned with gold braid. The underlying fabric was white, but so heavily embroidered, primarily in scarlet silks, that very little of it showed. Lady Mary's gaze swept down, noticing that murrey-colored netherstocks showed off well-formed legs, then up to concentrate on his face.

His beard was neatly trimmed, as was his short, thick, dark hair partially concealed by a small red velvet bonnet. The only thing ostentatious about the headgear was the jewelry holding its single white plume in place. This brooch was in the shape of a gold flower set with two rubies, two emeralds, and three pearls. Convenient collateral, Lady Mary could not help thinking, should he find himself in urgent need of money.

"Well met, my lady," Sir Robert greeted her.

She smiled slightly and continued to scrutinize him. He wanted something from her, but what?

"Of late, you met my wife."

Lady Mary acknowledged that truth with a regal nod.

"Is it possible you would come and sup with us in our humble abode, that we might in some small measure repay your kindness?"

What kindness? Lady Mary knew she'd helped Susanna Appleton very little, and she suspected Sir Robert realized that. On the other hand, it was out of the ordinary for her to receive invitations of any kind. And she had liked the woman.

"When?" she asked.

Clearly unprepared for an easy victory, Sir Robert had to clear his throat before he could recover his aplomb. "Lady Appleton has left London for a brief visit to our country seat in Kent. I am uncertain when she will return."

"She might be wise to remain there," Lady Mary remarked. "There are rumors of plague spreading through France. 'Twill be but a matter of time before it reaches our shores."

The court would move to a less populous area in the hope of avoiding infection, and any London resident who had property in the country would also evacuate. In an epidemic, a city was the most dangerous place to be.

"My lady wife fears nothing," Sir Robert said. "Least of all some vague threat from across the Narrow Seas. She will return betimes, and I am certain she will be most pleased to entertain you."

"I await her invitation with great anticipation." Lady Mary meant her words, but a few minutes later, as she watched Sir Robert walk away, she felt a growing disquiet.

He did want something from her, and she could not convince herself 'twas anything so innocent as a friend for his wife.

29

The county of Essex did not lie on any direct route between Kent and London, but a visit to Peregrine Marsdon's estate added only two days to Susanna's journey. A fine May morning found her entering the courtyard at Spur Hall. A man, of middling height and unremarkable features, but a gentleman by his dress, came out from the mews to greet their small party. A faint tinkling sound followed him from the small bells tied to the feet of some of the birds within.

"Master Marsdon?" Susanna asked. "I am Lady Appleton. Sir Robert's wife."

The man beamed at her from behind a bushy beard. He moved quickly past several stone blocks, each one with a falcon chained to it, to reach her side. "We have been expecting you. I am Christopher Beckett, Lady Appleton. Marsdon's steward and friend. Sir Walter Pendennis wrote to tell us of your mission."

"And to warn you I might turn up unexpectedly?" She took an instant liking to this man while at the same time wondering when Sir Walter had learned to read her so well.

"Aye." His smile did not falter and his eyes twinkled. "Shall I take you to the suspect at once or may I offer you some refreshment first?"

"To Master Marsdon, by all means. Let us complete this business without delay." Peregrine Marsdon had been a long shot, at best. Sir Walter's letter and Beckett's behavior seemed to eliminate him from her list, but she had questions to ask, and would meet the man to decide for herself.

Jennet, Fulke, and Lionel all trailed along when Beckett led the way toward a nearby meadow. They knew too much of the story now to allow their mistress to place herself in any danger. Susanna was torn between pleasure that they cared so much and annoyance at the way they hovered, seeking to protect her from some unknown danger.

"Do you know much of falconry?" Master Beckett asked.

"Only a little," Susanna told him. Among the nobility, hunting with birds and dogs was more sport than quest for food. She did recall that the type of hawk or falcon a man carried on his wrist reflected his rank. A king carried a gyrfalcon, and an earl the peregrine. Beyond that, her knowledge was limited. She had never cared to know more.

At her first glimpse of Marsdon, Susanna's steps faltered. He was immense. Such a man could break a woman's neck with as much ease as a goodwife wrung a chicken's.

"Wait," Beckett cautioned. "Watch."

A falcon sat on Marsdon's wrist, hooded and leashed.

"See how his assistant hands him the lure? 'Tis a pair of crane's wings tied together with a leather thong, held in the position they'd have if they were folded on the crane's back. Now he removes the hood, at the same time singing to the bird.'' A faint melody reached Susanna's ears. " 'Tis the same tune he uses every time he feeds her.''

Marsdon kept hold of the jesses while the falcon tasted the meat in the lure. His assistant, an elderly, stooped fellow, but spry, then took the lure, carried it to a place some distance away, placed it on the ground, and withdrew. As Susanna and the others watched, Marsdon released the bird, letting the line that held her run through his fingers until she landed on the lure.

"He rewards her with meat," Beckett explained unnecessarily, "then recaptures her and repeats the training, teaching her to come back to his wrist at his call. A good falconer must be patient above all, but also needs acute hearing and vision, a daring spirit, an alert mind, and an even temper."

Marsdon was as gentle as a nursemaid with the bird.

"I did not think gentlemen served as falconers," Susanna remarked.

"Master Marsdon is a most unusual gentleman." Beckett was laughing at her, she thought, but she was not sure why.

"This amuses you?"

"Your pardon, Lady Appleton. Not only is it unique for a gentleman to train his own birds, but most authorities agree that the best falconers are men of medium size, not too large to be agile but not too small to be strong. Those are the same folk who believe the only good birds come out of Dansk or sundry places in the East and are to be had only at excessive prices. The truth is that we have right here in England the lanner and the lanneret, the tercel and the goshawk, the sparrowhawk, hawk, and even some few merlins.''

"Though this talk of birds is most illuminating, Master Beckett, I came here to learn all I could of another Peregrine. You need not delay me further. Sir Walter warned me that Master Marsdon prefers to avoid women. He told me Marsdon's betrothed left him for another.''

"You need have no concern for your safety, Lady Appleton. Master Marsdon has mellowed in the years since, and found contentment here, in the life he now leads.''

"How long ago did she jilt him?" Susanna asked.

Beckett thought a moment. "Five years? No. More than that.''

After Lora's death, then. If Marsdon had killed her, it had not been in retribution for that particular betrayal.

"I never go to London," Marsdon himself told her a short time later. He was a soft-spoken man, for all his giant stature. He and Beckett sat side by side on the remains of the corner of a wall of an abbey dissolved and razed in the days of King Henry. Susanna perched at a right angle to the two men, with a clear view of both.

"You knew Lora Tylney?" she asked.

"I knew of her. I knew she was the quarry that night at Whitehall, though I did not have much interest in finding her.''

"Because you were betrothed?''

Marsdon smiled. "I do not deal well with women, unless they be safely married, as you are, Lady Appleton.''

"You have sisters, I am told.''

"Aye. Six of them.''

"Big strapping girls," Beckett put in. "Not a tiny, dark-haired lass among them."

"And all married now." Marsdon's pride in that accomplishment was evident. "I have Spur Hall to myself at last."

He sounded sincere.

"Tell me about that night at Whitehall," she urged him.

"There is not much to recount. We behaved like drunken fools and were evicted from the premises."

"Evicted?"

"Aye. One of the keepers caught us. An old man." He frowned. "Might have had a servant with him. I cannot recall, but I do remember how distraught the fellow was on behalf of the Office of Revels. Doubtless he thought we meant to break up the scenery. Lord Robin sent him away, but the fun had gone out of being there by then. We left right after."

"This keeper . . . might he have come back?"

Marsdon laughed. "Anything is possible. And now that I think on it, it must have been that same keeper who discovered the body the next day."

In that case, Susanna thought, she had no hope of speaking with him. According to Sir Walter, the old keeper had died some time ago. She took what consolation she could from knowing she could therefore also eliminate him as the murderer.

30

"Lady Appleton believes knowledge is always a good thing."

"You do not seem so sure of that." Mildly amused by the fact that Jennet had arrived unescorted at the Sign of the Smock and asked to speak with her alone, Petronella had suggested a stroll in the garden. At this time of day, the walkway was deserted. Only the ducks on the small artificial pond could overhear their conversation.

"I think she may have put her own life at risk," Jennet said. "I think Sir Robert was the one who killed all these women. And I fear that when he realizes that his wife is still asking questions . . ." Her voice trailed off, as if she could not bear to voice the possibilities aloud.

"Has she found something?" Petronella demanded, thinking of Diego. "Some evidence?"

"No. But Sir Robert's behavior has been most odd. Fulke has noticed, too."

"And who is Fulke?"

"A groom. He went with Sir Robert to Scotland. And again into Spain. And more recently into Hampshire."

"Sir Robert has been to Spain?"

"Aye. This past year. And now he is up to something." She lowered her voice. "He's been visiting the goldsmiths. Fulke told me that, too."

Sir Robert was no doubt involved in something he'd not want the world to know, but Petronella was not convinced it was murder, or that Lady Appleton was in any danger . . . from her husband. Still, Jennet might be right to fear the killer.

Petronella shivered, even though the morning sunlight was warm. For the last few days, she'd once again felt that she was being watched. Stalked. If the man who had already murdered seven women broke his pattern, it might be to kill Lady Appleton, but it seemed to her as likely he would not bother to wait until next April to make sure Petronella kept silent. Her interest in the murders was far more widely known than the gentlewoman's.

"This is a dangerous business," she agreed, "but I do not see how either of us can convince your mistress to change her mind."

"You could," Jennet said, boldly meeting her eyes. "You could pretend to discover proof that the Spaniard is guilty. She'll believe evidence you unearth. She trusts you."

Inordinately pleased, Petronella smiled weakly. Such a solution would not work, but she had to admire Jennet's audacity in suggesting it.

She might have pointed out that, if Sir Robert was guilty, this plan would leave him free. Or that it seemed clear Lady Appleton did not think her husband was the murderer. Instead she asked a question.

"You are more to her than a maidservant, are you not?"

Jennet drew herself up a bit straighter, smoothing both hands down the front of her dark blue bodice and skirt. "I am the housekeeper at Leigh Abbey. My husband is the steward there. And here in London, where the house is small and there is little to do, I am as much friend and companion as servant. I have been with Lady Appleton for many long years. She depends on me."

"And yet you would betray her."

Shocked, Jennet sputtered a denial.

"I speak the truth. You came here without her knowledge. You would stop her, thwart her."

"Protect her!"

"She would, I do think, most strenuously object to your efforts if she were to learn of them."

Angry, Jennet would have stalked off had Petronella not caught her arm, pulling at her until they stood face to face once more. Jennet was a bit taller and much rounder, and her eyes flashed dangerously, but Petronella was no weakling. She clung to the other woman's sleeve, determined to have her say.

"The only way all of us will be safe is if we discover this madman's identity and end the killing."

"All of us? Whores?"

"Women!"

Nearly nose to nose, they stared at each other for a long moment before Jennet blinked. When she stepped back, Petronella released her. To her surprise, the other woman made no further attempt to leave the garden.

"How can you and Lady Appleton be so like?" Jennet wondered in a whisper. "Think so like?"

Petronella found she was smiling. "As your mistress did, I received a good education. I was brought up to run mine own business." She gestured behind her, toward the Sign of the Smock. "My inheritance."

Reluctant fascination showed on Jennet's face. "Is that how all brothelkeepers gain their posts? Generations of. . ." She flushed, hesitant now to risk giving further offense by repeating the word whores.

With a wry chuckle, Petronella shook her head. "In my case, yes. But we come to it in many ways. Why, there is a brothelkeeper here in Southwark who was born a gentlewoman. Old Heloise. She's something of a legend hereabout. Ran away from her family back in King Henry's day and went to work in a brothel. Just for fun, the way she tells it. Now she owns the place."

Jennet's eyes went wide with astonishment and— was it possible?—admiration.

"It is not an easy life," Petronella felt compelled to add. "Most girls do not end up so well. There are . . . risks." Diseases, in particular. The French pox. The chaudpisse.

"There are ways to prevent childbearing," Jennet blurted, surprising her yet again. "Lady Appleton—" She broke off, embarrassed, then added in a mumble, "Potions and such."

Petronella resisted the wicked urge to trade preventives with this country goodwife. Here at the Sign of the Smock they'd found sponges soaked in vinegar to be most effective, though some of the girls also engaged in a bout of hard pissing after each customer left, since this was believed to prevent the spread of disease, as well. And Long Nell had always insisted that a large nutmeg, pickled in vinegar and thrust up into the whibwob, was the most certain way to prevent conception.

"Go back to Lady Appleton," Petronella said instead. "Keep watch over her if you fear for her safety. Enlist the aid of other servants, for I sense they are all most loyal to her. But help her in her quest. Only when this villain is caught and executed will any of us be safe."

Jennet chewed on her lower lip for a moment, but in the end she was forced to agree. She was almost at the garden gate when she turned to give Petronella a long, assessing look.

"Did you choose," she said, "you might set yourself up in the country as a gentlewoman and none would be the wiser."

Petronella decided, after a moment's thought, to consider that a compliment. She was still chuckling to herself when she went back inside the house. She jumped a foot when a deep, masculine voice, slightly accented, spoke from the shadows.

"She speaks the truth."

Hand to her lips, she faced Diego Cordoba. "You heard?"

"Only the last of it, from just inside this convenient window. Have you given thought to retirement? You might move away from Southwark. Start a new life."

With Diego, she might consider it.

Appalled by her weakness where he was concerned, Petronella forced a laugh. "Never! What would I do in the country? And gentlewomen lead dull lives."

He stepped closer, taking her in his arms. "I must leave England soon," he whispered. "I will return to Spain. You could come with me."

Her heart began to beat faster, but she warned herself not to hope. He meant to take her along as his mistress, nothing more. She'd lose her independence and gain nothing. And 'twas still possible Diego was the murderer. She could be certain only that he was not the person who'd been following her of late. Vincent would have known of it had Diego left the

Sign of the Smock, just as he'd known when Diego moved in. Petronella's Spanish lover had not left the premises since he'd informed her she must hide him in her house.

Toying with the buttons on his doublet, she stared at his ruff, not daring to lift her head far enough to meet his eyes. "I would be a fish out of water in a strange land."

"You'd adapt, *mi corazon*. You already know some words of Spanish."

Love words, she thought. And a few crude expressions.

"You will be safe with me. And you will travel thither as the attendant of a royal lady. Your acceptance as a gentlewoman will be assured when we reach Madrid."

Startled, Petronella looked up. "Royal lady?" she echoed.

"Say you will go with me and I will tell you everything."

She was tempted. Oh, so tempted. "Does Sir Robert Appleton play a role in this?" she asked. "Is he to travel to Spain, too?"

With apparent reluctance, Diego nodded.

Separating herself from his embrace, she drew in a deep breath. "How can you ask me to go with you, if he goes, too? What if he is the killer? He'll be in Spain with us. Come next St. Mark's Day, he'll not have far to look for his next victim."

"I will protect you," Diego swore, but her questions seemed to provoke second thoughts. When they adjourned to her chamber, he made love to her with great passion and thoroughness, but he did not mention again the possibility of taking her with him into Spain.

31

The second time Francis Elliott visited Catte Street, he came alone. He found Susanna in her garden, industriously weeding the raised beds. Lionel worked a short distance away, similarly occupied.

"I have come for the medicine you promised my father," he said.

She made a production of straightening, dusting off her apron, and removing her work gloves. That wayward curl had come loose from beneath her cap again and she poked it back into place with one bare finger. All this to cover her surprise at his words. She'd not thought, from the way Jerome Elliott reacted when asked about his son, that he would confide in the younger man. Shortsighted on her part, she realized now. Certes, he would broach the subject, if only to give Francis a moment's unease.

How much of her purpose in going to Bermondsey did Francis Elliott guess? Had the old man sent his son for the electuary she'd promised, or was that just an excuse for him to come here? Aloud, she asked only, "How is your father's health?"

"Much the same as when you spoke with him, Lady Appleton."

She gestured toward a small stone bench shaded by the garden's only tree. Apple blossoms had come and gone, but there did not appear to be great promise of fruit. "I have been away, Master Elliott, obliged to oversee a domestic matter at Leigh Abbey."

"I am told you have a most excellent stillroom there." Elliott's smile charmed her. He seemed neither angered nor worried by the knowledge she'd been poking around in his personal life. That might mean he had nothing to hide. Or that he, like others who had served the duke of Northumberland, had learned to be very good at concealing his true feelings.

"Did Robert say so?" she asked, stalling for time while she tried to read him.

He shook his head, his smile a little more broad. "Walter Pendennis. He is most impressed by everything about you, Lady Appleton. He believes you are a clever woman, having compiled two herbals, and admires that quality in a female."

"And you, Master Elliott? Do you find the workings of my mind appealing or appalling?" She framed the question in a way that he might take as teasing, even flirtatious, but she was interested indeed to hear his answer.

Her curiosity was doomed to remain unsatisfied. The cat chose that moment to leap onto the bench between them, demanding attention.

Elliott chuckled and reached out, allowing Ginger to sniff his fingers before he rewarded her with a scratch behind the ears. He seemed relaxed, as if he had not a care in the world beyond stroking her cat.

Indeed, man and cat appeared to have much in common as they shifted to absorb more of the daylight. Master Elliott extended his long legs in front of him and rested his shoulders and the back of his head against the apple tree. Ginger, on his lap now, began to purr. Master Elliott's eyelids drifted down as if he, too, might consider curling up to nap in the sun.

Susanna cleared her throat. "This electuary gently purges the belly and doth comfort the stomach and aid digestion."

"Most excellent medicine. Will he complain about the taste?"

"The ingredients are made into a fine powder and mixed with honey. 'Tis not unpalatable."

"But medicine ought to taste bad," Elliott said with a grin. "Ah, I have it. I will take him your soothing nostrum but also gift him with a copy of your cautionary herbal. That should torment him sufficiently. He will find it passing difficult to trust a woman who knows hundreds of poisons."

"You must do as you will," Susanna told him. "He is your father." She meant the words as both reminder and reproach, but Elliott only grinned more widely.

For a moment they shared a silence broken only by the purring of the cat.

"Why are you still asking questions?"

"I am not satisfied with the answers I've heard so far. It is convenient to blame the Spaniard, but if he is not guilty then another young Englishwoman will die in less than a year."

Elliott's eyes opened fully at that statement and he sat up straight, dislodging the cat. With a feline huff, Ginger leapt to the ground and stalked off. "How can you be so certain? The death of three women on the same day of the year does, I grant you, seem an unlikely coincidence, but—

"Seven women."

"W-what?" He seemed taken aback. "Who? I . . . I—" He broke off and drew in a steadying breath. "You astound me, Lady Appleton. Your husband told me only of a possible connection between Lora Tylney and the beautiful Diane and some Southwark doxy."

In a crisp, no-nonsense manner, Susanna enumerated all the victims and the places of their deaths.

"But why think any of us at court when Lora was killed had aught to do with these other murders?"

"Because all these victims were similar to her in appearance. When she was killed, a number of men were questioned most closely about her demise. Most of those men could have killed each of the other women. Even you, Master Elliott, for all that your father says you spent the night before Diane's death in his house in Bermondsey."

He smiled at that, a wry expression containing little humor. "Had you told him what you suspected, no doubt he'd have lied and said I was never there. You'll have noticed there is little love lost between us, Lady Appleton."

"You might have crept out of your father's house before dawn," she informed him, though she smiled back to soften the words, "and returned again to break your fast with him none the wiser."

"What an imagination you have, Lady Appleton."

"I do but try to keep an open mind."

"So, you suspect Pendennis and myself and the Spaniard and your own husband."

"And Lord Robin. And Peregrine Marsdon."

"And Lord Robin." His voice was solemn, but his expression mocked her.

"Seven women have been murdered," she

reminded him, struggling to contain her growing irritation at his attitude.

"Four of them prostitutes."

"Does that make their deaths less important?"

For a moment he did not reply. Then he said, "Gentlewomen are not supposed to know of such things."

The intent behind his mild words was difficult to gauge. A man might speak so if he sought to soothe a fractious child. On the other hand, this might be another attempt to tease her, to charm her out of what must seem to him the wayward notion she could discover a killer's identity. He did not, after all, know her very well.

Now it was her turn to remain silent and think. From the street beyond the gate came the sounds of London. Susanna had grown accustomed to most of them now and scarce heard the churchbells or the hawkers' cries. She concentrated on the man beside her. For all that Master Elliott seemed to lack respect for her reasoning, he might prove a useful sounding board. He presented no threat to her person even if, as seemed unlikely given his father's testimony, he was the murderer she sought. Lionel was nearby. Other servants worked within shouting distance.

"All of you gentlemen have been known to visit houses of pleasure," she said bluntly, making her companion wince. "On the night the woman was murdered in Duke Humphrey's Rents, 'tis a known fact that many courtiers were nearby, in attendance on the queen."

"Aye. And I believe I saw Cordoba that night, too."

"So you *were* there?"

"Aye. As you say, all your suspects could have committed any of the crimes. That particular night, hundreds of courtiers accompanied Queen Elizabeth from Whitehall to Baynard's Castle. I do not remember being with Pendennis or Lord Robin or your good husband, but I recall now thinking I recognized Cordoba in the crowd. I discounted the sighting, and forgot all about it until now, for we knew very well, or thought we did, that Cordoba had left England long before."

"When? Did Cordoba fight at Saint-Quentin?"

A negative shake of the head answered her. Elliott looked completely serious now. "The king sent him . . . somewhere. He left court shortly before we went to France. Shortly after Lora's murder. I assumed he'd gone back to Spain."

"When did you return from the war?"

"With Lord Robin. The battle was in August. By late September we were disbanded and dispatched home."

"Pendennis too?"

"Pendennis was wounded at Saint-Quentin. He came back earlier." He cocked his head, his gaze sharpening, boring into her. "You did not know that?"

"No." The thought of Sir Walter injured made her clasp her hands together tightly in her lap, but she was quick to regain control of herself. "Then all of you were in England in time for the next murder, that of Little Alice."

"You speak as if you knew these women personally," he muttered.

If he'd said they were of no importance, being whores, she'd have struck him, but Francis Elliott wisely kept any thought concerning that aspect of the murders to himself. She watched him watch her as they both mulled over what they knew.

"It is all very well to suspect the gentlemen you do," he said after a time, "but there are also many

lesser men who had equal opportunity to do harm
to any or all of those women. Lord Robin's servants.
Other menials with posts at court. And those not so
menial."

"Does Lord Robin have the same servants now as
then?"

"He may."

She would find out, Susanna decided. Sir Walter
would know.

"These posts at court—are they not filled anew at
the beginning of each reign?"

"Ah, there you are mistaken." He seemed inordinately pleased to have caught her in an error. "Many
newcomers do receive their rewards in the form of
appointments to serve the new monarch, but others
stay on. The Master of the Queen's Horse has a permanent staff of more than sixty. Some have been working
in Royal Mews since they were first converted to stables in old King Henry's time."

He was right, and in truth she'd already known
that. Had not Sir Walter told her that the old keeper
of the storage room where Lora had died had been
there when Edward was king? And that he'd died
only a year ago?

Something else flickered in her memory, but she
could not grasp it.

Forehead creasing in the effort, Elliott came up
with another example. "Thomas Keyes," he said.
"Sergeant-porter, keeper of the queen's water gate
at Whitehall. He's been there at least since Queen
Mary's reign." He chuckled. "One can scarce miss
him. He stands a head higher than any other man I
know, and is burly besides."

"And I should suspect him?" Susanna asked in dry
tones. She remembered noticing the fellow during
her recent visit to Whitehall with Sir Walter. He was

as large a person as Elliott indicated. Bigger than Peregrine Marsdon.

"I did not mean to imply that," Elliott assured her. "Indeed, Keyes is the kindest of men. A widower with young children. He shelters travelers caught in bad weather in his own lodgings above the gate and has been known to host many a merry gathering there. My point is that you cannot suspect only those of us who figured most prominently in events leading up to Lora Tylney's death. Rather, you must suspect every man who was at court then."

At last seizing upon the elusive thought she'd been trying to capture earlier, Susanna narrowed her eyes. "Your father?"

Elliott laughed. "Aye. My father. Not such an unlikely villain. He was a clerk to the Master of Revels under Queen Mary. He might well have gone back to the storage room that night. It was part of his responsibility to make sure all the scenes and machines were returned to their proper places."

"Gone back?"

"Have you not learned that, Lady Appleton? He came in with the keeper and caught us there. He did not see me. I moved into the shadows to avoid him."

"And suggested leaving in case he did return?" So much for his chivalrous behavior toward Lora.

"My father has a temper," Elliott allowed. "I had no wish to be embarrassed in front of my friends."

Had Jerome Elliott gone back after his son left? Was he the murderer she sought? Susanna could not ignore the possibility. Even after he'd given up his post at court, he'd lived near London. Very close to both Southwark and Deptford. Could he have attracted a young woman like Sabina Dowe? He might have, she conceded, if he'd made her think he had money and power and a place at court. Or perhaps she had simply been on her way to meet some young lover when Elliott waylaid her. Susanna found it tempting indeed to visualize the unpleasant Jerome Elliott in the role of villain.

"What did your mother look like?" she asked abruptly.

"Like an angel."

For a moment, Elliott seemed to lose his composure. Some powerful emotion flickered in his eyes, but it was gone again an instant later. He drew in a deep, steadying breath. "You are thorough, Lady Appleton. My mother was a small woman. But she had fair hair, the same color as this." He touched a golden lock. "I cannot prove it, more's the pity. Father had her portrait painted in miniature, but he destroyed it after she left us."

"Did your father kill her, or was it suicide?"

Again, she'd caught him by surprise. Again, he recovered himself. "You should not listen to gossip, Lady Appleton."

Ginger returned and Elliott scooped her up, concentrating fiercely on eliciting a purr as he spoke of the painful events of his youth.

"My father, a knight's younger son, married a distant kinswoman to secure an inheritance. My mother was born in Westmorland. She was most unhappy living in Bermondsey. She ran away during my thirteenth year, returned to the north, and tried to have her marriage annulled. Angered, my father gave out that she had died and forbade the mention of her name in our house ever again. He may have wanted to murder her for leaving us, but he did not kill her. Some years later, she and I were reunited and I saw for myself that she was content with life apart from Father."

Placing Ginger gently on the ground, he stood to

take his leave. His expression cold and unrevealing, he met Susanna's eyes. "My father is not the murderer you seek, Lady Appleton. He was in Bermondsey when Diane St. Cyr was murdered. As was I."

32

"I wish to visit the Spanish embassy," Susanna announced.

Robert gaped at her, appalled by the suggestion. He had thought, in the week since her return from Leigh Abbey, that she had lost interest in catching a killer. On the other hand, he'd spent only one night in the Catte Street house in all that time. It was possible she'd unearthed all manner of secrets.

Concealing a deep-rooted concern with an air of nonchalance, he forced himself to lean back against the inside of the casement, put his feet up on the window seat, bite into the comfit he held in one hand, and ask why.

"I have questions about Diego Cordoba. If he was, as you claim, the man who murdered all these women, then it seems possible someone there will have noticed odd behavior either before or after he killed Diane St. Cyr."

Did a man's manner alter fresh from such a kill?

Robert was not convinced of it. He'd seen soldiers slaughter their fellows, in battle and in the aftermath. He'd watched two hotheads fight with sword and buckler over a matter of honor. But killing women to a pattern was different. Mayhap there had been signs.

"He held a post at the embassy but a short time," he said aloud. "As Ruy Vierra."

"What name he used makes little difference. He cannot have moved about Durham House unnoticed. He may have made friends. And I would speak with his immediate supervisor. He may have noticed something." Susanna crossed the solar as she spoke. Hands on her hips, she stared down at him. He could feel her eyes boring into him, but resisted meeting her gaze.

"And if he did, why should he tell an English-woman?" He swallowed the last of the comfits.

"Because you will be with me, Robert, and you will ask."

It was the utter assurance with which she spoke the words that galled him most. Did she think she controlled him? "You waste your time on such a mission. We already know Cordoba is guilty."

"You may think so. I am not convinced." Shoving his feet aside, she sat where they had been and placed one hand on his forearm. "I only wish to see justice done, Robert." A small smile played about her lips. "Mayhap there is some reward in it. Prove Cordoba guilty and no suspicion attaches itself to you . . . or to Lord Robin."

A visit to Durham House, Robert thought sourly, could also verify he'd been at mass the morning Diane died. 'Twas a lesser crime than murder, 'twas true, but one he could not risk having exposed. Not at this juncture.

He thought he could count on the discretion of the ambassador's servants. And if he went with Susanna, he would have some measure of control over both questions and answers. Although his wife had studied Spanish, she could only read the language, not converse in it. She would have to rely upon him to translate.

"This visit to Durham House will persuade you Cordoba is guilty?" he asked. There were risks involved, but if this was the only way to stop Susanna from going there on her own, then he supposed he must yield to her persuasions.

"I will not know the answer to that question until I go, will I?"

Impossible woman! He jerked his arm free, handed her the empty comfit box, and rose from the window seat. "I will see what I can do," he promised, and left before she could make more demands.

For three days, Robert put her off, while his schemes moved ever closer to fruition. But in the end, he bowed to the inevitable. He had done all he could to ensure that she received the proper answers, but he worried because he did not know precisely what the questions would be.

They traveled on horseback, proceeding at a decorous pace through Ludgate and along the Strand, the main highway between London and Westminster. Great houses lined this thoroughfare—Paget Place, across from the church of St. Clement Danes, then Arundel House, Somerset House and the Savoy, a long, narrow, impressive building that extended all the way back to the water's edge. On the far side of Ivy Bridge Lane they came to a series of gardens, then reached the embassy's imposing gatehouse.

"Durham House has changed little since Northumberland's day," Susanna murmured as they

passed through the first courtyard and into the inner
court. It was a high and stately house, the parlor
block alone rising to four stories. The main range of
buildings was distinguished by marble pillars. The
crenelated and buttressed great hall lay straight
ahead.

Robert took care not to glance to his left, toward
the chapel, but he knew it was there. Running parallel
to the hall, it connected by a north-south range to
the high end of Durham House.

" 'Twas a great occasion when last we were here
together," he said.

A glance at his wife was enough to tell him she was
remembering. He recalled above all the richness. The
Lady Jane had been gowned in gold and silver brocade sewn with diamonds and pearls. Even her hair
had been plaited with pearls. Her sister, the Lady
Catherine, had also been married that day. She'd
been in cloth of silver. And Lady Katherine Dudley,
the third bride, one of the duke of Northumberland's
daughters, had been attired in cloth of gold.

"All the state rooms at Durham House were draped
with gold and crimson tissue," Susanna murmured.

"Your thoughts echo mine."

"Do you remember the altar front? 'Twas sewn with
pearls."

To match the Lady Jane's gown, he'd thought at
the time. A whimsical notion, but back then he'd
been giddy with grandiose plans, believing he'd be
serving King Guildford through a long and prosper-
ous reign.

"I do not know which sister I pity more," Susanna
whispered as one of the ambassador's servants
escorted them to the ground-floor business rooms.
"The Lady Jane and Lord Guildford were executed,
but the Lady Catherine's life has scarce been happy."

"There's irony in it," he answered cryptically, knowing Susanna would understand his meaning.

On that long-ago day here in Durham House, the Lady Catherine had been married to the earl of Pembroke's son. She'd made no objection to the union. The Lady Jane, however, had much protested her marriage to Lord Guildford, claiming a prior betrothal to Lord Hertford. Three years ago, that first marriage long since annulled, the Lady Catherine had disgraced herself by eloping with the same Lord Hertford.

Robert felt no pity for the Lady Catherine, but he was grateful for her folly, which had opened the way for his own current endeavor. While in Spain, he'd learned that the young woman's impulsive actions had ruined the plans King Philip had made for her. Although the widowed queen of Scots claimed to be rightful queen of England, the Grey sisters had a better right, having been born in England. King Philip had intended to abduct the Lady Catherine and marry her to Don Carlos. The scheme had been well advanced when she'd spoiled it by eloping.

No chance of that with the Lady Mary, Robert thought. God knew what monsters they'd breed, the dwarf and the imbecile, but if there was the smallest hope of a healthy male heir to the English throne, his efforts would be worthwhile.

Once he had accomplished the Lady Mary's kidnapping, he'd be richly rewarded. No matter what the future brought, he'd have, at the least, a title and land and a new life in Spain.

But first he must satisfy his wife's curiosity and lull her into a false sense of security.

33

Susanna remembered a great deal more about Durham House than the ceremony that had united three young brides with their grooms. There had been the celebrations afterward, and the moment when she had gone into the garden for a breath of air and come upon Robert already there.

He had not been alone.

She'd retreated in haste and made excuses for what she'd seen. In hindsight, she supposed she'd known even before she married him that he was not the sort of man to be faithful to one woman. Back then, she'd still dared hope she was mistaken.

"He says he cannot recall seeing Ruy Vierra on the morning Diane died," Robert translated.

His words brought her back to the present with a jolt that left her disoriented.

"He is the fourth to tell us the same story," Robert grumbled. "Are you ready to give up?"

She considered it. In the hour they had been at

Durham House they had found no one who knew anything about the missing Spaniard. His possessions had vanished with him, and everyone denied being aware that Vierra was not his real name. He'd been a hard worker but had apparently never spoken to anyone about his personal life.

"Well?" Robert prompted.

"Sir Robert," interrupted a new voice.

Fascinated, Susanna watched Robert's face blanch. He recovered himself quickly, greeting the ambassador, Alvaro de Quadra, who was also bishop of Aquila, and introducing him to Susanna, but she had to wonder what could have provoked such an extreme reaction.

The bishop presented another puzzle. In spite of a harried look about him, he seemed determined to play the host, insisting in English that they accompany him to a private chamber for refreshment.

When they were settled comfortably in a big, airy room overlooking the gardens to the east, she explained her reasons for inquiring into Ruy Vierra's past. The ambassador became gratifyingly expansive, though from time to time he shot almost furtive glances into the shadows at the corners of the room, as if he thought someone might be lurking there to listen.

"Did you know Vierra was not his real name?" she dared ask.

"So direct. So charming. I did know and was also privy to the fact that Diego Cordoba stayed in this country after King Philip left, although I did not take up my duties as ambassador until some two years later. I fear I cannot share details with you, dear lady. You understand this, I am sure."

And she did, given her own husband's profession.

"Can you tell me anything of Cordoba's background?" she asked.

"Very little."

"Has he family in Spain?"

"He was, I believe, orphaned young."

"Does he have a title?"

"No, Lady Appleton. Cordoba made his own way. He fought for honors." De Quadra chuckled. "It is said that is how he lost an eye, in a tournament."

"Do you think the story is true?" At the ambassador's confused expression, she clarified her question. "Could the eye patch be false, part of some disguise?"

"I have no reason to think so."

Impatient, Robert broke in on their dialogue. "Have you any reason to think Diego Cordoba did not slay seven women and flee to avoid being charged with those crimes?"

De Quadra sipped Spanish wine from a goblet of enameled glass set in a silver-gilt foot. He appeared to consider carefully before he answered. "It may well be that guilt made him run." He glanced at Robert, then back at Susanna. "I have heard ere now Sir Robert's case against Cordoba. Should not a wife be guided by her husband's opinions?"

"Only, I do think, when the husband's argument is irrefutable."

The ambassador shook his head, as if despairing of her reason. Susanna posed more questions, but he deftly deflected them and made it clear that the interview was over. A servant appeared on cue, eager to show them the way out.

"He is not what I expected," Susanna murmured as she and Robert followed the liveried manservant through a long gallery.

"Rumors abound that he is deeply in debt," Robert

whispered back. "Perhaps you should have offered him a bribe."

Susanna did not think indebtedness explained the Spaniard's odd demeanor, but she said no more, distracted by the luxurious decor of the embassy. Even as they were being hurried out, she could not help but admire the many fine portraits hung along the inside wall.

Highlighted by the sunshine streaming in through the windows on the other side of the gallery, a detail of one portrait, the last before the exit, caught her eye. She skidded to a stop on the tiled floor, grasping Robert's sleeve as she did so.

"Who is that man?" she asked, pointing to the subject of the painting. By its location alone, she thought she knew.

"King Philip," Robert said, confirming her guess.

"But he is fair-haired."

Robert looked at her as if she had lost her mind.

"I thought he would be dark," she explained, still staring at the portrait. "Spanish looking."

"He resembles his Flemish ancestors," Robert said.

Apparently she had jumped to a mistaken conclusion about his appearance, based on the fact that he was king of Spain. King Philip's short, pointed beard and his hair, distinguished by a receding hairline, were yellow. He had large eyes with dark circles beneath and thick, close brows above, an unremarkable nose, a broad forehead, a large mouth, and a protuberant lower lip.

Robert waited until they were out of Durham House and riding along the Strand toward home before he commented on her error. "You thought King Philip might look like Cordoba?" he asked.

"I assumed so, since they are both Spaniards."

Robert was much amused by her misconception.

He made matters worse by choosing to lecture her in an annoyingly superior tone of voice. "Spain is a large country. The darkest Moors lived there, but Vikings invaded Spanish soil, as well. A noble nose. The color of the eyes. A shock of brilliant hair. All may crop up to show a child's distant origins. You would know this if you had traveled as much as I have, Susanna. Seen as much. Done as much."

"One may learn a great deal by observing the inhabitants of a single village," she said drily.

The undercurrent of nastiness in his answering laugh irritated Susanna. "True enough," he conceded, "and therein some poor cuckolded peasant might find ample proof of his wife's unfaithfulness, did he but have the wit to see it."

"Are women always to blame, then?"

"Always," Robert arrogantly declared. "Why, never would Adam have sinned had Eve not tempted him."

If she'd thought he was teasing her, Susanna might have held on to her temper, but she sensed he was serious. He believed the drivel he was spouting. It was too much to bear. Before she could control her hasty words, she blurted out the announcement she'd meant to save for a better time. Once uttered, the words could not be called back.

"What did you say?" Robert demanded.

"That proof of *your* fatherhood may be found in your daughter's countenance," she repeated. There was no help for it now. She had to tell him the rest. "A woman named Eleanor gave birth to the girl last December and named her Rosamond. Should you wish to see for yourself, they now reside at Appleton Manor."

34

Thunder crashed outside the windows of the Crowne Inn. Flashes of lightning streaked across the sky. It was only three in the afternoon, but the day had turned dark as night and the storm raged all around, making the superstitious wonder if the end of the world was nigh.

Robert drank deep and ignored the howl of the wind and the fury of the thunderstorm, though it lasted nearly an hour. The rain continued to pour down after the lightning stopped, but he was scarce aware of it.

He had a daughter.

He'd known of her existence for less than twenty-four hours, and did not believe he would ever meet her, but the mere fact of her had made him doubt himself, doubt everything in his life that had led up to this moment.

He'd wed Susanna because the duke of Northumberland had ordered it, but she'd been comely enough.

And her dowry had been extensive. Only after they were wed did he realize she had a razor-sharp mind and a stubbornness that equaled his own.

Not an easy woman to live with.

He'd needed Eleanor and others like her. A man had to have someone to admire him, praise his prowess, encourage his efforts. Oh, Susanna was agreeable enough when it came to helping him advance at court now, but under Queen Mary she'd nearly ruined everything by allowing men of the New Religion, those forced to flee into exile to avoid arrest, to shelter at Leigh Abbey on their way abroad. It did not matter that Robert had professed to be of that faith when Edward was king. Everyone had abandoned Catholicism then. Religion was a political issue, as far as he was concerned, but Susanna had never wavered. She had been brought up in the faith King Henry made and had kept to its tenets even during the five years of Mary's reign.

He'd be a good Papist in Spain. Robert grimaced. King Philip had the Inquisition to enforce piety. That alone was reason enough to leave Susanna behind.

Susanna.

He'd ordered her to London, insisted she return as quickly as possible from the brief trip to Leigh Abbey, because she gave him a respectable image and an excuse to leave Whitehall without explaining his absences. His friends at court believed he went home to his wife every night. No one questioned his movements, even when he vanished for several days at a time.

Susanna insisted she wished only to clear his name, but if that were true, she'd have accepted his arguments for Cordoba's guilt. Damn Eleanor for going to Leigh Abbey. Damn this child for being born. Susanna's behavior was naught but her way of taking revenge. Why else would she so stubbornly pursue the matter of Diane's death?

He drank more ale and brooded.

Her resentment went back to the beginning of their marriage. She had never liked being under his control, had demanded and gotten unheard-of rights from him in a weak moment. Mayhap now she'd decided she'd prefer to be a widow.

But if he were executed for murder, or for treason, she would not get control of his entire estate. Everything he owned would be forfeit to the Crown. Scowling, Robert drained his cup and refilled it. She'd have her dower rights. And the profits from those damned herbals she kept writing. She'd also have her wits.

Aye, widowhood would suit her. And the way Pendennis danced attendance on her, she could marry again if she chose.

She would not do so, he thought. His lips twisted into a wry grimace. She'd rather exist in poverty than subject herself again to the whims of a man. Under the law, widows gained the rights to manage their own estates and to choose to marry again or not.

Unless they were royal. He chuckled into his ale. Any royal lady had to get the queen's permission to wed or she ended up in the Tower of London. Unless some kindly soul kidnapped her. He toasted the air and drank again, renewing his vow to complete what he had begun. He would use Susanna's name to lure the Lady Mary into the trap. Aye. She'd help him, though she'd know it not.

The court would be on the move soon. It could not be soon enough to suit Robert. Then he would leave England.

But he would return one day. Nothing had ever altered his desire to see a king on the throne of his homeland. Lord Guildford Dudley would have been ideal, but Lord Guildford was long dead. Now the only choice left was a Spaniard. Either King Philip would come with an armada and conquer this island nation, or a child born to the Lady Mary by Don Carlos would claim the throne when Queen Elizabeth died.

Or was assassinated.

Yes, he would return . . . and still be legally bound till death to Susanna.

There was a sobering thought, especially when Robert realized that, in spite of the antagonism between them, he would probably miss her while he was in Spain.

She was a challenge. Someone he could never quite comprehend. It confused him that she'd waited to tell him about his bastard daughter. And yet she had taken steps to make sure the child was not in want. Susanna was not a vindictive person. She had already given mother and daughter a home.

Why hadn't she told him about Rosamond sooner? Had she been saving the information to use when it would most hurt him?

It wasn't as if he'd ever flaunted his women in his wife's presence. The last few years he might have grown insensitive where her feelings were concerned. He was not proud of that. But he'd never set out to hurt her.

This was all Diane's fault.

He drank deeply, then drank again.

The Frenchwoman had presented a danger to his plans, making demands on his time and energy, directing unwanted attention to him. He was glad she was dead. Her murder had solved a problem for him. Too bad it had created more.

At the thought of that night with Diane, a loneliness descended, an almost unbearable need for the kind of comfort only a warm female body could offer. Not Susanna. God, no. He wanted as far her opposite as he could get.

"Small and dark," he muttered, and laughed.

A memory stirred. He knew where to find one such, one who had not yet been listed on Susanna's tally of victims. Was she still there, or had she fled, alerted to the danger she was in by Susanna's investigation?

Robert had imbibed far too freely to be deterred by the downpour. He slammed out of the inn chamber, calling for someone to saddle his horse.

35

"Three nights past, during the great storm, your husband came looking for me at the Sign of the Smock."

Petronella's words worried Susanna. She'd known something was amiss the previous morning, when she'd received a note from the brothelkeeper requesting permission to come to her in Catte Street to discuss a matter of utmost urgency. They had not met in person since Susanna's return from the country, at Petronella's request, but had kept up a correspondence, largely to report no progress at all in their search for a murderer. Susanna had also stayed in touch with Sir Walter and with the Lady Mary Grey, with the same results.

Susanna had not suspected Robert would be the reason for this meeting, though she'd been careful to schedule Petronella's arrival at a time when she knew her husband planned to be closeted with Sir Walter Pendennis in Blackfriars.

"Robert did not hear your name from me," she told the other woman.

"He did not remember my name. He remembered what I look like."

Susanna conducted her guest through the solar and into her bedchamber, where they could be private even from Jennet. "What happened?"

"He arrived dripping wet and prodigious cup-shotten. I came out to see what the commotion was about when Vincent attempted to evict him from the premises."

"Robert saw you, then?"

"Aye. And spoke to me."

"To say what?"

" 'Well met, mistress. 'Tis good to see you are still alive.' "

Susanna's stomach lurched, but her words came out in a firm voice. "Whatever his reason for saying that, 'twas not because he has killed all those women, or means you to be next."

Compassion shone in Petronella's eyes. "I cannot be so certain of that as you are, Lady Appleton. Someone has been following me for weeks, since before your friend Diane was killed."

"Diego Cordoba?" she asked. "No. That cannot be. Robert said he'd fled the country."

"Not Diego," Petronella said.

In the little silence that stretched between them, the two women looked deeply into each other's faces, seeking truth, seeking trust. At last Susanna spoke. "You know Cordoba well. As well as I know Robert."

"I have known Diego for a long time," Petronella amended.

That was not quite the same thing, Susanna realized, but most like more accurate in both cases. "I wish to prove my husband innocent. You wish to do the same for Diego Cordoba."

"Yes." Petronella seated herself atop Diane St. Cyr's traveling trunk, which Susanna had moved into her chamber.

"Then we must no longer hold back any information. Only if we both know everything will we have a hope of finding the real murderer. It was Cordoba who told you about Lora, was it not?"

"Yes."

"And you have already said you knew all of them at about the time Lora was murdered."

"Before that, Lady Appleton."

Briefly, she gave an account of how they'd been accustomed to come to the Sign of the Smock in King Philip's time, all of them but Marsdon, and revealed that Diego Cordoba had continued to visit her through the years.

"I never felt any sense of danger until shortly before Diane's murder. Since then I have again had the feeling of being watched. In Duke Humphrey's Rents when I visited my friend Isabel. And in Southwark, these last few weeks."

Susanna was not sure what that meant. Possibly it made Cordoba's guilt more likely. Had he been saving Petronella, murdering other women who looked like her first? Or had Diane had been murdered by mistake, as she'd thought at the beginning?

Perching at the foot of her bed, Susanna watched her guest closely. "If the killer we seek is not Cordoba or Robert, we are left with Marsdon, Pendennis, Lord Robin, and Francis Elliott. But Elliott suggested to me that a servant might have been responsible, or some functionary at the court, a person who is always there, blending into the background."

"If that is true, we will never discover the killer's identity."

"Thanks to Sir Walter, I have eliminated a few. Lord Robin has no one man who was with him at court from the time Lora died to the present, and on one St. Mark's Day, Lord Robin himself was absent, having gone from Windsor to his manor at Kew instead of returning with the queen to Whitehall." Susanna did not believe she'd need to question him in person, after all.

Petronella's expression was glum. "If we consider every man who provides a service at court to be a suspect, the list will be endless."

"But we can take a closer look at Master Jerome Elliott, Francis Elliott's father. He was employed by the Office of Revels under Queen Mary and lives now in Bermondsey. He and his son vouch for each other's whereabouts when Diane was killed, but they could be lying."

"I do not know this Jerome," Petronella said, "but what reason would either father or son have to think Diane a whore? Assuming she was not murdered in mistake for me."

Her words reminded Susanna that the killer had left a feather to mark his victim as a Winchester goose. "Elliott escorted Diane to the inn where she spent the night before her death," she mused aloud. "Did she do something during the short time she spent with Elliott to make him think she would sell herself for a price?"

"I do not believe Master Elliott has any dislike of those in my profession. He is a regular patron of the Castle-on-the-Hoop." Petronella's tone of voice carried a hint of disdain. At Susanna's lifted brow, she explained that this particular bordello was not a well-kept, reputable establishment like the Sign of the Smock. She shook her head dismissively. "Men ofttimes have peculiar tastes."

"Do you have firsthand knowledge of Master Elliott's . . . tastes?"

A laugh answered Susanna's hesitant question. "In Elliott's case they must have developed over time. He was easy enough to please when I knew him."

"Were any of them . . . difficult to please? In bed, I mean?" Susanna felt her face flood with color. She could discuss midwifery, lecture other women on preventing conception, but she had never before thought much about, let alone openly discussed, the sexual appetites of men.

Taking pity on her, Petronella did not go into detail. "No one was violent. None were impotent."

Susanna sighed. "We must start over, then. Consider everyone's background. Assume any or all of them may have lied to me."

"What is it you hope to find in the killer's past?"

"A woman, I think. Does it not seem likely that something a woman once did to a man is responsible for his desire to take revenge on other women?"

Slowly, Petronella nodded. "Men have been known to take out their frustration with one female on another. While 'tis true that under the law a man may beat his own wife, a whore makes a convenient substitute when there are reasons why he should not."

Shocked, Susanna stared at her. She had voiced a theory. Petronella spoke from experience. Her words made Susanna wonder if Robert's inability to control her had ever driven him to vent his anger on another woman, a woman who did not dare fight back.

She did not think so, but how could she be sure?

Abruptly, she hopped off the bed and fetched ink, pen, and paper to start a new list. A few minutes later she threw down her quill. "This is impossible! They were all wronged or deserted by some woman!"

Petronella studied what Susanna had written. "Marsdon was jilted at the church door. He resented his sisters but he married off all six of them. Jerome Elliott's wife, who was also Francis Elliott's mother, deserted the family when Francis was thirteen. Cordoba's mother died when he was a boy. Lora, his mistress, flirted with other men. What have you crossed out by Pendennis's name?"

"A woman in his past killed herself. I have no details."

"I think," Petronella said gently, "that you must ask for them. What of Sir Robert? How old was he when his mother died?"

"Three. And he'd lost three stepmothers by the time he was fifteen."

"Any chance his father killed them?"

With a rueful smile, Susanna thought of all the stories she'd heard about Sir George Appleton, the father-by-marriage she'd never met. "Only if it was through overuse. He was reputed to be a lusty fellow, and he took a fifth wife, too."

Jane had been her name, Susanna remembered. She'd once been intended as Robert's bride.

Susanna had never revealed to her husband that she'd heard the rest of the story of his aborted betrothal from Mark and Jennet, who had stayed on in Lancashire after Susanna left and become friendly with the neighbors. It seemed that Robert, at nineteen, had not wished to marry Jane. He'd claimed he desired to enter the priesthood and therefore would not wed. Since that part of Lancashire clung to Catholicism even after it was made illegal in England, he'd been believed. Susanna was uncertain why he'd then been sent to the Dudley household, where the

New Religion was ostentatiously practiced. Perhaps to cure him of such a wrong-headed notion. Perhaps as a ploy to allow Sir George to continue to worship as he pleased while his son convinced those who counted that the family was loyal to the Crown.

Whatever the reason, Susanna did not for a moment believe Robert had experienced any calling to the religious life. That had been an excuse to get out of the betrothal, nothing more. The man she'd married was not the devout type. Since she'd known him, he'd always attached himself to whatever faith was most politically expedient at the time. If Turkish pirates conquered England, he'd happily turn Mussulman.

"What more can you tell me of Señor Cordoba?" she asked, dismissing this aspect of Robert's past as irrelevant. "Has he ever talked to you about his childhood? And what about his eye? Did he lose one or is the patch part of a disguise?"

"He lost an eye." Susanna heard the pain in Petronella's voice and realized she cared more deeply for the Spaniard than she wanted to admit. " 'Tis most terrible to look at. Scarred and puckered."

"How did he lose it?"

"In a tournament."

So he said, Susanna thought. But what if a woman had been to blame? "He is a fighter, then? A killer?"

"He is always most gentle with me."

Resigned, she told Susanna what little she knew. Cordoba had been born into the lower level of the Spanish aristocracy, a second son whose parents had both died when he was young. He'd entered tournaments to earn money and gain the attention of royalty, and his performances had pleased King Charles, King Philip's father. When he'd lost his eye, he'd been offered an opportunity to serve the younger man.

The decision to leave him in England had been made because Diego Cordoba genuinely liked the English people. He was comfortable with them, and could pass for a fellow countryman with a minimum of effort.

"He charms them," Petronella said.

"Every man on this new list, save for Jerome Elliott, is a most charming fellow. We seem to be at an impasse."

"Are we?" Petronella challenged her. "What of your husband, Lady Appleton? Is he a paragon of virtue at home?"

"No, he is not. Robert resents me for being well educated and clever. He holds the queen in much the same contempt, but he is careful not to let her see it. He no longer cares what I perceive, which makes me believe that if he meant to kill any woman, it would be me."

"Or the queen," Petronella murmured.

"He is not a violent man. Not with women. He simply does not like to give them much credit."

They shared a sad smile at that truth.

"Shall we stop asking questions?" Petronella asked. " 'Tis possible the man who did this has gone away and will not return until next St. Mark's Day. Indeed, much of London prepares to flee."

"Robert told me some time ago that we will not remove to the country until the queen leaves Whitehall for Greenwich." Sometime within the next two weeks, she thought. The first plague crosses had already gone up in the city.

"The queen," Petronella murmured. The odd look on her face drew Susanna's attention.

"I do not think Robert means to kill the queen," Susanna said, forcing a smile. "That would be treason, and my husband has the best of reasons to know that attempts to disrupt the succession can be fatal. He was once a follower of John Dudley, duke of Northumberland, who paid with his life for his attempt to put one of the Grey sisters on the throne.''

36

On Monday, the fourteenth day of June in the year of Our Lord 1563, the Lady Mary Grey received a most peculiar missive, a letter signed by Susanna, Lady Appleton. It asked the Lady Mary to come to the Appletons' Catte Street house. Alone. A postscript reinforced the importance of this meeting and the need for secrecy. It also suggested that she plead illness in order to avoid leaving Whitehall aboard the royal barge with the queen. She might, the note suggested, requisition one of the queen's coaches for the journey.

Lady Mary had learned to be careful. She still had the earlier missive Lady Appleton had sent to her, the one requesting a meeting at the Lady Mary's convenience. She compared the handwriting and saw at once that two different people appeared to have written the letters. The penmanship was similar. Both wrote with a clear Italian hand, easy to imitate. Lady

Mary knew she might be mistaken, but some instinct told her she was not.

She considered carefully. She was curious, and had often regretted the lack of adventure in her life. She spent an hour deciding how to rid herself of her tiring maid, and finally did so by sending her with the court to look after the belongings Lady Mary took with her from palace to palace on each move.

As the letter recommended, she pleaded illness and asked for the loan of a coach. Then she took the precaution of sending a note of her own to Lady Appleton in Catte Street to say she was on her way. If, in fact, the invitation sent to Lady Mary was a ruse, she reasoned that message would alert Lady Appleton and prompt her to investigate.

Nothing untoward happened at first. The coach was brought for her. The horses drew it smoothly enough through Whitehall's precincts and reached the place where the driver must guide his horses north toward the Strand and London and, ultimately, Greenwich, or southwest through Westminster and into the countryside.

The door beside her opened.

"Good morrow, my lady," Sir Robert Appleton greeted her, polite as always as he climbed into the coach and took the seat opposite her.

"Sir Robert."

"May I beg a ride with you, since we travel in the same direction?"

There was something about the way he spoke that she did not like, but she had little choice about allowing him to stay. The coach was already moving again.

It pulled past the royal coachman, lying unconscious . . . or dead. Whatever man had taken his place turned the horses away from London.

"And where is it," she asked politely, "that we are going, Sir Robert?"

He smiled. "To Spain, my lady. I am going to make you a queen."

37

When the plague struck a house in London, a white paper was attached to the door. Beneath a painted blue T, which was supposed to represent a headless cross, it bore the words Lord Have Mercy upon Us. Every morning, each parish clerk had the onerous duty of making sure none of these quarantine signs had been defaced or removed during the previous night.

Except for those confined to their homes, most of the city turned out to watch the royal progress from Whitehall to Greenwich. Susanna Appleton and her household walked to Thameside to view the great, gilded state barges from a spot near the Custom House. Propelled downriver by rowers, they were filled with important personages. When the sun glinted off the glitter of jewels on their apparel, the crowds roared their approval, most especially when they caught a glimpse of the queen. She was an awesome sight, all in green and gold and white, the Tudor colors. Even from a distance she had a regal air about her, a presence.

Susanna returned to Catte Street in a cheerful mood, ready to finish the last of the packing, but in her absence a most strange message had arrived from the Lady Mary Grey. It implied that a royal coach should already be standing in front of the house. Susanna read the missive twice through, puzzled and growing alarmed. She had never invited the noblewoman to visit her, and had she ever thought to, it would not have been when she was about to remove to the country.

Something was very wrong.

Her uneasiness grew when she realized Robert had taken Fulke with him that morning. Fulke, who had accompanied him to Scotland and to Spain, but had always before stayed near Catte Street when the Appletons were in London, assigned to look after Vanguard and Lady Appleton, in that order.

She was in Fulke's sleeping quarters, staring at the empty space where the groom's belongings had been kept, when Jennet came in with Lionel.

"He's gone, madam." Lionel's face had an odd, crumpled look, as if he fought not to give way to unmanly tears.

"Gone where?"

"Foreign parts," Lionel told her. "He did not tell me what land, only that he does not want to go."

"He is with Robert, then." Susanna spoke to herself but Lionel answered her.

"Aye, madam. With Sir Robert."

Confusion warred with concern. She'd long since given up expecting Robert to confide in her, but he usually paid her the courtesy of telling her when he was about to go abroad. She feared this oversight was more than mere slighting of a wife. What was he involved in? And what did the Lady Mary have to do with it?

Susanna had just confirmed that Robert's clothes and jewelry were missing when Sir Walter Pendennis arrived. Colorful curses greeted the news that Robert was not there.

"What is it, Walter?" she demanded, so far forgetting herself as to drop his title and grasp his arm. "What has Robert done?"

Murder, she half expected to hear.

"Treason," he said in a stone-cold voice.

"No." The idea was unthinkable. Beyond belief.

Or was it? With a deepening sense of dread, Susanna drew the letter from the Lady Mary from the deep placket in her skirt and stared at it, then turned it over to Sir Walter. "Does it have aught to do with this?"

No sooner had he read the missive than he was turning to go. Again Susanna caught his sleeve. "Take me with you."

To his credit, Sir Walter hesitated only a moment. "You will have to ride in front of me."

She nodded. His horse waited in the street. Within moments they were mounted and riding through London. Susanna gritted her teeth and said nothing, but this position was not comfortable, physically or otherwise. She perched sideways, crushed between the saddle horn and Sir Walter. This enforced intimacy did not matter, she told herself. It could not matter. The only thing that did was finding Robert without delay. If she was quick enough, perhaps this situation could still be salvaged. Amends made. Mistakes undone.

"What does he intend?" she asked, looking up into Sir Walter's stoic countenance.

"The Lady Mary is heiress presumptive. If he has

her, he means to take her to Spain. Marry her off to some Spanish princeling that Spain may claim the throne when Elizabeth dies."

"You suspected Robert was plotting something. Why did you not try to stop him sooner?"

"Your husband is a clever man, Susanna. It was not easy to guess what his plans might be. We had to wait until he acted."

They fought their way through crowded streets, but Susanna paid no attention to pedestrians, or to the shouts of abuse they leveled at the horseman in their midst. Sir Walter stopped at the city gate only long enough to inquire if a coach had passed into London in the last few hours. None had.

"Cordoba," Susanna murmured. "Does Cordoba have aught to do with this?"

"Aye. Your husband met with him several times in recent months."

"And did Cordoba leave England?"

"No, though I do think Robert believes he has. Cordoba was being watched. He went only as far as a brothel called the Sign of the Smock, where he has been ever since."

Susanna accepted the news that Petronella's establishment had been under surveillance with mixed emotions. Watchers afforded the brothelkeeper some measure of protection, and might even explain her conviction that she was being stalked, but Susanna had to wonder what else Sir Walter's men had seen and reported. Had Susanna herself been recognized? Had Jennet?

The Royal Mews, used for stabling the queen's horses, was located at Charing Cross, north of Whitehall. There they found the royal coachman, William Boonen, holding his aching head. Sir Walter's men seemed to materialize out of thin air to keep everyone else away while the Dutchman blurted out his story.

The Lady Mary's coach had been stolen by two men, one of them a gentleman. The words tumbled out in a mixture of English and his native Dutch, but the gist of the tale was clear. Robert had taken the coach Boonen had brought over from Holland three years earlier . . . and the Lady Mary, as well.

Swearing Boonen to silence, Sir Walter commandeered the remaining royal coach, an earlier model acquired during Queen Mary's reign. While two horses were brought out and hitched to it, fastened first by a strap fixed to the shaft and attached to their horse collars and then by traces attached to swingletrees, Sir Walter's men discovered that a maiden-hair-colored velvet saddle and an Andalusian jennet were also missing from the queen's stables.

Susanna stared at the vehicle with distaste. High, ornamental pedestals surmounted by the queen's heraldic devices, sat upon front and back axletrees. The body of the coach hung suspended by means of leather straps attached at the tops of these pedestals, an arrangement that struck her as perilous at best. One of Sir Walter's men climbed to an even more precarious perch, sitting on a stool placed upon a board with a footrest attached to the front of the triangular underframe.

"Are you coming?" Sir Walter asked, opening a door situated between the wheels. Like the panels at side, front, and back, it was elaborately decorated with scrolls and other figures. "Where one coach can go, another can follow."

She got in.

"As they have done, we'll bring mounts with us." Two outriders trotted up alongside the coach, leading

Sir Walter's horse and another, a little gray mare. "We will finish the journey on horseback if need be."

The coach lurched into motion.

How extraordinary, she thought, that Sir Walter had agreed to bring her with him. Did he hope she would have some influence over Robert when they caught up with him? Or was there some other reason for this unexpected concession?

Unable to find an answer immediately, Susanna resolved to consider Sir Walter's motives at some later date. For the present, she was grateful he could tolerate her presence. She vowed not to cause him any delay.

"Do you know where Robert is headed? Other than Spain." England had no shortage of coastline.

"South," Sir Walter said without hesitation. "He'd make himself too conspicuous trying to circle London to reach other ports. And lose too much time."

Susanna tried to clear her mind, to think. Would Robert confound them and head north? Toward Appleton Manor? Then she remembered something Fulke had mentioned weeks before. "Hampshire," she said aloud. "Did you send him there, Sir Walter? Just before I arrived in London?" And perhaps afterward, too. Was Hampshire where he'd gone all the times he'd seemed to vanish for days on end?

"No," Walter said. "If he went to Hampshire, he had private business there." He nodded, as if her question had confirmed his own conclusions. " 'Tis a likely route. The road called the London Way is a principal thoroughfare. Even a coach can get through, at least as far as Winchester."

But he stopped at the Lambeth horse ferry, to rule out the possibility that Robert had crossed the Thames there and was making for the southeast coast with which he was most familiar. Once Dover and the other Cinque Ports had been ruled out, they continued on toward Staines.

Susanna had never ridden in one of these newfangled coaches before. Few people in England had. There was space enough inside for two people to sit side by side, back and front, but even with cushions padding the wooden benches, every rut and bump in the road jarred the passengers viciously. More than once she was bounced high enough to bang her head on the underside of the roof and drive her teeth together with a painful jolt.

The farther from London they traveled, the less likely they'd be to find the highway in good repair. Once the road surface began to deteriorate, Susanna feared, the coach would become a bone-rattling torture chamber. If a wheel broke, they'd be stuck.

But she could see the method in Robert's choice of this vehicle to transport the Lady Mary. Behind the drawn curtains, occupants remained hidden. Folk who saw a coach pass by would assume that some prestigious person traveled within, perhaps the queen herself. All would give way.

At each crossroads, Sir Walter stopped and asked questions. By the time the coach crossed the Thames at Staines Bridge and traveled the few miles to Bagshot, where the road diverged, one branch leading to Winchester and another to Southampton, he seemed certain which way Robert had chosen.

" 'Tis likely he'll journey as far as Winchester in the coach, then abandon it to travel one of the narrower byways to the coast. To Southampton or Portsmouth, or any of a hundred little hamlets along Southampton Water and the Solent."

Susanna had been silent a long time, thinking. At last she spoke. "If we catch Robert, he'll be hanged, drawn, and quartered as a traitor." If he had been as disloyal as Sir Walter claimed, not just to her but to queen and country, no one could save him. The most they could hope to achieve was the Lady Mary's rescue.

Sir Walter turned to look at her, a desolate expression on his face. "He is my friend, Susanna. I take no joy in this pursuit." He seemed about to say more, then shook his head.

They did not stop for the night, but kept doggedly on. Twenty, even thirty miles a day was a reasonable distance to cover on horseback, but a coach could not go that fast. The slow-speed chase continued, night bleeding into day and day turning again into night as their journey took them ever southwest. They clattered through Guildford, then another ten miles to Farnham, and from there Winchester was still a full day's journey.

The first coach had gone before, for people noticed it, but Susanna began to wonder if Robert might not have perpetrated some elaborate hoax. Did an empty vehicle lead them astray while Robert and the Lady Mary, mounted on fresh, fast horses, rode hard for the coast?

They drew near Winchester just as the morning curfew bells began to ring in the city. "Every day at four," Sir Walter told her as she jerked out of an uncomfortable doze and blinked in the darkness. "And again at eight at night."

How like him, she thought, to know such little details.

Flint-surfaced streets gave them a brief respite from rough roads, but Sir Walter wasted no time asking his questions. Once he had answers, he chose not to hire local guides, instead relying on milestones to guide them on the road south from Winchester.

The London Way had often been used for large

baggage trains and royal progresses, but not so the road they now traveled. Twisting and turning, it led them deep into the Hampshire countryside. Sir Walter insisted upon as much speed as they could manage and in the early morning light the outriders soon called out that they'd spotted dust rising in a great cloud ahead, the sure sign of another vehicle. They came up behind it a few minutes later.

Leaning precariously out of the opening above the door, Susanna strained to see, then pulled herself back inside and spoke to Sir Walter. "Fulke is driving. He cannot have had much experience with the vehicle. And he does not want to leave England." Vanguard and the Andalusian jennet were tied to the back of the coach.

With a nod of agreement, Sir Walter took his turn to lean out and look, shouting commands to the driver before he resumed his seat. "Hold tight," he warned, grasping two straps attached to his side of the interior. Susanna did likewise on hers. "We'll draw abreast and try to force Fulke off the road."

They thundered on, dangerously fast even if they'd been on a major highway in good repair. On this road the effort seemed suicidal. Susanna prayed they did not encounter a farm wagon coming the other way. There might be just room for the two coaches to drive side by side. There would be none to spare.

Inch by inch, they pulled level with the other vehicle, until Susanna could look directly into Robert's coach. She met the Lady Mary's frightened gaze first, through the drawn-back leather curtain. Then her attention fixed on her husband.

He produced a pistol, primed and ready to fire. For a moment, Susanna did not think he recognized her, for he lifted the weapon, aiming it toward her.

Only when he looked her straight in the eye did he falter. He froze in the act of firing.

That delay cost him dearly. A moment later, a rough patch in the road flung the two coaches together. Wheels connected with a horrifying, grating noise and a screech of protest. They bounced apart, then came together a second time with a resounding crash.

Propelled off the hard bench seat, Susanna struck her head on the doorframe hard enough to produce stars. Dazed, she was still in a confused state when the coach began to tip, to tumble. Before she could gather breath to scream, it had left the road, turned over, and come to rest tilted halfway over on its right side.

Susanna lay still, sprawled awkwardly on the seat, every muscle in her body aching. The sky, she thought, looking out through a window that was now above her, appeared to be in entirely the wrong location.

"Susanna? Susanna, are you all right?"

Walter's concerned voice washed over her like a wave, forceful, tugging at her, yet nothing she wished to respond to.

The feel of his hands caressing her face, then running lightly over her body to check for broken limbs, could not be as easily ignored. "Stop fussing, Walter."

She meant to snap at him, but the words came out as a mere whisper. Susanna frowned. She did not believe she was seriously hurt. Just winded. No more bruised than she'd already been. To prove that to herself, she struggled to an upright position.

Pain lanced across her scalp, but it did not last. Gingerly, she felt the lump that contact with the side of the coach had made on her forehead.

Then she looked at Walter. He was much the worse for wear, a long tear in his once pristine doublet. His bonnet missing entirely. But he was smiling at her in relief. "Praise God," he murmured.

The sound of a shot shattered the moment, and then a shout.

"Sir Walter!" One of the outriders called out. "He's getting away!"

"Robert," Susanna whispered, and watched Walter's grim expression return.

He scrambled out of the wrecked, upended coach and she followed, needing assistance only for the last leap to the ground. The other vehicle had ended up against a tree on the opposite side of the road. The Lady Mary was just emerging from within.

"He's on Vanguard, madam," Fulke's familiar voice said.

"The horse was not hurt in the crash?"

"Tether broke."

The horses attached to Susanna's coach struggled in the traces, and one appeared to be injured. Fulke and Walter turned their attention first to freeing them, then to catching Walter's gelding and the mare he'd borrowed for her from the queen's stable. Both were loose and spooked, released by the outrider when he'd fallen from his horse while trying to get out of the way of the coaches.

Robert had shot the other outrider, wounding him badly enough that he could not continue his pursuit. Susanna did what she could for him, while the men dealt with the horses. In short order, Walter was ready to ride after his old friend.

"Not without me," Susanna told him.

"I need you to stay with the Lady Mary and the wounded man."

"The Lady Mary," that noblewoman said staunchly, "rides with you." Her eyes glowed with excitement. If she had suffered worse than the same bumps and bruises the rest of them had endured, there was no sign of it.

"We have no time to lose," Walter reluctantly conceded, "and I am loath to leave you women here unprotected."

They went on—Walter, Susanna and the Lady Mary, Fulke and one of the outriders—while the coachman stayed behind with the injured man. Fulke lost no time telling them all he knew, but Robert had revealed very little beyond their ultimate destination. Spain.

"Where did he mean to abandon the coach?" Walter asked him.

"In a cave near here. Big enough to drive right into, he said. Said no one but the smugglers would ever know it was there."

"He must have a ship waiting at anchor," Walter decided. "No doubt he meant to take the Lady Mary aboard in the guise of a wife. Give out that she was ill and 'twould be no great matter to explain keeping her out of sight."

The Lady Mary could add only a bit more to the story, but she shuddered visibly when she got to the part about her marriage to the king of Spain's mad son.

Robert did not go into the port of Southampton, but instead rode along the east side of Southampton Water, past Netley and Hamble, known smugglers' strongholds according to Walter, eluding his pursuers all the way onto Titchfield land, near where the New Forest began.

"Burseldon ferry can take him across Southampton Water to Calshot Castle," Walter said grimly. "He might arrange passage there, his most logical destination Brittany. Once across the Narrow Seas, though, he can easily journey on to Spain."

"Why assume he has abandoned his original plan?" Susanna asked. "If he had a ship waiting to take him all the way to Spain—"

"That, too, is possible. Both Spithead anchorage and St. Helen's Road anchorage lie off the coast to the east, and smugglers lurk in every bay and creek, both on the mainland and on the Isle of Wight, ready to take a man to whatever port he desires, so long as the pay be sufficient."

Robert rode as far as Titchfield Haven, then boarded a passage boat. It had already begun its crossing, carrying both Robert and his horse out onto the choppy waters at the mouth of Southampton Water, by the time Susanna's party arrived in pursuit.

Walter soon arranged for another boat, but when they reached the wide mudflats on the opposite shore, only Vanguard remained to be apprehended.

Robert was well away once more, this time all alone in a small, sturdy rowing boat. Susanna watched in dismay as it bobbed on the rough water, slowly making headway against the waves.

"The prevailing winds blow toward Southampton from the southwest," Walter said. "It takes a good breeze from the east before most ships set sail, and missing that wind can cause a delay of weeks, even months, if a ship sails with an escort."

"What are you saying?"

"That the wind is favorable. Many vessels are leaving port just now. He might board any of them. Or be struck and capsized in traffic. Come. We will be able to see more from above."

Calshot Castle was little more than a small blockhouse with a round tower, surrounded by a gun terrace. It had been built by the queen's father, old Henry VIII, to guard the Solent against invasion.

The waters below seethed with activity. Ships setting

off on long ocean voyages filled the vista with their great square sails. Some were white, but most were brown, and a few appeared to be a blackened gray. Over the water came the sharp sounds of boatswains' whistles, combined with the creak of masts and the clank of more anchors being lifted from the depths.

Robert's rowboat skimmed across the water now, moving rapidly away from shore. When Susanna shielded her eyes against the sun and squinted, she could see that he had his feet braced and was putting his back into pulling the oars in long, steady sweeps. If he had been jostled in his coach even half as much as she had over the last few days, every stroke must bring excruciating pain.

Spray struck him full in the face as he glanced over his shoulder to judge the distance between himself and the nearest ships in the Solent. His destination? She could not tell.

"Salt water flows north just here, creating a channel between the mainland and the Isle of Wight. The Solent is rife with strong eddies and powerful currents. If that boat does capsize, Robert will surely drown."

The words were said with a flat finality, but Susanna did not accept them. Could not accept them. "He knows how to swim."

" 'Twill matter little."

They could no longer see well. Too much distance lay between land and fugitive, and larger vessels now emerging from Southampton Water on their way out to sea blocked Susanna's view of the rowing boat. Was Robert attempting to overtake one of the departing ships, some of which were now moving rapidly, the wind behind them? Or was he bound for some smuggler's haven, as Walter had suggested? Five miles away from Calshot Castle, across the water, she could just make out what appeared to be two small stone block-houses on the north coast of the Isle of Wight. Hills rose behind them, creating the illusion that the island was larger than it was.

When Susanna looked again at the Solent, searching for Robert, her heart lurched. She could no longer locate the rowboat. "Where is he? Did it capsize?"

But Walter had also lost sight of his quarry when larger vessels blocked it from view. Though they strained and squinted, neither they nor the others in the chase party ever caught sight of the small boat again.

To all intents and purposes, Sir Robert Appleton had just vanished off the face of the earth.

38

Robert touched shore. In spite of aching muscles and throbbing bruises, he leapt from the boat and dragged it and himself into cover. He'd fetched up exactly where he'd wanted to on the Isle of Wight, but with Pendennis in close pursuit, he dared leave nothing to chance.

He hated to give up the jewels. He could live for a year on what the brooch would bring. But he knew no one would believe he'd willingly part with it and therefore it must be sacrificed. He set the scene, wrecking the small craft that had carried him to safety.

One hand on the leather pouch that contained his gold, he ran for the cave where he'd arranged to hide until one of the local smugglers came for him. Food and blankets had already been stowed. He'd hoped not to need them, had planned to be aboard a small caravel by now, with his "wife" secured below in a cabin, but he'd made not one but two contingency plans during several visits to this area in recent months. He was glad now that he had.

Not until he was one with the concealing blackness inside the cave did Robert fully comprehend all that he had lost. He'd been forced to leave his horse behind. Lady Mary was still free and on English soil. And now he was a man without home or country. His mission a failure, he could expect no rewards from Spain. He had burned his bridges in England.

This was all Susanna's fault! The sight of her in the pursuing coach had shaken him to the core. And with Pendennis! Damn the man. Robert wished he'd shot him. He should have killed them both. What did one or two more deaths matter?

Cursing his wife, Robert hugged himself for warmth and waited for his disreputable confederate to appear. He still had his gold, he reminded himself. He had suffered no serious physical damage.

He would survive. He would return. Somehow, he would regain all he had lost.

39

"A brooch was found caught in the splintered planks of a rowboat washed ashore on the Isle of Wight," Diego Cordoba said. "The Lady Mary Grey and Lady Appleton both recognized it as one Sir Robert was accustomed to wear on his bonnet."

Petronella watched her lover carefully, trying to judge his feelings. He'd told her everything: the plan to kidnap the queen's heiress; Sir Robert Appleton's scheme to leave England, and his wife, and live in Spain; Diego's own decision to stay secretly in England when Sir Robert had bade him flee the country.

He had left the Sign of the Smock, for the first time since coming to her to hide, on the morning of the day the queen's barge sailed downriver to Greenwich. Appleton's plan, Petronella now knew, had been to convey the Lady Mary to a secret rendezvous near Southampton and take his prisoner and their horses aboard a smuggler's ship for the voyage to

Spain. Appleton had scouted the area and made contacts well in advance.

"You think he survived," she said. Diego had been on the scene, in disguise, following Pendennis's men, an easy enough task for one who had spent so many years in England.

"Yes. I think he left the brooch to be found. But whether he can make good his escape from England, that is another question. He'll dare not show his face."

"Will he try to reach Spain?"

"I do not think so. Not now. Nor will I."

Puzzled, she frowned at him. "Had you meant to be aboard the same ship as Sir Robert?"

"I meant to come back for you if he was successful." Petronella's heart began to race. "At first, I thought to take you with us, to serve the Lady Mary on the journey to Spain. Then I decided to wait rather than risk your safety. When I realized Sir Robert's scheme had been thwarted, I might have ridden on, taken ship in some port farther west, but that thought brought me no pleasure. I followed my heart instead, and returned here, to you."

Had he come back for a final farewell? Or was he proposing something quite different? Petronella warned herself not to hope for too much.

"Were you serious when you suggested I could pass as a waiting gentlewoman?" she asked.

"*Sí, mi corazon.*"

She knew what the words meant. My heart. But she had difficulty believing he could envision her as anything more than what she was. She attempted a light tone, as if this were all a great jest. "My name alone gives away my background, Diego. Petronella is no gentlewoman."

" 'Tis not your birth name, either. You were christened Mary, and still called Molly by some when I first knew you."

"You remember that?"

"I remember much more than you will ever guess, and from the beginning I knew you were the only woman for me, but pride kept me from admitting it, from speaking to you then of love. Because of what you were, what I was, I saw no future for us. Later I pursued a woman of gentle birth, Lora, because she looked like you. I might have married her. Our posts at court made such a union acceptable. But she was not you."

Flattered, astonished, she could not think what to say to him. She was still struggling to grasp the significance of all he'd told her when he moved close, taking her into his arms.

"After Lora died, I saw the truth. No other woman could ever take your place. That is why I returned here, to you, year after year."

"I am scarce unique," she whispered. "There were others very like me."

"I never met any of the other small, dark women who were killed. And no woman I encountered in my travels, of any description, was your equal. I want to marry you, *querida*. I should have asked you long ago."

"I am a whore, Diego!"

"You will be my wife when we are wed. Your past will be of no more importance than mine. Turn this place over to Vincent. I have money enough for us to live on. We will find a small house in the country, far from London, and both of us will be reborn. We will take new names, new identities. Become exactly what we want to be."

Was such a thing possible? Could they start over? When she looked into her lover's eyes, she saw that he believed every word he'd spoken. Her heart tripped double-time. "Yes," she whispered.

"I am accustomed to answering to the name David when I travel in the English countryside," Diego said.

A smile blossomed as she curtsied to him. "Good day to you, David. My name is Molly Bainbridge."

"Bainbridge," he repeated, nodding his approval. "A good English name. Shall we keep it, for both of us?"

"I would like that," she said.

"I love you, Molly."

Tears of joy began to flow as she melted into his arms. "Oh, David," she managed to say between sniffles, "I love you, too."

She suspected she always had.

40

The Catte Street house interested Lady Mary, not only because it had been the home of Sir Robert and Lady Appleton for some months, but also because she had experienced very few opportunities to see how ordinary folk lived. She had spent her entire life in mansions and palaces, surrounded by wealth, luxury, and power. She owned an exotic parrot brought from foreign lands, and a lap dog. Lady Appleton kept a ginger-colored cat who did not seem to make any distinctions between the heir to the English throne and the housekeeper who'd opened the door to them when they arrived in London after their arduous journey to and from Southampton.

Lady Appleton was telling this woman everything, as if her servant were her equal. Was this a typical gentlewoman's household? Lady Mary thought not. When the order had been given to bring them hot, spiced wine and fetch meals for everyone from one of the nearby cookshops, Lady Appleton's housekeeper had joined them in the solar and sat right down with her betters.

Sir Walter seemed to think nothing of it, nor did he trouble to censor his words around the woman. Jennet, Lady Appleton had called her. Like the small Spanish pacer Lady Mary had ridden after the wreck of her coach.

"We must talk about this situation, Susanna," Sir Walter said.

"We have talked. Endlessly. Nothing changes the fact that Robert committed treason. All he has is forfeit to the Crown, even his life."

Poor Susanna, Lady Mary thought. She would not believe her husband had drowned. There was no way any man could survive that wild current, those terrible waves. And there was no reason that the good woman he'd left behind should be made to suffer for what he had done. Neither Queen Mary nor Queen Elizabeth had punished Lady Mary's mother for the treasons committed by her husband, Lady Mary's father, even though both parents had been hand-in-glove with the duke of Northumberland, plotting to put Jane on the throne instead of either Tudor princess.

Lady Mary frowned. Queen Elizabeth as yet knew nothing of what had transpired. Word had been sent to her that her cousin's arrival at Greenwich would be delayed. Nothing more.

Why trouble her now with events past and done? No harm had befallen kinswoman or country. For the most part, except for the jouncing and bruising she'd received riding in that wretched coach, Lady Mary herself had enjoyed the adventure, although she had been heartily glad to be rescued. She'd had no desire to visit Spain, and less to marry a man about whom she'd heard most frightening tales. At the same time, it had been pleasant, for a change, to be wanted.

With her most imperious air, Lady Mary put down her wine and stood. "Sir Walter," she said in a loud, carrying voice that made his eyes widen and riveted his attention. She could sound exactly like the queen when she chose. They were, after all, closely related.

"Yes, my lady?" Since she had stood, he was obliged to rise also. Lady Appleton and the servant followed suit, Lady Appleton rather more stiffly. Lady Mary stifled a sympathetic smile.

"Both coaches have been repaired and returned to Whitehall, have they not?" Their party had stayed in Southampton long enough to allow for that. Lady Appleton had refused to leave until they'd conducted a thorough search for her husband's remains, but in the end she'd had to accept that a body might be swept out into the Narrow Seas and never be seen again.

"Aye, my lady," Sir Walter agreed.

"How many persons know what happened to me, all or in part?"

"My men. Fulke. Master Boonen. Those of us in this room." He'd dealt with others at various stages, but they'd been told very little. They'd answered questions or followed orders without needing to know Sir Walter's purpose. None were likely to have recognized Lady Mary or guess she had been taken from Whitehall against her will. Only Sir Walter's trusted outriders knew the identity of the man they'd sought with such diligence.

"Are your men loyal?" Lady Mary asked. "Can they be sworn to secrecy? Or bribed? Can Boonen be persuaded to say nothing?"

She saw he divined her intention and that he dared hope they could manage what she proposed, for Lady Appleton's sake.

"I see no reason to reveal what really happened,"

Lady Mary continued. "Let it be given out that when I recovered from the illness that required me to remain behind at Whitehall, I accepted an invitation to visit my friend Lady Appleton, and have stayed all this time with her here in London."

"And Sir Robert's death?"

"Have you not just sent him on some mission abroad, Sir Walter? I am aware of what power you wield."

She took smug satisfaction from Lady Appleton's covert glance in his direction and Jennet's open look of confusion. It was gratifying to be in possession of knowledge few others shared.

"You may have begun as just another intelligence gatherer, but you are much more than that now. You do not report to any of the great men at court, but only to my royal cousin. And you choose what to tell her and which things she has no need to know."

"Is this true, Walter?" Lady Appleton looked worried. "Is that why you suspected Robert of wrongdoing all along?"

He took her hands in his. "True enough, but I am in your debt for any favors I have earned at court. You know that well."

Lady Mary did not, but was too fascinated to plague them with questions. She had found their relationship most interesting to study during the three-day journey back to London from Southampton.

"Robert did not realize his reports from Spain went directly to me," Sir Walter said. "Word sent by others from that hostile land obliged me to keep a watchful eye on him after his return to England. I did not know his intentions, but 'twas clear he was plotting something. He visited Durham House repeatedly, even attended mass there."

Startled, Lady Mary interrupted. "He was a Catholic?"

"He was born in Lancashire," Lady Appleton said quietly. "A great many people keep to the old religion there, even now."

"Is that why he threw in his lot with Philip of Spain? He wished to restore Catholicism to England?"

"I think," Lady Appleton said carefully, "that he was more concerned with getting a male heir for England. Begging your pardon, my lady, but the plan was to marry you to the Spanish prince, was it not? Had Queen Elizabeth died and King Philip enforced your claim, Robert would have seen Don Carlos rule as King Charles and any child you bore him would inherit both thrones. Robert had expected to rise to power under King Guildford. He never got over the failure of Northumberland's scheme. Though he was careful what he said in public, in private he chafed at serving women, first Queen Mary, then Queen Elizabeth. For a time, he clung to the conviction that his great friend Lord Robin would one day marry our sovereign lady, share the throne with her, but when that last hope died ..." Her voice trailed off. She did not need to say more.

"What else did your men observe Sir Robert to do?" Lady Mary asked Sir Walter. Clearly they had not followed him everywhere or she'd have been at Greenwich ere now and Sir Robert lodged in the Tower.

"Sir Robert met frequently with a clerk at the Spanish embassy named Ruy Vierra. My men failed to recognize him as Diego Cordoba. They had no reason to take particular notice of him and neglected to mention to me that this Vierra had but one eye."

Lady Appleton drew in a sharp breath, shaking herself out of her misery over her husband's treason and probable drowning as a thought struck her. "Did you have Robert under surveillance the morning Diane died?"

"Aye. And Cordoba, as it happens. They crossed paths at Durham House, your husband entering as Cordoba left. Neither could have been in Southwark at the time the woman was murdered."

"But you let him blame the Spaniard. And you let me believe Robert might have committed those terrible crimes."

"It was necessary," Sir Walter stated.

Lady Mary heard the quiet desperation beneath the insistent words. He had used Lady Appleton's quest for justice to further his own ends. The gentlewoman's investigation had complicated Sir Robert's plans and Sir Walter had hoped that fact would make him act in haste, make him vulnerable. Lady Mary could not fault his logic, but she felt sorry for her friend, and fortunate indeed that Sir Walter had come to Lady Appleton when Sir Robert finally made his move.

Lady Mary cleared her throat and addressed Sir Walter. "You will give out that Sir Robert died abroad, in the service of the Crown. His widow will inherit everything."

"But I am not a widow," Lady Appleton objected. "We found the boat, the brooch caught in the planks. We did not find a body, or any other evidence."

"Even if he is not dead," Sir Walter said, "he cannot risk returning to England. To avoid charges of treason, he must leave the country, and no doubt already has. You will never see him again. Better to believe him drowned, Susanna, for even if he lives, he is dead in all the ways that matter."

Swept out to sea, Lady Mary thought. No doubt of *that*. Perhaps, one day, Lady Appleton would be able to accept the truth. In the meantime, there was no reason why she should not *call* herself a widow.

"I must travel to Greenwich," she said abruptly. "Sir Walter, you will escort me. By water, I do think."

"Of course, my lady." He turned back to Lady Appleton. "Will you go to Leigh Abbey?" He did not ask her to travel with them, but Lady Mary sensed he wanted to.

"Soon," Lady Appleton said. She waved a vague hand, indicating the disarray in her house. She had been packing for the journey when Lady Mary's letter arrived. "I have a few matters to attend to first."

41

Susanna studied the note Petronella had left for her with mixed emotions. She must be glad, she told herself, that the other woman had found happiness. According to what was written here, she was going to marry Diego Cordoba and start a new life with him. In Spain, Susanna supposed.

"She left London two days ago," a voice said behind her. Vincent. Petronella's doorkeeper. Her friend. And now, apparently, the new owner of the Sign of the Smock.

"I am happy for her," Susanna told him, "and relieved to have proof now that neither Diego Cordoba nor my husband is the murderer we sought."

"Someone was watching her. Following her."

"Following?" Susanna had thought Sir Walter's men accounted for Petronella's unease, but they'd only have followed Cordoba. It seemed they'd even failed to do that, losing track of him during Sir Walter's absence in Hampshire.

"Aye," Vincent said. "The killer."

Susanna drew in a deep breath. She had to finish this. She could not retire to her "widowhood" in Kent leaving this undone. She was relieved Petronella was safe, but if she did not uncover the murderer's identity, come April another woman would die. She had thought and thought, if only to take her mind off Robert's perfidy, and it seemed to her that, unless Peregrine Marsdon was accustomed to make an annual journey in from Essex for the express purpose of killing, the most likely candidates were Francis Elliott and his father.

"Petronella told me that Master Elliott visits another bankside brothel with some regularity," she said to Vincent. "Is it possible to find out which girl he favors? Talk to her?"

Vincent gave her a long, hard look, then said, "Elliott keeps lodgings near the Castle-on-the-Hoop."

"Is that unusual?" Her heart began to beat faster. It sounded suspicious to her, but she did not know the customs of Southwark.

"He has a room at court, does he not? And his father's house in Bermondsey to go to? Why a third place? And no one has ever seen a woman visit him there. I asked."

So, he shared her suspicions. "I think, Vincent, that you must take me there. Now."

A short time later, accompanied by the escort she had brought from Catte Street, consisting of Jennet, Fulke, and Lionel, Vincent led Susanna through the dank and dirty streets of Southwark to a tenement more foul than anything her nightmares could have conjured. Elliott's rooms were situated on the top floor.

No one answered her knock. For a fleeting

moment, Susanna contemplated turning away, fleeing into Kent and forgetting all about murder, all about treason. Then Vincent lifted one ham-handed fist and broke down the door. Her heart full of trepidation, she went in.

The proof she'd sought was not difficult to find. In a chest, carefully preserved, were seven triangles of cloth. Susanna recognized one of them, black brocade, as coming from Diane's sleeve.

A supply of feathers, exactly like the one she'd found by Diane's body, was kept in a separate box.

The most damning evidence sat on the table next to the bedstead. It was undoubtedly the miniature Elliott had spoken of. Jerome had not destroyed it. And the woman in the portrait was dark haired, not blond.

"Helen," she murmured, picking it up to study more closely.

The name provoked a startled look from Vincent. "Who is she?" he asked.

"Francis Elliott's mother. She deserted the family when he was thirteen. Ran away to the north. Or so he told me. Is it possible he killed her? A boy."

"At thirteen? Old enough, but—"

Before he could finish the thought, a sound at the door diverted their attention. Francis Elliott stood there, shock blanking his handsome features for a moment when he realized he had been found out.

Then he flashed the same charming smile he'd displayed in prior meetings. "Lady Appleton. I am honored."

Ignoring his broken door, he advanced into the room and came right up to her. With Vincent at her side, Susanna did not feel unduly alarmed. Lionel and Fulke stood near the room's one tiny window, alert and watchful. And she heard the rustle of Jen-

net's skirt as she moved to stand just behind her
mistress.

"Your mother?" she asked, holding the miniature
toward Master Elliott.

"Aye." He took it without glancing at it.

"You lied to me, Master Elliott." Odd, Susanna
thought. Damning as the evidence seemed, she clung
to a small hope that she was wrong. Could Francis
Elliott provide another explanation besides the obvious? Had he lied to protect someone else? His father?

Then she looked directly into his eyes and saw there
that she was not mistaken. They were as cold as death
and filled with hatred.

"Time to finish what I've started," he muttered.

He made no attempt to harm Susanna. Instead,
hugging the small painting to his breast, he turned
and dashed through the open doorway, catching
them all by surprise.

"Stop him!" Jennet cried, the first to recover her
wits.

Fulke and Lionel sprinted after the escaping villain,
but Vincent went to the window. "I know where he
is going," he said.

The view encompassed little more than the decrepit
house across the road. A sign swung, creaking, above
the door, marking it as the Castle-on-the-Hoop.

"He did not kill his mother," Vincent said. "Not
yet."

"Helen Elliott is the gentlewoman Petronella told
me of?" Jennet's voice rose in astonishment. "The
one who went to work in a whorehouse for fun!"

"Aye. I do think so. Transformed herself from
Helen into Heloise. 'Twas Heloise I went to in search
of names of victims, and thought nothing of it that
she had so many questions of her own. But Elliott's
a regular visitor there, and she'd have told him of

my Molly's interest. I put her in danger by saying too much."

Molly? Petronella's real name surprised Susanna. It seemed so . . . ordinary. She touched Vincent's arm. "Molly's safe now. Safe and far away. But we must do what we can to keep Francis Elliott from claiming another life. He is mad, surely, killing women who resemble his mother when she is the one he's wanted to murder all along."

She would have hastened to the woman's aid, but Vincent held her back. "No need to fear for Heloise, madam. Her son's the one who deserves our pity now."

"I must see for myself."

Over everyone's protests, Susanna insisted on entering the Castle-on-the-Hoop. It was a far different sort of establishment than the one Petronella had run, but Susanna did not allow herself to think about what she saw. Not then. She stored fleeting impressions away to contemplate later.

At the sounds of shouts and cries of pain, they rushed up the stairs to the rooms Heloise occupied. They found there an immense woman, her once-black hair turned gray, her formerly tiny body grown gross and bloated, her flabby throat marred by fresh red marks. As she shrieked orders to her henchmen, the two burly guards wrestled Francis Elliott to the rush-covered floor. One of them began to stab him repeatedly.

Horrified, Susanna tried to intervene, but Vincent prevented her. He held her arms until Elliott lay limp and bloody and his murderers had fled, ordered by their mistress to hie themselves to safety.

Slowly, Susanna turned to face the woman who had given birth to Francis Elliott, abandoned him and his

father, and now chose to let the men who'd killed
him go free. "He was your son," she said. "How could
you—"

Bitter laughter cut short the question. "I have no
son," Heloise declared.

"Not anymore."

"You are the gentlewoman who has been conspir-
ing with Petronella," Heloise said with a derisive twist
of her lips. "Lady Appleton. You should have stayed
at home and tended to your own concerns."

"As you did, Helen?"

Again the woman laughed, but this time there
might have been grudging admiration in the sound.
"I like you," she declared. "And in the end you have
rid me of a most annoying problem. I always knew
he'd try to kill me one of these days."

Aware she must tread warily, that Heloise might
well be as mad as her son, yet Susanna felt an overwhelming need for answers. This terrifying woman
was the only one who had them.

"Why did he kill them?" she asked. "Why did he
want to kill you?"

"Because I was not already dead." Her tone was
almost conversational as she sank into the cushioned
recesses of a large, padded chair and reached for the
container of ale on a nearby table. She drank deeply,
smacking her lips, then belched. "He thought I was
dead until some eight years past. Then, one night
after a visit to the Sign of the Smock, he came here.
Recognized me." She drank again. Burped once
more. "He was never the same after that."

"What do you mean?" Susanna asked.

"Francis became impotent." She gave a nasty
chuckle. "My girls think I must have been responsible
for that. The whores at the Sign of the Smock found

him lusty enough . . . until he discovered who I was. What I was.''

Fighting a shudder of revulsion, Susanna took a step closer to Heloise. This unnatural mother had taunted her son with his loss of manly prowess. Heloise appeared to have reveled in Francis's failures.

''Was Lora Tylney the first he killed?''

''Aye.''

''Why?''

Again that horrid laugh. ''A madness overtook him, or so he said. She was the first woman he met following our tender reunion who looked like me. He came here the day after he killed her and told me what he'd done.'' Her grin was ugly, a ribald sneer.

''Why did he leave a feather by Lora's body?''

''You know the answer to that. He thought it appropriate. His private message that the girl was no better than she should be. The first kill excited him,'' Heloise bragged, ''and he knew his action had impressed me.''

''And St. Mark's Day?'' Susanna asked. That, too, had become part of Francis Elliott's ritual after Lora's death.

Heloise's face lit with another ghastly smile. ''The feather was a random thing, plucked from a pageant wagon on impulse, meant to show everyone Lora Tylney was no better than a Winchester goose. Killing her on St. Mark's Day was also by chance. Only afterward did Francis realize how appropriate that had been. 'Tis my birthday.'' Her expression widened into a grotesque parody of pleasure. ''After that, each dead girl became his annual present to me. A trophy. Proof of his manhood.'' She shrugged, not caring why he'd killed, only that he'd done so because of her.

Her son's murders had given her a sense of power, Susanna thought, sickened by the idea.

"He searched out women who were small and dark. He'd keep careful watch over the chosen one until April, that he might find her easily and kill her when my special day came around again."

By implication, mother and son had maintained regular contact after their reunion. Had simply learning what she had become driven Francis Elliott mad? Or had it been her taunts? There was no doubt in Susanna's mind that he *had* run mad. No sane person could have behaved as he had, enacting what he longed to do to Heloise with others who only looked as she had when she was young.

Susanna was sure now that Francis Elliott had intended to kill Petronella. Perhaps he had mistaken Diane for her. Or he had chosen to make the substitution at the last moment. Diane must have sensed something threatening about him when he took her to the inn. That would explain why she'd seemed so fearful when she came to Catte Street.

But Heloise's role in the murders, the way she'd encouraged her son to commit them, was more chilling than anything Francis Elliott had done. And her henchmen would not have slain her son, Susanna realized, a man who must have been well known to them, unless she'd ordered them to kill.

Concern for her own safety and that of her retainers urged Susanna to end the interview quickly. This woman was evil, and she had the advantage here in her own house.

"You will want to see to your son." Susanna felt a moment's pity for Jerome Elliott, though she thought he'd been more fortunate than he knew when his wife left him.

"Aye. We'll dispose of him," Heloise said.

Susanna did not like the sound of that, but she did not argue. Only when they were outside, walking briskly along Maiden Lane, did she turn to Vincent and speak of her concern. "Is it not our duty to call the constable and the coroner?"

The incredulous look he gave her spoke volumes.

"She will get away with murder."

"She already has."

He kept walking, past the brothel that now belonged to him, escorting Susanna and her party all the way to Paris Garden Stairs. He signaled to a passing boat, which immediately veered toward shore to pick them up.

"Lady Appleton," Vincent said in a firm voice that brooked no argument. "The man who murdered seven women is dead. Killed to prevent him from murdering an eighth. There will be no more St. Mark's Day victims. We know Heloise bears some guilt for these killings, but she has long paid bribes to all the local officials to look the other way no matter what she does. In her own sphere, she has money and power and influence."

"And I am just an ordinary gentlewoman, easy to ignore."

"Leave it be, Lady Appleton. You have done what you set out to do."

Yes, Susanna thought as she stepped into the wherry and was borne away from Southwark. She had done what she had set out to do. She had cleared Robert of any suspicion of murder. A bitter victory. She had even, through her fortuitous acquaintance with the Lady Mary, kept her husband's name clear of charges of treason. That triumph, she thought, tasted more bitter still, for she must present herself henceforth as a widow, living a lie.

Swallowing bile, she steeled herself to return to Catte Street, pack, and make the journey back to Leigh Abbey. In a month or two, according to the plan the Lady Mary had devised, Sir Walter would visit her there to bring word of Robert's death.

42

Three Months Later

Accompanying her mistress from the chapel, Jennet walked close to her side in the hope of shielding her from questions. And from an excess of sympathy. Sunday services gathered everyone together. There was no escape from neighbors and friends.

Jennet was surpassing glad they had left London behind. All summer long, stories had filtered out into the Kent countryside to tell of the vicissitudes brought by the spread of the plague. Fires burned in the streets every Monday, Wednesday, and Friday, in an attempt to correct the corruption in the air. Any dogs or cats found running loose were slaughtered, for fear they carried the disease. And the Spanish ambassador had died of it in August, though some said worry about his debts, and other matters, had been what really killed him.

Now it was autumn again, the harvest season. In

the past, Sir Robert had been accustomed to leave them at this time of year, bound on one mission or another. Jennet was glad he was gone for good.

All but a few trusted members of the household believed he had died abroad, of the plague. A nice touch, that. Sir Walter's doing.

"I wonder if we will ever know what happened to him?" she mused a short time later.

Alone with Lady Appleton, Jennet helped her remove an elaborate black headdress. A widow was expected to wear mourning for the remainder of her life. Unless she remarried. Not likely, Jennet thought. Except for the unrelenting use of black in all her clothing, the death of a husband gave a woman complete freedom of choice.

"I think we will," Lady Appleton said.

For a moment Jennet stared at her blankly, having forgotten she'd asked a question.

"He'll turn up one day, when we least expect it." Lady Appleton managed a sad smile and spoke with what sounded suspiciously like fondness. "Knowing Robert," she said, "he'll even find a way to land on his feet.

Please turn the page
for an exciting sneak peek
at Kathy Lynn Emerson's
next Susanna, Lady Appleton, mystery
FACE DOWN BENEATH THE ELEANOR CROSS
* * *
coming soon from Kensington Books!

1

Back again, eh? 'E's gone on without ye. In a powerful hurry, 'e were, too.''

Susanna Appleton broke off her survey of the tavern known as The Black Jack to stare at its proprietor. Until a moment ago, she'd never set foot in the place, but there might be some use in letting his misconception stand, especially if the mysterious '' 'E'' turned out to be the man she sought. "How long ago did he leave?''

The tavernkeeper was shorter than she, a small, wiry man in a canvas apron. When he took a step closer, Susanna smelled garlic and stale, spilled wine, a pungent and unpleasant combination when trepidation had already made her queasy. A pockmarked face and brown teeth did nothing to alleviate her first, negative impression.

"Come and sit with old Ned, sweeting," he invited, leering at her, "and I'll tell you everything I know. But let's see what's under the 'ood this time."

Before she could stop him, he flipped the heavy wool away from her face, narrowing his eyes to get a better look. As he leaned in, the stench of his breath nearly made her gag.

Repulsed, Susanna backed away. Beneath her cloak, she fumbled for the small sharp knife suspended from the belt at her waist. She could expect no help from customers who frequented a place such as this, and for once she did not think it likely she'd be able to talk herself out of trouble.

The Black Jack Tavern was as disreputable as the lowest tippling house. A smoky fire burned in the chimney corner, spreading its murky light over four rickety trestle tables in a windowless, low-ceilinged room. Around them, occupying rough-hewn benches and stools, with not a chair in sight, were more than a dozen patrons, men who appeared down on their luck and potentially dangerous. A few of them were eating, but most ignored offerings of cheese and meat pies in favor of beverages served in black jacks, wooden cans treated with pitch on the inside.

To Susanna's relief, a call for more beer distracted Ned. The moment he turned away, she fled, escaping into the narrow street outside.

Frigid air lanced through her like a thousand ice-tipped arrows. Hugging herself beneath her warm wool cloak, Susanna left the slight shelter of the building's overhang and started walking. Her heart was racing, but she no longer had any immediate fear for her safety.

When she reached the corner, she glanced back at the tavern. Its sign, showing a crudely painted black jack, creaked as a chilly gust of air set it swinging. A second pole bore a picture of leaves, proclaiming that wine, as well as beer and ale, could be found within.

Shivering and stamping her booted feet to keep warm, Susanna considered what to do next. She'd arrived almost an hour late, delayed by this uncommon cold weather. The Thames was frozen solid. She'd planned to hire a boat to take her across. Instead, she'd been obliged to walk, or rather to slip and slide, until she reached the opposite shore.

For whom had the tavernkeeper mistaken her? One cloaked and hooded woman looked much like another, she supposed, especially in a poorly lit room. But why would Robert have been with someone else when he was expecting her?

Her lips twisted into a mockery of a smile as Susanna silently answered her own question. With Robert, there always seemed to be another woman.

Their marriage had been arranged as soon as Susanna turned fourteen and solemnized when she was eighteen. Robert, then twenty-seven, had expected to acquire a quiet, obedient spouse, one content to remain in the background, to stay in the country while he was at the royal court. For the most part, at least in the early years, she had obliged him.

A door opened a few feet from where Susanna stood. Giving her a suspicious look, a shopkeeper hung out a lantern containing a candle. A hook had been set into the doorframe for that purpose.

The action served as a pointed reminder of the foolishness of remaining where she was when the sun was about to set. She'd come alone, as Robert's coded message had instructed. Now she was acutely aware that she was in a strange neighborhood without the protection of servant, friend, or husband.

Susanna was tall for a woman, and sturdily built. Along with a sharp mind and an inquisitive nature, both characteristics had been inherited from her father. Neither, however, made her any match for footpads or cutpurses. The fact that she had on her person a pouch containing the gold coins Robert had requested she bring with her rendered her even more conscious of her vulnerability.

Where was he?

Why had he not waited for her, especially if he was in need of money? Susanna was torn between relief and disappointment and beset by the same anxiety that had settled over her five days earlier, when she'd first opened the letter and realized it had come from Robert, a man most people supposed to be dead.

Leaving the environs of The Black Jack, she began to walk toward Charing Cross, in the north part of Westminster. She'd suspected all along that Robert had not drowned eighteen months earlier. Seeming to do so had provided too neat a solution to his problems at the time. And to her own.

Susanna had allowed others to persuade her to declare him dead and go on with her life. She'd had no real choice, and it had scarce been a hardship, not when the result was complete control over all Robert had owned. She was honest enough with herself to admit she enjoyed the freedom her false widowhood entailed. In her opinion, the advantages of the married state were much overrated.

During the previous year and a half, while waiting for some word of or from her "dead" spouse, Susanna had come to the conclusion that Robert must have planned well, secreting funds sufficient to spirit him safely out of England. She'd begun to think she'd never see him again. On the other hand, she had not been unduly surprised to receive what amounted to a demand that she secretly come to him and bring with her a considerable sum in gold.

Despite the acrimonious nature of their relationship, she and Robert knew each other well. He'd have had no doubt she'd obey. Her sense of honor compelled her to comply with his wishes, no matter how much she resented doing so.

She had made certain vows when they wed. Robert might hold them in little regard, but Susanna had always been a woman of her word. As long as her husband lived, she was bound by her obligations to him. For that reason, she had come to Westminster in secret, and she had not betrayed Robert's whereabouts to his enemies.

This would be their last meeting, she'd decided on the long, cold journey from her home in rural Kent. They would clear the air between them. She'd remind him that he had a most pressing reason not to be seen by anyone who might recognize him. Then she would explain that the money she'd brought, invested wisely, should be sufficient to allow him to live comfortably for the rest of his life. If he followed her advice, he'd have no need to contact her again.

At Charing Cross, where King Street met the Strand and both noisy thoroughfares were crowded enough to make Susanna feel safe, she paused in front of a bookseller's shop and contemplated her next move. The buildings directly across from her comprised the Royal Mews. In spite of the name, which implied the presence of falcons and other hunting birds, this mews housed the queen's horses. Robert had been wont to leave his own mount there when he was in attendance on Queen Elizabeth. On such occasions, when he could not secure a bed in the palace or impose upon the hospitality of friends with lodgings in the vicinity, it had also been his custom to take a room in a nearby inn called The Swan.

She would spend the night there, Susanna decided.

It was possible that Robert, following her logic, would look for her at that inn. If he did not, then in the morning she would return to Leigh Abbey. She had, she assured herself, obeyed every instruction in the coded letter. After a dozen years of betrayals, her sense of obligation was worn thin. Any true affection for Robert Appleton had long since withered and died.

Susanna had just turned toward The Swan when she heard a commotion erupt behind her. Shouts and laughter drew her attention to the ornate Eleanor Cross at the center of the intersection.

Like similar memorials in Cheapside and thirteen other locations throughout England, this Eleanor Cross had been erected by King Edward I to mark one of the stopping places of his beloved queen's funeral cortege. A tower of Caen stone, decorated with sculptured scenes from the life of Christ, and with Eleanor of Castile's image and arms, rose above a flight of stone stairs.

In the last rays of the setting sun, Susanna saw a man, apparently much the worse for drink, struggle to climb them. His slow progress was marked by considerable weaving and stumbling. To the delight of the jeering, hooting crowd that quickly gathered to watch him, he suddenly clutched at his throat and tottered, his footing precarious on the icy surface of the top step.

Beset by an uneasy premonition, Susanna joined the throng moving toward the cross. She was too far away to do more than gasp when the man seemed to lose control of his legs. Before anyone could aid him, he tumbled headfirst down the stairs, losing his bonnet on the way and striking his unprotected skull several times before his limp form came to rest at the base of the monument.

A sudden hush fell over the spectators. The man lay still, sprawled face down at the foot of the stairs. Bright blood stained the back of a bald head. That, together with the unnatural angles of his limbs, made it likely he was beyond human help.

All the same, Susanna stepped closer. She was a skilled herbalist. A healer. If any spark of life remained, she felt obliged to do what she could to ease the fellow's pain and suffering.

Another would-be Samaritan reached the body ahead of her, turning it over only to recoil in revulsion.

At first, in the rapidly fading twilight, Susanna did not recognize the dead man. She did not know anyone who was both completely bald and clean shaven.

Then someone brought a lantern forward. Silhouetted by its light was a familiar profile of brow and nose and chin.

Susanna heard a choked sound and realized with a dull sense of surprise that she had made it. She squeezed her eyes tightly shut, struggling to exert some measure of control over her rapidly fluctuating emotions. . . .

The dead man was her husband, Sir Robert Appleton.

ABOUT THE AUTHOR

Kathy Lynn Emerson lives in Wilton, Maine. She has written many novels, including romantic suspense and children's mysteries. You can visit her website at *www.kathylynnemerson.com*

<u>BOOK YOUR PLACE ON OUR WEBSITE</u>
AND MAKE THE
<u>READING CONNECTION!</u>

We've created a customized website just for our very
special readers, where you can get the inside scoop on
everything that's going on with Zebra, Pinnacle and
Kensington books.

When you come online, you'll have the exciting
opportunity to:

- View covers of upcoming books

- Read sample chapters

- Learn about our future publishing schedule
  (listed by publication month *and author*)

- Find out when your favorite authors will be visiting
  a city near you

- Search for and order backlist books from our
  online catalog

- Check out author bios and background information

- Send e-mail to your favorite authors

- Meet the Kensington staff online

- Join us in weekly chats with authors, readers and
  other guests

- Get writing guidelines

- AND MUCH MORE!

Visit our website at
http://www.kensingtonbooks.com

Get Hooked on the
Mysteries of
Jonnie Jacobs